# RED
# BURNING
# SKY

Kensington novels by Tom Young:

*Silver Wings, Iron Cross*

*Red Burning Sky*

# RED
# BURNING
# SKY

## TOM YOUNG

**KENSINGTON**
PUBLISHING CORP.

www.kensingtonbooks.com

KENSINGTON BOOKS are published by

Kensington Publishing Corp.
119 West 40th Street
New York, NY 10018

All Kensington titles, imprints, and distributed lines are available at special quantity discounts for bulk purchases for sales promotion, premiums, fund-raising, educational, or institutional use.

Special book excerpts or customized printings can also be created to fit specific needs. For details, write or phone the office of the Kensington Special Sales Manager: Attn. Special Sales Department. Kensington Publishing Corp, 119 West 40th Street, New York, NY 10018. Phone: 1-800-221-2647.

The K with book logo Reg. US Pat. & TM Off.

Library of Congress Card Catalogue Number: 2021948129

ISBN: 978-1-4967-3294-1
First Kensington Hardcover Edition: March 2022

ISBN: 978-1-4967-3295-8 (ebook)

10 9 8 7 6 5 4 3 2 1

Printed in the United States of America

In memory of my father, Bobby W. Young

# RED
# BURNING
# SKY

# CHAPTER 1
# Into the Maelstrom

*Over Central Europe, June 1944*

AT THE BOMBARDIER'S STATION OF *MISS CAROLINE*, BILL BOGDON-avich aimed through his Norden sight and toggled the bomb release. Turbulence rocked the B-24 Liberator as heat rose from fires below. Shrapnel raked the fuselage. Bogdonavich's target, the refineries of Ploesti, Romania, fueled the Nazi war machine, and he knew the Germans would defend them with vicious zeal. But that didn't begin to describe the storm of explosives and sharp metal hurled up at the men and machines of the Fifteenth Air Force.

"Bombs away!" Bogdonavich called. He couldn't judge his accuracy well. The bombs from *Miss Caroline* disappeared into a cauldron of smoke and fire, as if they had dropped into a burning lake.

Bogdonavich looked up from the Norden, through the aircraft's Plexiglas nose, and saw a wide-angle vision of hell. Smoke boiled from a burning refinery, the work of bombs dropped by aircraft ahead in the formation. Both the earth and sky seemed to burn. Antiaircraft artillery rounds exploded into black puffs and slashed the air.

Up on the flight deck, the aircraft commander, Lieutenant Wilson, switched off the autopilot and racked the Liberator into a steep left bank. Now the goal was survival: escape the flak storm and turn onto the egress route over Yugoslavia. Clear the Dinaric Alps and cross the Adriatic to get back to base in southern Italy. Chalk up another mission toward completing the tour. For the crew of *Miss Caroline*, this was number eight. At least twenty-two more to go, assuming they managed to return to base.

Once the Liberator cleared the target area, the flak fire vanished. Bogdonavich heard Wilson ask for a damage report.

"Minimal," Sergeant Bowers, the flight engineer, answered. "Sheet metal damage in the bomb bay. And oil pressure's a little low in number four."

*Miss Caroline* had made it through the bomb run nearly unscathed, but that didn't mean the danger had passed. German fighters prowled egress routes, looking to exact vengeance. A bomber shot down meant a bomber that would never again threaten the Reich.

"All right, people," Wilson called. "Use those eyeballs."

Bogdonavich scanned the blue ahead of him. The cruciform figures of twenty B-24s dotted the sky, three of them trailing smoke. Next to Bogdonavich, Lieutenant Greenbaum, the navigator, shook his head. Bogdonavich knew what the nav was thinking: Those three stricken aircraft would probably never make it back to Italy. Bogdonavich had already counted four Liberators blown out of the sky—just the ones he'd seen. Each downed plane meant ten men dead or missing.

Below, forested hills rolled along like green ripples. In the valleys, the patchwork of fields and hedgerows offered little evidence of combat. Germans occupied most of that ground, but sheep grazed as if conflict never reached this far into Balkan farmland. Bogdonavich imagined families at their tables, blissfully ignorant of the destruction just over the horizon.

But he knew better. Yugoslavia wasn't only at war against Nazi occupiers. Yugoslavia was at war with itself; a civil war within a world war. Bogdonavich's father had emigrated from this land to the United States at the end of the Great War. The nation his father called the Old Country was tearing itself apart. Chetniks led by General Draza Mihailovich battled with Partisans led by Josip Broz Tito. The stories reaching Bogdonavich's dad back in Pittsburgh were horrifying. Whenever Tito's Communist-leaning forces took new territory, they conducted swift and public executions of anyone suspected of aiding the Chetniks. There were also reports of Chetnik massacres of Croats, Muslims, and Partisan prisoners of war.

A call from the flight engineer brought Bogdonavich back to immediate problems.

"Bandits at two o'clock high," Bowers said.

Bogdonavich looked up and to his right. At first, he saw only the B-24s, heavy four-engine bombers lumbering toward home. But then dust motes appeared among them. The specks darted and turned. As *Miss Caroline* drew closer, the specks took the form of Messerschmitt Bf 109s.

Built for destroying bombers, a Bf 109 carried a pair of twenty-millimeter cannons. Bogdonavich had seen a 109 practically rip a Liberator in half. One of the 109s—there were at least eight of them—banked toward *Miss Caroline. Balkenkreuz* crosses marked its wings. The fighter's guns began to flash. Bogdonavich felt hot all over.

"Here they come," Wilson said. "Gunners, look alive."

Bogdonavich reached for the .50-cal in the nose compartment. But when Wilson rolled the Liberator into a hard right turn, Bogdonavich lost sight of the fighter. Evidently, Bowers saw it, though. His top turret guns hammered away.

The Liberator shuddered. Bogdonavich felt the wings flex and tremble. In the same instant, the turret guns went silent. Disoriented, Bogdonavich tried to understand what was happening.

"Right wing's on fire," someone said on the interphone. Maybe one of the waist gunners.

"Engineer, how's it looking?" Wilson asked.

No answer.

"Engineer, pilot," Wilson called.

Still, no answer.

Runnels of blood, droplets pulsating with the thrum of the engines, oozed into the nose compartment. Horror gripped Bogdonavich as he realized what that meant: When the 109 raked *Miss Caroline*, the rounds must have torn through Sergeant Bowers in the top turret. Blood seeped through joints and crevices above the nose section. Vibration shook loose beads that spattered the navigator's table and the bombardier's control panel. *It's raining blood,* Bogdonavich thought.

"Feather number three," Wilson said.

The aircraft commander was ordering the copilot to shut down a flaming engine.

"The fire's getting—" a gunner called out. He didn't get to complete his sentence because the interphone went dead.

*Miss Caroline* rolled hard to the left. With communication out, Bogdonavich had no idea if Wilson was taking evasive action or if he'd just lost control. From the navigator's table, Greenbaum looked over at Bogdonavich with eyes widened by fear. What now? By way of an answer, Bogdonavich tightened his grip on the nose gun. Nothing to do but man the weapons and defend the ship until the aircraft commander said otherwise.

The aircraft shuddered again, this time with a screech of rending metal. *Miss Caroline* seemed to roar in pain. Bogdonavich felt himself grow light in his seat. The aircraft was descending. Fast.

Over the cries of bending steel came the clangs of the bailout bell. Bogdonavich let go of the gun. He and Greenbaum disconnected their oxygen masks and unplugged their interphone cords. Greenbaum opened the hatch at the bottom of the nose compartment. The slipstream's howl assaulted their ears. Far below, green hills flowed underneath the plane.

Without another word or look, Greenbaum placed a gloved hand on his rip cord and disappeared through the hatch. Bogdonavich hesitated just a moment. Every instinct screamed against leaping from an airplane. Would his chute open? Would he slam against the airframe and die from the impact?

But Bogdonavich knew what happened to crewmen who waited too long to bail. He placed his hand on the rip cord and rolled through the hatch.

The tumble through space overwhelmed his senses. Earth and sky swapped places over and over again. A rush of wind deafened him. The bright blue blinded him. When the chute inflated, the opening shock yanked Bogdonavich hard. His limbs flailed as the risers snapped tight.

The world went silent. In an instant, the engines' reverberations vanished.

Under the canopy, Bogdonavich floated alone. He twisted in his harness to look around. He saw no other parachutes and no aircraft. He scanned the ground for a crash site, but found no telltale column of smoke. Perhaps *Miss Caroline* had drifted out of sight in a slow descent before striking the ground. Perhaps his crewmates all got out before him and had already touched down. For a moment, Bogdonavich felt as if he'd dropped to Earth from another planet.

He had no memory of pulling the rip cord. No matter. He had a good canopy, and now he needed to think about landing.

What had his instructors told him? Don't brace, don't anticipate the ground. When your boots hit, become a rag doll and roll with the impact.

Bogdonavich placed one boot over the other. Maybe that would keep a tree limb from striking his crotch. He folded his arms and placed his hands in his armpits. That served two purposes: It protected his fingers, and it shielded the arteries under his arms. He hoped his leather A-2 jacket could absorb some of the cuts and scrapes, too. He tucked his chin and closed his eyes.

And then the beating started. Something struck his shins and wrenched him to his left. Something hit him in the back. Something scratched his face. Leaves showered him.

When everything stopped moving, Bogdonavich opened his

eyes. He found himself hanging in dappled shade, two feet above the forest floor. He looked up to see his parachute tangled in an oak. Pain radiated all over his body, but nothing felt broken.

He unclipped one of his releases. The effort left him swinging by his right shoulder, inches off the ground, with a strap digging into his scrotum. Bogdonavich unclipped the other release. He thudded to the dirt. His hip bone slammed into his .45 Colt. That hurt, and he stifled the urge to shout curses. He looked up through the branches at the sky, the deep blue from which he'd fallen.

For a moment, Bogdonavich's predicament overwhelmed him. Just minutes ago, he'd flown miles above the earth at nearly two hundred miles per hour. Enemy fighters had threatened high-speed death by fire and metal. The thin, cold air of high altitude had forced him to breathe oxygen simply to remain conscious. Now he faced different dangers: on the ground, motionless and alone, in the thick, warm air of summer, in territory held by the enemy. He crept to the edge of the woods, where a pasture pitched downhill.

Three figures appeared on the slope. They trotted uphill toward Bogdonavich, accompanied by a large dog. Bogdonavich dropped his hand to his side. Unclipped his holster, gripped the pistol. But as he watched the people advance toward him, he realized they were not German soldiers. They were civilians: a woman, an old man, and a boy.

Bogdonavich wondered about their loyalties. Were they patriots or collaborators? Maybe neither. Maybe they were only hardworking farmers who just wanted to be left alone.

Over the next few minutes, Bogdonavich realized, fate would have to take its course. He couldn't shoot civilians, and he sure as hell couldn't read their minds. He rose to his feet. Held his arms outstretched with palms open, to look as unthreatening as possible.

The civilians hurried toward him. Bogdonavich spoke some Serbian; he'd learned the language from his dad. He'd resented it, though, and had learned only because his father insisted. To

Bogdonavich, the Old Country meant old ways and old superstitions. Backwardness and poverty. Something to put behind you, not celebrate. Bogdonavich considered himself purely an American and a man of the modern age. Why should he care so much about a place he'd never even seen?

For the moment, however, he didn't try to remember his Serbian. He simply pointed to a patch on his jacket. The patch displayed the wings of the U.S. Army Air Forces, with a *15* to designate the Fifteenth Air Force.

"American," Bogdonavich said in English. "I'm an American."

The dog began barking. Its teeth flashed. The animal was a fierce-looking thing of indeterminate breed. A spiked collar encircled its neck, and scars covered its nose. A farm dog for protecting livestock, Bogdonavich guessed, and wounded in battles with wolves.

The old man uttered a single syllable, and the dog hushed. The man smiled, revealing gaps in his teeth. His white beard hung to his rib cage, and he wore a traditional *šajkača* atop his head—the brimless Serbian hat. He grasped Bogdonavich's hand.

"Friend," the man said.

Bogdonavich nodded and smiled. "Pleased to meet you," he said.

"Friend," the old man said. It seemed to be the only English he knew.

*I could have heard worse words,* Bogdonavich thought. *Like "hands up" or "halt." Or anything in German. But of all words for a non-English speaker to know, why this one? And who taught it to him?*

The boy stared at Bogdonavich's pistol. The woman avoided eye contact. She looked to be in her twenties. Fairly attractive, with a face tanned from work outside. A kerchief covered her black hair. Perhaps the old man's daughter and grandson.

Bogdonavich searched his pockets for some small gift. In his jacket he found a pack of Beechnut gum. He handed it to the boy. The boy unwrapped the gum and tore it in half. Popped one half into his mouth and gave the other to the woman. *Not the first time he's seen gum,* Bogdonavich thought. The man smiled and pointed toward the farmhouse. He gestured for Bogdonavich to follow.

They led him across the open pasture, with no effort to hide him. Apparently, they didn't worry about Germans spotting them. Maybe they knew no Germans were around. Or maybe they were so tight with the Nazis that they were leading him into a trap.

# CHAPTER 2
## Second Chances

*Bergstrom Army Airfield, Texas, June 1944*

LIEUTENANT DREW CARLTON SPENT THE MORNING PRACTICING takeoffs and landings with a student. After each touch-and-go, the C-47 lifted into a turbulent sky. A twenty-knot wind bounced the aircraft. The rough ride did nothing to improve Drew's mood. Instead of bringing the fight to the Germans from a bomber base in England, where Drew had once been stationed, he was stuck on a training base in Texas. At Bergstrom Army Airfield, he taught new pilots to fly the C-47 Skytrain. The C-47 was a lumbering cargo aircraft, the military version of the DC-3. In Drew's view, it was the least glamorous, least lethal, and least important aircraft in the United States fleet. That's why they'd put him in it.

The weather at least presented a training opportunity. Drew talked his student through a dozen crosswind landings. He demonstrated how a pilot could maintain a straight final approach path by crabbing the aircraft into the wind. Just before touchdown, Drew pressed on a rudder pedal to kick the plane out of its crab. The plane touched down first on its right main wheel, then on its left. The white centerline stripes tracked directly under its nose.

"Very nice," the student said. "I'll never do it that smoothly."

"Sure you will," Drew said. "It just takes practice."

Drew believed his flying proficiency was the only thing that had saved him the further disgrace of a discharge. The military kept him because he was a skilled pilot, if not a daring one. The U.S. Army Air Forces felt he could serve the war effort best as an instructor.

The other officers at Bergstrom never asked him about his brief combat tour. But he felt reproach in their eyes whenever he entered a room. Most of his fellow instructors had completed overseas tours, flying in the Pacific or North Africa. His own tour had ended in disgrace. Other men from his hometown of Columbus, Ohio, were earning Bronze Stars, Air Medals, and Purple Hearts. Their sweethearts and family members were worried and terrified, but proud. Drew's parents had no reason for any of that. He had even considered placing the muzzle of his .45 against the roof of his mouth and letting the weapon end his pain. But a suicide would only compound his family's humiliation. If only for that reason, he remained on duty, among the living.

During a break, he found some of the instructors in the squadron ops office, huddled around the radio. This time, no one looked at him. The news on the radio held their undivided attention.

"What's going on?" Drew asked. He'd not bothered to turn on his Philco that morning. The last news he'd heard had come from Italy. Rome had fallen to the Allies.

"Shhh," someone hissed. Drew got no other answer. But he recognized the voice on the radio: NBC commentator H.V. Kaltenborn. Kaltenborn's reporting told him all he needed to know. The big invasion everyone had expected was on. The newscast described how troops had come ashore at Normandy and tanks were breaking through Hitler's so-called Atlantic Wall. Winston Churchill had addressed the House of Commons to say everything was going according to plan.

Other broadcasts offered prayers for Allied troops, and reactions from London, Washington, DC, and Moscow. One report discussed the air operations that supported the invasion. Bombers and attack aircraft had hit German targets in France. The homely C-47 had played a critical role, too. During the night, Skytrains had dropped paratroopers to seize key roadways and cut off enemy reinforcements.

Drew would have given anything to be there, in any role. He burned for action, for a chance to redeem himself.

Only a sense of duty kept him functioning for the rest of the day. *American soldiers are dying by the minute,* he told himself. *The least you can do is to support them from back home.*

That afternoon, a strange event appeared on the instructors' duty roster: *MANDATORY BRIEFING, 1430.* The roster offered no details. None of the other pilots had any idea what was up. Rumors could sweep through a squadron like fire through kerosene, but this time, no one had heard even the wildest guesses.

Thirty pilots filled the seats in the briefing room. The base commander introduced a man in civilian clothes. Colonel Overton, the commander, did not give the man's name or title. He did not say which agency or department the man represented. Overton said only, "This gentleman flew in from Washington today, and he has some important things to say to you."

The civilian wore a gray pinstripe suit with a matching waistcoat. His bald head shone under the lights of the briefing room. The man looked to be in his late fifties. Training posters decorated the wall behind him. One displayed silhouettes of Focke-Wulf and Messerschmitt fighters. Another showed a schematic of the C-47's electrical system. A third declared: *When you ride alone, you ride with Hitler! Join a car-sharing club today!*

"Good afternoon, gentlemen," the man began. "This briefing is classified. None of what we say here today goes outside this room. I represent an agency that reports directly to President Roosevelt. I'm here because we need volunteers. We're looking for C-47 pilots to take on a dangerous mission."

The man emphasized that there would be no shame in not volunteering. If a pilot did not sign up, his career would continue as planned. If a pilot did sign up, there was no guarantee of anything but high risk.

Drew sat up so straight in his chair that his shirt didn't touch the backrest. He placed his hands on his knees and hung on every word from this mysterious civilian. *Is this a chance to win back some self-respect?* Drew wondered. The civilian opened the briefing to questions, but he cautioned that there were a lot of questions he couldn't answer.

A pilot in the front row raised his hand. "Sir," he said, "if we volunteer, where are we going?"

"Europe," the man said. "For now, that's as close as I can narrow it down."

Drew raised his hand. "Sir," he said, "can you tell us anything about the kind of flying we'll be doing? Are we dropping troops?"

As he asked his question, he thought he saw one of his fellow instructors roll his eyes. *I know what you're thinking,* Drew thought. *Like yellow belly's ever going to sign up for this.*

"This is not an air assault mission," the man answered. "All I can tell you is that the operation will likely involve short-field takeoffs and landings in German-occupied territory."

The room fell silent as the civilian's words sank in. Flying *over* enemy territory was dangerous enough. During Drew's short stint with a bomb group, he'd seen proof of that. *But this guy is asking crews to fly into a hostile area and* land *there,* Drew thought.

"How long will this assignment last?" someone asked.

"Unknown. There is still a lot we don't know about the location and scope of the mission."

"Will we return to our regular units after it's over?" another instructor asked.

"Unknown."

The man sounded as if he'd given no thought to what the volunteers would do when they got back. *Maybe he doesn't expect the crews to get back at all,* Drew considered.

"Sir," a pilot asked, "if we volunteer, when do we need to let you know?"

"I need the names by the end of the week," the man said. "Colonel Overton will forward a list to me. If you sign up, you can expect new orders to be cut immediately."

Today was Tuesday. Drew had three more days to think about it.

He didn't need three more *minutes*. He knew what he'd do before he even left the briefing room. The only question was whether he'd be accepted for the mission.

After an afternoon training sortie with another student, Drew went straight to Colonel Overton's office. According to the briefing, Overton would have full discretion on which volunteers to accept for this secret mission. Drew didn't know the commander well; he knew only that Overton was a reservist called to active duty, and that he'd been a minister before the war. Flying and preaching seemed a strange combination of skills, but Drew hoped that strange combination would work in his favor. *Of all people*, Drew thought, *Overton should believe in redemption.*

In front of the commander's desk, Drew reported in and stood at attention. Overton said, "At ease." Drew glanced at the diploma on the wall: Yale Divinity School, 1926. Beside the diploma hung a framed photo of a Curtiss JN-4. In younger days, Overton had flown the "Jenny" biplane.

"Sir, I'd like to volunteer," Drew said.

"I figured that's why you were here," Overton said. He lifted a manila folder from his desk. "I've gone over your file."

Drew felt a knot twist in his intestines. Perhaps he'd let his hopes soar too high about another chance to prove himself.

"Yes, sir," Drew said.

"Lieutenant, why do you want to do this?"

"Sir, I'd give anything to get back in the fight."

Overton regarded Drew without expression. Drew wondered what that blank look meant. Was it disbelief? Or, worse, pity?

"But you *were* in the fight."

Drew weighed his words with care. "Sir," he said, "I may have made some bad calls in the past. But . . . they were gray areas. I think I'll make different decisions next time. I want to be a different kind of officer."

Overton raised his eyebrows, pursed his lips. "Ah," he said, "the zeal of the converted."

*Converted to what?* Drew wondered. *From cowardice to bravery? No, it's not like that.* But it would do no good to argue. Instead, Drew said, "It sounds like this operation will require some precise flying. I can land a C-47 anywhere they tell me to put it. Please, sir, you know I'm a good pilot."

"You are," Overton said. He flipped open the folder and adjusted his glasses. "I see you've never failed a check ride."

"Never."

"But here's my question: You're a pilot, but are you a warrior?"

Drew nodded. "I want to be, sir. There's nothing I want more."

"Very well," the commander said, "I'll approve your transfer. But it's against my better judgment. I have to say, I'm reminded of an old proverb, and it's not one from the Bible: 'Be careful what you wish for; you just might get it.'"

Drew thought he understood the commander's meaning. Now he had a second chance, and second chances didn't come often. He realized there were people who believed he couldn't handle risk, that he took counsel of his fears. He wondered if he actually agreed with them.

There was only one way to find out.

# CHAPTER 3
# Liquid Fire

*T*HE SERBIAN FAMILY THAT HAD FOUND BOGDONAVICH LED HIM across the pasture toward their home. They spoke to him in their language, but he could follow only part of it. Now Bogdonavich wished he'd practiced Serbian with his dad more often. He'd have to get by with what he could remember. He gathered that the family intended to shelter him.

"You stay in our barn," the old man said in Serbian.

Three outbuildings stood near the house, and one was bigger than the others. Bogdonavich figured the large structure for the barn, and he guessed the others were chicken coops or toolsheds. The two-story barn sat on a stone foundation. Rocks, most likely pulled from nearby fields, made up the walls of the first floor. The second floor was built of logs, and a wood-tiled roof topped the building. Beside the barn, a pitchfork rested in a haystack taller than a man's head. In a fenced pasture adjacent to the barn, a milk cow chewed her cud and flicked her brown ears at buzzing flies. Three goats romped on the other side of the pasture. Yellow and white wildflowers sprinkled color through the grass along the fence line.

Bogdonavich ducked to enter the barn's stone first floor. As his eyes adjusted to the darkness, he saw a collection of farm tools: a plow, a hay rake, shovels, hoes, and axes. A ladder built of tree limbs lashed together led to the upper floor. The old man pointed, and Bogdonavich climbed the ladder. The effort hurt; his joints and tendons remained sore from his bailout.

Upstairs he found a hayloft. The straw smelled like freshly cut wheat, with no hint of mildew.

The hayloft seemed as good a place to hide as any, though not perfect. Bogdonavich figured he could burrow into the straw to hide from casual observers. But if the Krauts brought dogs or started probing the straw with bayonets, it was game over.

"*Hvala vam,*" Bogdonavich said. Thank you. Then he added, "The boy. Your grandson?"

"*Da,*" the old man said. "His mother is my daughter. His father is a freedom fighter."

That sounded good to Bogdonavich. He couldn't guess the local politics, whether his benefactors were Partisan, Chetnik, or something else. But apparently this man's son-in-law was fighting against Germans in one capacity or another. Bogdonavich remembered how his father had followed events closely: In 1941, the Belgrade government signed onto the Tripartite Pact, joining the alliance of Germany, Italy, and Japan. Two days later, a coup d'état overthrew the Axis-leaning government and installed King Peter II, a mere teenager. The coup invited Hitler's wrath. But if German soldiers had believed they'd easily defeat an "inferior" Slavic people, they were learning a different lesson in the hills of Yugoslavia.

"Have you seen many other fliers like me?" Bogdonavich asked.

The old man made a dismissive gesture. He climbed down from the hayloft and left Bogdonavich to himself. Bogdonavich burrowed into the hay, but not so deeply that he couldn't hear noises from outside. He also kept his boots on in case he needed to beat a hasty exit.

A short time later, the old man came back with a bottle and two glasses. The man sat down with Bogdonavich in the hay, and he poured an amber liquid into the glasses. Handed a glass to Bog-donavich.

"Drink," the old man said in Serbian. "To your health and to your country."

Bogdonavich smiled and raised the glass. He recognized the aroma of *rakija*, a plum brandy. The first sip went down warm and strong; the stiff drink nearly watered his eyes. The brandy's heat spread down his throat and through his innards. For a moment, he felt safe. Maybe it was the alcohol talking.

But then a noise brought Bogdonavich back to reality: a high-pitched whine, soft at first, then louder. An airplane. But not the growl of a four-engine bomber, and certainly not the thunder of a B-24 formation. This sounded more like a single-engine fighter. The engine's song carried a particular timbre. This was no Mustang or Thunderbolt. Probably a Messerschmitt or a Focke-Wulf.

*Is it looking for me?* Bogdonavich wondered. Entirely possible. German pilots probably marked the positions of bombers they'd shot down. More than likely, they'd scour the ground looking for survivors.

The old man shifted his eyes upward, as if he could stare through the ceiling and spot the German aircraft. His fear, plainly evident, reminded Bogdonavich there were no safe moments. Anyone who sheltered him took long chances.

And yet, here he was. This little family was risking everything for him. He supposed he owed their assistance to some Serbian code of honor as strong as their Orthodox faith. Bogdonavich had seen hints of it in his father: the way Dad brought food to a sick neighbor, helped a cousin fix a truck. Dad would do anything for a friend or relative.

But that was back in America, where such kindness, though admirable, called for little sacrifice. A fancy, sweet cocktail with a hint of *rakija*. Now Bogdonavich tasted the pure version, straight up. Liquid fire.

The light yellowed in the barn as the sun began to set. The old man left Bogdonavich alone with his thoughts. Shafts of dying sunbeams shone through chinks in the log walls and lit dust motes floating above the straw. Just in case the worst happened, Bogdonavich checked his pistol: a round chambered, hammer cocked, thumb safety on. He lay in the hayloft, wondering how this might end.

*Will the family keep me up here indefinitely?* he asked himself. *How long before I wear out my welcome? How long before Allied forces take this area?*

Bogdonavich found no answers to those questions. He realized he could remain on the ground in hostile territory for days, weeks, or months. Nothing for it but to take one day at a time. One minute at a time, for that matter. He would simply have to try his best not to do anything stupid and get these people killed.

Life here was dangerous enough even in peacetime, Bogdonavich considered. If you cut yourself while chopping wood, where was the nearest doctor? If drought killed your crops, what would you eat? His dad's nostalgia for the Old World—and Bogdonavich's disdain for it—had always caused tension between them. But he had to give his father credit for escaping this life of never-ending hardship. *If Dad hadn't left,* Bogdonavich thought, *this would be my world, too.* He wondered how soon his parents would be notified he'd been shot down. How would they take the news? More than likely, they'd be told only that he was missing.

Bogdonavich drifted off to sleep with his hand still on his Colt.

Fiery images came to him in the night: Liberators burning, smoking, and spinning. Splashes of flame as they struck the ground. Targets blazing in his bombsight. Tracers ripping the sky.

A noise joined the scenes of conflagration, a series of rapid impacts. Bogdonavich imagined cannon rounds from a Bf 109 slamming into his wings. As the sounds continued, his mind pulled him out of the dream state. The noise was real, not just in his head.

He opened his eyes, found himself wide awake in full darkness. He raised his wrist. The luminous dial on his watch told him it was after midnight. What was that sound?

Not cannon rounds but hoofbeats.

Bogdonavich sat up, rolled out of the straw. On his knees, pistol still in hand, he crawled to the wall. Through a slit between the logs, he peered outside.

He saw men on horses. Men on foot. Men with torches. Men with guns.

# CHAPTER 4
## Consider Yourself Dead

*T*HE AFTERNOON SUN SCATTERED DIAMONDS ACROSS THE SURFACE of the Adriatic as Drew began his descent toward San Pancrazio Airfield. Off the C-47's left wing, the city of Brindisi, Italy, offered little hint of the war that raged to the north. Whitewashed walls of homes and shops beckoned from the hillside above the port. Two freighters lay at anchor in the harbor.

"Doesn't look anything like Sicily, does it?" Drew asked his co-pilot.

In the seat to Drew's right, Lieutenant Alfredo Torres shook his head. Drew and Torres, along with the rest of the five-man crew, had flown from the United States to Italy in several hops. Their previous leg had taken them to Sicily, which still bore scars from the Allied airborne and amphibious invasion the year before. Scorched tanks and destroyed aircraft had dotted the country-side.

The Italian army had collapsed in Sicily, and the Germans had withdrawn. But Hitler's armies still held parts of Italy and much of Europe, and plenty of hard fighting remained.

Drew still understood little about his part in the battles ahead. He knew only that he'd volunteered for something called Opera-

tion Halyard. He'd be landing in a remote area. Probably somewhere with the enemy nearby. Drew felt a mix of anticipation and
dread.

San Pancrazio tower cleared the C-47 to land, and Drew
banked onto final approach.

"Gimme one quarter flaps, please," Drew said.

"One quarter flaps," Torres said. He reached for the flap
handle.

"Gear down."

"Gear down."

In the air, Torres seldom said anything that didn't involve flight
procedures. A quiet kid from a farm in New Mexico, he was all
business from engine start to engine shutdown. If he knew anything about Drew's history, he didn't let on.

After they landed, the plane rattled onto a ramp built of PSP:
pierced-steel planking. This was no permanent base built by the
Royal Air Force, like some of the airfields in England. Combat engineers had thrown this one together with PSP, tent stakes, and
bubble gum. A makeshift place for warplanes to rearm, refuel,
and take off again to go blast the Third Reich.

The crew shut down the aircraft and checked in at base opera-
tions. Drew's team included an aerial engineer, Sergeant Jimmy
Montreux. The engineer had grown up working on boat motors
along the bayous of Louisiana, and he knew how to make a Pratt
& Whitney Twin Wasp engine sing. Drew's radio operator,
Sergeant Vince Calvert, came from Havre de Grace, Maryland.
His navigator, Lieutenant Ronald Chisholm, was the son of a
Montana rancher. Chisholm had completed a master's degree in
philosophy at the University of Montana before joining the
USAAF.

An orderly from base ops directed the sergeants to a tent for
enlisted crew members. Then he led Drew and the other two lieu-
tenants to the officers' quarters. It was a wall tent, staked in a row
of ten similar tents. The orderly drew back the flap to reveal a
shelter with eight bare cots and a plywood floor. Beside each cot

sat a folded army blanket and a bedroll tied with twine. The air felt hot and close, but at least the canvas offered shade. Everything about the base, from the tents to the pierced-steel planking, gave the feeling of impermanence. It was as if the army had built the place as a foothold and a jumping-off point, a stepping-stone on a journey all the way to Berlin.

"Home sweet home," Chisholm said.

"It'll do," Drew said.

Drew opened his duffel bag, and the men arranged their clothing and personal effects in the footlockers provided at each cot. They had no idea how long they'd stay here, but they'd traveled light. Just a few changes of uniform and underwear, a couple of flight suits, and their shaving kits.

By the time they got unpacked, airplane engines thrummed overhead. Drew opened the tent flap. A pair of P-38 Lightnings overflew the field and rolled onto a modified downwind leg.

A fuel truck idled along the perimeter track. Ground crewmen carried chocks and toolboxes. Officers appeared on the railing outside the glass-paneled control room on the top level of the tower building. They shaded their eyes and pointed into the sky.

*Sweating them in,* Drew remembered from his previous overseas deployment, brief as it was. The men were counting the airplanes coming back, praying it was the same number of airplanes that went out. All too often, those numbers didn't match.

From somewhere across the airfield, a siren keened. Drew stepped outside the tent and donned his sunglasses for a better look. A crash truck and an ambulance sped along a taxiway and took up positions near the departure end of the runway.

An enlisted man pedaled by on a bicycle.

"What's going on?" Drew asked.

The man looked back and called out, "Tower says we got a wounded pilot coming in."

Drew felt a spike of cold down in his gut.

The first Lightning extended its landing gear and banked onto

final approach. Sunlight glinted off its windscreen. The propellers appeared as twin discs, translucent circles on either side of
the central nacelle that housed the cockpit. The second aircraft,
wingman to the first, remained on a high base leg. The lead ship
settled to the pavement; then number two dropped its gear.

After the second Lightning landed, a third appeared in the sky.
At first, only a speck to the north, the aircraft grew larger until
Drew recognized that one of its engines had failed or had been
shot out. The left propeller did not spin like the one on the right.
It stood motionless, blades feathered to minimize drag. Other
than that, Drew saw no obvious sign of trouble. No flames, no
smoke trail.

This kind of predicament gave Drew night sweats during his
bomber deployment. Coming in with a crippled airplane, perhaps struggling to control your ship while suffering from a griev-
ous wound. Or not even getting that far. Dying in a ball of fire at
twenty thousand feet, or feeling yourself ripped apart by cannon
rounds.

Sweat oozed on Drew's arms and palms, and not from the heat.
Torres and Chisholm joined him outside the tent. Torres donned
his aviator's glasses and watched the stricken aircraft enter the
traffic pattern. He folded his arms and showed no emotion as the
emergency unfolded before him.

"I wonder if he was in a dogfight," Torres said.

"Don't know," Drew answered. "They're probably getting a lot
of ground attack missions, too."

"Doesn't matter," Chisholm said. "In the end, it comes out the
same."

Drew wondered what the navigator meant by that. He was still
getting to know the men who would fly beside him into harm's
way. For most of the training flights he'd conducted back in
Texas, he hadn't flown with a full crew. No need for a navigator or
a radio operator to fly touch-and-go landings all day with a student pilot. But for hard-core combat airlift, he'd need all the help
he could get.

On the turn from base leg to final approach, the Lightning pilot lowered his landing gear. Whatever he had faced, however he had performed, his ordeal was about to end, one way or another. Maybe that's what Chisholm had meant: In a war zone—or even in peacetime, for that matter—there were so many ways to die. Drew wondered what the navigator's schooling in philosophy had to say about the arbitrary nature of death in wartime.

Ever since Drew had volunteered for this assignment, he'd done a lot of thinking and reading on the nature of courage and fear. He'd found a line from Mark Twain that he liked: "Courage is resistance to fear, mastery of fear—not absence of fear." Hemingway called it "grace under pressure." Drew had also heard an interesting take on the issue from a paratrooper in an Officers' Club bar. The guy said, "Consider yourself already dead. Then you can stop worrying and focus on the job."

All that was well and good in the safety of a dusty library or over a highball glass with a double Scotch. Harder to apply when you got where bullets flew and bombs exploded.

The P-38 was on short final now, and Drew noticed two things wrong: It was too high; the aircraft was going to land long. And only one of the two main landing gear struts had extended.

"Go around," Drew muttered under his breath. The Lightning pilot needed to abort the landing and climb back up to pattern altitude. Cycle the gear or follow whatever procedures the P-38 had for emergency gear extension. A go-around was tricky on one engine, but better than landing like this.

The pilot did not go around. Maybe in a state of blood loss and semiconsciousness, he hadn't noticed his gear problem. Maybe he had no strength to shove the right throttle forward and jam his right boot into the rudder pedal to counter the asymmetric thrust. For whatever reason, he landed halfway down the runway with only one main gear hanging.

The left wing dragged the pavement. Sparks showered from the wingtip, and the aircraft veered off the runway. When the plane dug into the dirt, the left wing separated. A fuel tank broke open and spilled gallons of one-hundred-octane gasoline.

The fuel ignited so violently that it blew the left tail boom high into the air. Flames engulfed the P-38. A column of black smoke rose into the cloudless blue Italian sky. Crash trucks raced toward the wreckage.

Drew stood motionless. For long minutes, he watched the aircraft burn.

# CHAPTER 5
# Risen from the Grave

*T*HE U.S. ARMY AIR FORCES HAD TAUGHT BOGDONAVICH TO DO many things: to operate the highly classified Norden bombsight, to find his way by the stars, to build a fire and survive in the woods. Unfortunately, they had not taught him to ride a horse.

Bogdonavich gripped the horn of his saddle, and he struggled not to fall off. Just mounting the horse had been a challenge; his companions had laughed at his clumsy efforts to place his boots in the stirrups. By now, he'd given up holding the reins. He'd found the slightest tug could make the horse turn or stop when Bogdonavich didn't want to turn or stop. The horse, a handsome brown mare, had apparently concluded her rider was an idiot. She'd quit responding to the reins and simply followed the other horses.

That was fine by Bogdonavich. The five men who'd come for him at the barn rode ahead of him. He had no idea where they were taking him. They seemed to mean him no harm. However, they looked for all the world like cutthroats: long hair and thick beards. They were practically dripping with weapons and ammunition—everything from pistol rounds to shotgun shells. Beefy guys used to hard labor. Not one of them spoke a word of English. Bogdonavich's attempts at Serbian won him points with these guerrillas. In this forced immersion, more of the language was coming back to him.

He won even more points when he managed to convey that their leader, Draza Mihailovich, had made the cover of *Time* magazine a couple years earlier. Bogdonavich's Serbian wasn't good enough to go into details. But with gestures and halting words, he told the guerrillas that the article likened their general to an eagle who swoops down on his prey. They loved it.

"You are a mighty eagle, too, my cousin," one of them said. "Eventually you will return to your unit, and you will fly and fight again."

While he rode, Bogdonavich tried to remember more about the *Time* story that made the fighters so happy. The piece said that with 150,000 men, Mihailovich had managed to tie up as many as ten Nazi divisions. Bogdonavich had no way of confirming that; his own little corner of the air war kept him busy enough. But he knew from his officer's courses that a committed insurgent force could make life miserable for a conventional army.

At an oak grove on a hillside, the guerrilla band halted for lunch. Sunlight shafted through the branches as the men dismounted and tied their horses. One Chetnik stroked a stallion's neck for a moment, then poured grain for the animals to eat. The men unwrapped bread and cheese, along with a few scraps of salt pork. Bogdonavich thanked them for the food, meager as it was. The salt from the pork clung to the back of his throat until a fighter gave him water from a German canteen. The taste of the salt pork and the smell of horses put Bogdonavich in mind of wars from the previous century. His leather flying jacket seemed entirely out of place.

"How much farther?" Bogdonavich asked in Serbian. He felt exhausted and entirely out of his element, but he tried to keep his tone upbeat. He doubted these guys would have much patience for any sign of weakness.

The burly insurgent who led this little band leaned an M1903 Springfield—an American rifle from the Great War—against a tree. "Just a few kilometers," he said. "We will bring you to a church. The priest will take care of you from there."

"Thank you," Bogdonavich said. "I am sorry; I missed your name."

"I am called Stefan," the man said.

As Stefan spoke, he waved his right hand. The gesture revealed a disfiguring injury: His index finger was missing. Only a quarter-inch stub remained. Perhaps a German bullet had torn away the digit, or maybe Stefan had slipped with some sharp tool. The sight reminded Bogdonavich of old-timers in Pennsylvania: Practically half the farmers and mechanics had lost fingers to crunching gears or whirring blades. They didn't let it stop them from working, and neither did Stefan. Presumably, he used his middle finger to fire his weapon. *Well, that's fitting,* Bogdonavich thought.

Bogdonavich took another bite of pork and washed it down with warm water. "I appreciate your help," he said.

"We are happy to do this," Stefan said. "Sometimes it seems the Americans are our only friends."

Stefan's words puzzled Bogdonavich. He knew about the Chetniks' struggles against the Partisans, the civil war in the middle of a world war. *But in the fight against the Nazis, aren't all the Allies in this together?* he thought. *The Brits, the Aussies, the Canadians, and all the rest?* He decided to risk asking. Besides, he needed to improve his Serbian, and every conversation helped.

"What about the other countries on our side?" Bogdonavich asked. "Like Britain?"

That question produced laughter from some of the men— laughter without mirth.

"Churchill wants to fight to the last Serb in Yugoslavia," one of them said. The man's biceps bulged inside his field jacket. Like Stefan, he carried a Springfield. On a web belt, he wore ammunition pouches and a leather sheath that contained a dagger. The blade must have been six inches long.

"The British have thrown in their lot with the Partisans," Stefan explained. "Maybe they don't want to offend the Russians."

"The Communists spread the lie that we are collaborating with the Germans," another guerrilla said. Bogdonavich had to think to translate all the words from Serbian to English. Some he figured out simply through context.

The complexities were starting to make his head spin. Now Bogdonavich wished he'd asked his dad more questions—but most of their discussions about the Old Country devolved into arguments. He'd known about the Yugoslav civil war, of course. But he hadn't realized it was causing divisions among the Allies. That figured, though. In Bogdonavich's experience, anytime anybody talked about Yugoslavia, it started a fight.

"Forgive me if I have offended you," Bogdonavich said. "I am ignorant."

Stefan pointed to the man who spoke so bitterly about Churchill. "That is Gregor," Stefan said. "We had a radio until he heard a BBC broadcast about Yugoslavia. They gave all the credit for killing Germans to the Partisans. Gregor got so mad, he smashed the radio."

The other fighters laughed, with less irony this time. Gregor shrugged.

"It is no wonder people in the West are ignorant," Gregor said. "The Communists say such garbage about us, and the British believe it."

"The British send us no supplies, and the Americans send us too little," Stefan said. "We could kill more Nazis if we had better weapons." He tossed a pebble at his outdated rifle. "Yet, we fight on with what we have."

Gregor told a story that explained why he walked around with so much rage inside him. He came from a town called Kraljevo. Back in 1941, before the split between Chetniks and Partisans became irreconcilable, a joint Chetnik-Partisan operation killed ten *Wehrmacht* troops. The Germans had formulated a policy to suppress resistance: For every German soldier killed, one hundred Yugoslav civilians would die. Fifty for every German wounded.

The Germans rounded up all the men in Kraljevo from ages fourteen to sixty, including Gregor, his brother, and his father. At the time, Gregor was sixteen. The Germans lined up the men in front of trenches and opened fire with machine guns. A bullet struck Gregor's arm, and he collapsed into a trench filled with corpses. A bulldozer covered the bodies with a thin layer of soil. Gregor placed his nose in the crook of his elbow to allow room to breathe.

Covered with dirt, he waited. He waited for the bulldozer to rumble away. He waited until he heard nothing. In the stale air, his lungs burned. And he waited some more.

When he could wait no longer, Gregor dug himself out of his grave. He emerged in darkness, bleeding, covered in mud and viscera. He said he must have resembled a ghoul from the folk tales, a vampire risen to feed on the living.

"I did, indeed, rise from the grave to kill," Gregor said. "But only Germans."

Bogdonavich did some quick math in his head. If Gregor was sixteen in 1941, that meant he was nineteen now. With his thick beard, the lines around his eyes, and the scar across his nose, he looked twenty years older.

"The Germans killed more than two thousand people in Kraljevo," Stefan said. "It is no wonder he rages when a broadcast suggests we are not serious about fighting Nazis."

Bogdonavich looked at the nineteen-year-old in the older man's body.

"I am so sorry for what happened to you and your family," Bogdonavich said.

Gregor nodded his head. Bogdonavich could imagine the fate of any German who came within reach of Gregor's rifle or dagger. But after hearing about the massacre, Bogdonavich could also imagine his own fate if the Germans caught him. If they would gun down innocent villagers, what would they do to someone who'd been dropping bombs on them? Bogdonavich was among friends at the moment, but he realized his life still hung by a thread.

After lunch and a brief rest, the men mounted their horses. As they rode through the forest, Bogdonavich heard engines, distant and high. He scanned upward past the screen of leaves but saw no aircraft. The rumbling reminded him that the air war was never far away, and it continued daily.

Just as Stefan had promised, a ride of only a few kilometers brought them to a village. The woods opened to a cleared valley, marked by the rounded cupola of a small Orthodox church. A few homes and barns surrounded the church. A single dirt street anchored the village. Fields and pastures spread beyond it. Sheep dotted one of the pastures. Milk cattle grazed in another.

The guerrillas tied their horses outside the church. Stefan knocked at the door.

The door groaned open to reveal a priest dressed in a black cassock. The man wore a crucifix on a long gold chain. His white beard extended nearly as far as the chain. The priest stood at least six feet tall, his spine straight despite his age—which could have been eighty. The priest spread his arms wide and welcomed Stefan with a kiss on both cheeks.

"Father Milos," Stefan said, "it is so good to see you."

"Greetings, my sons," the priest said. He did not seem at all surprised to find heavily armed insurgents outside his church.

Stefan made the sign of the cross, holding his right thumb and middle finger together. Bogdonavich crossed himself as well, and he followed Stefan inside. The rest of the guerrillas came in behind him.

"This man's name is Bogdonavich," Stefan said. "He is a Serb, like us, but from America. He speaks our language."

The priest gasped, kissed Bogdonavich on both cheeks. "Welcome, welcome," he said. "God's blessings upon you."

"Thank you, Father Milos," Bogdonavich said.

In the church's darkened nave, Bogdonavich needed a few seconds for his eyes to adjust. A dozen oaken pews, six on either side of the aisle, nearly filled the small building. Lantern light flickered beneath rows of icons. Bogdonavich recognized icons depicting Christ, John the Baptist, Mary, and several prophets and saints.

Three young men sat in the front left pew. When they turned, Bogdonavich saw they wore flight clothing.

"Bill!" one of them called out.

It was Greenbaum, the navigator from Bogdonavich's bomber, *Miss Caroline.*

# CHAPTER 6
## Reconnaissance in Force

*T*HE IMPRINTS OF GERMAN TIRES ALONG THE DIRT ROAD LOOKED fresh to Vasa Petrovich. As a farm boy, he knew the nature of soil. No rain for days had left the road dry and dusty. The soil, light as flour, would not have displayed tire treads for long.

Vasa explained his reasoning as he showed the tracks to Nikolas, his squad leader. At seventeen, Vasa considered himself fully a man. But Vasa knew he needed to prove his worth before others shared that opinion. He would take the hardest jobs, carry the heaviest loads, and make everyone know he was a fine Chetnik fighter.

"Very good," Nikolas said. "You are using your head."

Nikolas led a squad of Chetnik guerrillas that included Vasa and two other men, Piotra and Miroslav. Their detachment and others, under the command of General Draza Mihailovich, fought two enemies: the Nazi invaders and the homegrown Partisans, who sought to bring Yugoslavia under Communist rule. For now, here in this region of Ravna Gora, the Germans presented more of a threat than the Partisans. But Partisans were never far from Vasa's mind. They held his hometown of Velika, in Montenegro. He worried about what that meant for his father and for Aleksandra, the girl back home who'd won his heart.

One year younger than Vasa, the raven-haired beauty was the daughter of the largest landowner in the village. On Sundays after church, Vasa and Aleksandra would walk hand in hand to a hillside overlooking their village. She let him kiss her, even touch her breasts. But the intimacy went no further than that. She wanted to remain chaste so she could have a proper Serbian Orthodox wedding. He respected that wish; Aleksandra was worth waiting for.

But he would wait forever if her father had his way. Aleksandra had told Vasa of her tearful conversations with him.

"He is a good boy," her father had said, "but he has no money and few prospects. You must find someone who can support a family better."

*If I can win glory,* Vasa thought, *maybe I can change my prospects— and his mind.* Perhaps word of Vasa's exploits would reach his home village. It helped that his teammate Piotra was Aleksandra's cousin. But communication was difficult at best with the Partisans now in Velika.

Vasa's squad had received what was to him a new sort of mission. Not necessarily fighting the Germans—for now. Instead, the orders said to *find* the Germans. Learn where they are. What are they doing? How many? How heavily are they armed? If they discover you, by all means kill them. But try not to engage.

Reconnaissance in force, Nikolas called it.

Vasa liked the sound of that. There was so much more to soldiering than marching and shooting. And the new assignment, calling for more brains than brawn, helped keep Vasa's mind off his worries.

From overhead, Vasa heard the growl of engines. He looked up through the pines. At first, he saw only drifting clouds and patches of blue. Then, between the clouds, he spotted the American bombers. They flew so high, they appeared as mere toys. The machines moved in formation, a procession so stately that it put Vasa in mind of a church ceremony. Clouds obscured much of the formation, but Vasa counted nineteen aeroplanes.

The men in those machines were friends, Nikolas had told

him. If you ever encounter one, render him every courtesy. And meeting an American seemed increasingly likely. According to information from General Mihailovich himself, many Yanks had been shot down in Ravna Gora. The general hoped to gather them in one place and try to get them home. As their numbers grew, it was becoming harder and harder to keep them hidden from the Germans. To assure the fliers' safety, Mihailovich needed to know where the Germans were. That was the reason for Vasa's current mission.

Vasa, along with Nikolas, Miroslav, and Piotra, melted back into the forest. Now that they had seen fresh tire tracks and knew the enemy was operating in the area, they could focus their search more closely. They traveled through the woods, but kept within earshot of the road, so they would know if another vehicle passed.

Nikolas led the way. The team walked as quietly as they could. A carpet of ferns muffled their steps. Crickets strummed and birds chirped. The morning's sounds gave no further hint of war—no gunfire, no engines, no distant explosions. Vasa could almost imagine himself on a peacetime hunting expedition or nature hike.

He let his mind wander to thoughts of peace. What would he like to do after the war? Marry Aleksandra, to begin with. Perhaps start farming on his own. Save some money. Buy a cow, then a bull. Raise their calves in his father's pasture.

And learn a trade. His father said it was good for a farmer to have another skill. Vasa wanted to learn woodworking. Get a saw, a chisel, and some other tools and make a fine table for Aleksandra. Then build and sell furniture for all of Velika. Everyone needed chairs, tables, and beds.

Ahead, Nikolas stopped. He held out his arm, fingers spread. The team halted. Crouched low.

In front of them, the forest sloped downhill. Vasa could not see what lay in the little wooded valley, and he wondered what had alerted his team leader. He closed his eyes and listened hard. He thought he heard the babble of a brook. Yes, a stream probably ran through the vale down below. Perhaps enemy soldiers were filling their canteens.

And then he heard voices. Hard-edged words in German, which Vasa could not understand. Syllables like the scraping of a knife.

Nikolas motioned for his men to move forward. He gestured slowly, and Vasa took his meaning: move silently. Vasa gripped his Mauser, a weapon he'd taken from a dead German in an ambush a week ago. In addition to the Mauser, Vasa carried a big British Webley Revolver. The guerrillas made do with a motley assortment of whatever weapons they could scrounge. Vasa kneeled among the ferns with Piotra and Miroslav.

And there was the enemy. At least three of them. One man sat on his haunches, a cigarette between his fingers and a canteen between his knees. He placed the cigarette in his lips, nodded at something said by a comrade. Inhaled smoke, blew it out, and took a sip of water.

*I hold your fate in my hands,* Vasa thought. *I could send you to hell this instant.*

But he remembered his orders: observe and report.

*Note their weapons,* Vasa told himself. Two of the men carried Mausers, like the one across Vasa's thigh. The third had some sort of automatic rifle.

*What else here is important?* Their packs. The Germans had placed their knapsacks on the ground. Maybe they had taken a meal. The packs were not large. Perhaps that meant these soldiers were not on a long-range patrol. *They may have a camp nearby,* Vasa considered.

*Now what?* Vasa met his team leader's eyes. Nikolas held out his right hand, palm down. *Yes,* Vasa understood. *Now we do not move.* Safest simply to wait for them to go away.

Vasa's legs grew cramped, and his tendons burned. But he kept still, as instructed. The Germans continued talking and smoking, enjoying their rest. *Move on, you sons of whores,* Vasa thought. *Has Hitler granted you a holiday?*

After what felt like half a day, though it was probably less than an hour, the Germans finally picked up their gear. The enemy soldiers stomped through the woods with little concern for the noise they made. Perhaps they felt secure in their mastery of the region. Vasa would have loved to show them their error, to let fly a German bullet from a German rifle to fell a German invader. But he followed his orders and held his fire. The Nazis disappeared into the trees, and their footfalls grew fainter until they faded away.

Nikolas stared after them, gazed into the forest where they'd vanished. He pursed his lips like a man pondering a riddle. Vasa supposed his squad leader was trying to decide whether to follow the enemy. *Keep close behind them and try to learn more?* Vasa wondered. *Or hurry back to report what we already know?* War leaders of any rank had many hard decisions to make.

In a slow gesture, Nikolas crooked his middle and index fingers, beckoned the team forward.

*Very well,* Vasa thought. *We follow them.*

Vasa rose from his crouch. Felt the stiffness at the back of his knees from remaining motionless for so long. He reached down and massaged his right calf. His teammates stood as well, and they followed Nikolas down the slope, almost without making a sound. Only the occasional rustle of leaves marked the team's passage. A twig cracked under Vasa's boot, and he resolved to tread more lightly.

At the streambed where the Germans had stopped, the guerrillas scanned the ground. The Nazis had left nothing but footprints in a sandbar—no equipment or personal effects. The footprints led away from the stream and became invisible in the brush and fallen leaves. The team continued in the direction the Germans appeared to be heading.

Nikolas led on through the forest. The guerrillas lacked a proper map; in fact, part of their job involved *creating* a map. They needed to gather information about the local terrain, as well as the disposition of enemy forces. General Mihailovich, of course, knew Ravna Gora well. But he did not necessarily know every farm path and clearing. In the days ahead, the Chetniks would need that level of detail.

At the top of a wooded rise, the team came to a logging path. The path was little more than a tunnel through the vegetation. Two ruts, eroded nearly flat, defined the path. Grass and ferns grew down the middle. Nothing motorized had traveled this way for years. But the path did reveal a sign: A single German boot print pointed south. The team was still on the enemy's trail.

Nikolas held up two fingers. He pointed to the left side of the path, then the right. Vasa understood: Rather than simply blundering down the logging path and getting discovered by the Germans, the team would move alongside it—two men on one side and two on the other.

Miroslav and Piotra took the right side. They moved a hundred meters off the path, barely within sight of it through the trees. On the left side, Vasa followed Nikolas. He took a small measure of comfort knowing that the man in front of him carried the team's greatest firepower. Nikolas held his Thompson submachine gun at his waist, supported by a sling across his shoulder.

The men stalked as if hunting roebuck. From time to time, Vasa glanced to his right. Glimmers of movement assured him that he and Nikolas were keeping aligned with Miroslav and Piotra.

Vasa's concentration narrowed. Every cell of his being was focused on the forest ahead of him. From his limited exposure to combat, he knew the first side to spot the other usually won, the outcome decided in the first seconds. The rest of a small-unit firefight amounted to a bloody accounting of that decision.

With Vasa's attention directed so fixedly ahead, the noise behind him caught him off guard: a rustle of leaves, then the thumps of footfall.

In a single motion, Vasa whirled—and from a standing position, he spun to a low crouch on one knee. A drop of cold sweat trickled down his temple. *Surely, the enemy has seen me,* he thought. He imagined himself in the sights of a German infantryman.

He scanned the forest, expected a shot at any moment. He brought the Mauser to his shoulder, finger on the trigger.

The woods revealed nothing. The underbrush stood motion-

less. The oaks and birches threw shadows that might hide an entire platoon.

Then came another rustle. A flash of motion—not high, but
something low to the ground. Vasa looked for the curve of a helmet, the point of a bayonet, a sniper prone and aiming for the
kill.

Whatever made the noise blended perfectly with the trees. Vasa
almost wondered if he was encountering a *veela*, a mythical forest
nymph. The *veele*, as they were known in the plural, were female
and beautiful, with long, flowing locks. The old folk tales said the
*veele* could appear as wolves or hawks. In any form they took, they
could fly. When crossed, they could be very hostile to men. Con-
versely, they admired warriors, and they might offer help to a
hero proven in battle.

But Vasa's tormentor was no *veela*.

From behind the meter-wide trunk of an ancient oak, a wild
boar emerged. The animal's black eyes met Vasa's. Its yellow tusks
curved upward like miniature scimitars. Coarse hairs arched
along its back. The boar grunted, stamped its front hooves.

Vasa trained his rifle on the animal. He centered his sights on
the boar's head, but he did not press the trigger. A wild boar was
a dangerous creature, but not as dangerous as man. No sense firing a rifle and alerting the Germans, unless it was absolutely necessary.

The boar lowered its head. Swung its snout as if to slash with its
tusks.

And then it charged.

Starting from thirty meters away, the animal ran at Vasa. For
just an instant, Vasa wondered what to do. From early childhood,
he'd been taught to fear wild boars. Every instinct screamed for
him to put a bullet through the boar's brain.

But Vasa would not endanger his fellow fighters over a matter
of local wildlife. Instead of firing, he raised his Mauser like a me-
dieval war club. Brought the buttstock down hard on the boar's
head. The wood cracked into the creature's skull with such force
that it stung Vasa's hands.

The boar squealed. The animal dug its hooves into the ground at Vasa's feet, scrambled to regain its footing. Vasa swung the rifle and hit the boar again. The creature ran away into the brambles.

Vasa wiped his face with his sleeve. He looked over at Nikolas, who nodded in approval.

The forest stood silent once more.

And then from somewhere up along the logging path, gunfire exploded. Vasa dived for the ground, rib cage to the dirt. Like a storm of angry *veele* in high-speed flight, tracers cut through the trees.

# CHAPTER 7
## Wounds of War

*D*URING DREW'S FIRST FEW DAYS AT THE SAN PANCRAZIO AIR BASE, he learned—by official briefing and by unofficial rumor—several things. To begin with, this new Air Crew Rescue Unit that he'd joined wasn't just any regular part of the Fifteenth Air Force. The ACRU had ties to the Office of Strategic Services, a cloak-and-dagger agency tasked with all manner of secret missions. The OSS operated in the darkest corners—a world of deceit and disguise, spies and moles, turncoats and assassins. Its portfolio included bringing aid to resistance fighters and misery to German occupiers. The mysterious civilian who had first called for volunteers back at Bergstrom must have been an OSS officer, Drew surmised.

By answering that call, Drew had put himself within a chain of command that led to a figure who had already become legendary. The director of the OSS, William "Wild Bill" Donovan, had earned the Medal of Honor during the Great War. Word had it that when the French offered Donovan the *Croix de Guerre* for heroism under fire, he turned it down because the decoration was denied to a Jewish soldier who'd taken part in the same action. Eventually they both got the medal.

Drew felt honored to be attached to such a swashbuckling agency as the OSS, even if only as a glorified truck driver. He just hoped he could live up to its standards. He and his crew flew every day, practicing short-field takeoffs and landings. He understood he would fly some sort of rescue mission, but he knew few details. The intel officers said there were American fliers stuck on the ground in Yugoslavia. But the officers didn't know exactly where—or how many.

One morning, Drew checked the training schedule to find his sortie had been canceled for maintenance. That was strange; he knew of no maintenance problems on his C-47. Maybe the engineer, Montreux, had found something on a postflight inspection. With an unexpected day off, Drew collected his copilot, Torres, and his navigator, Chisholm. They signed out a jeep from the motor pool.

"Where are we going, boss?" Torres asked.

"Let's explore Brindisi," Drew said. "I got a feeling we won't have a lot of time off for touring while we're here."

"What about the enlisted guys?"

"They weren't in their tent. They must be working on the airplane."

Drew steered through the base's main gate and took a narrow two-lane road toward town. Beyond the vineyards and olive groves, a blue Adriatic stretched to the horizon. Seagulls glided on thermals rising from the ground, which reflected heat from the southern European sun. The sky opened cloudless and clear. Drew supposed that if he'd been flying his C-47 instead of driving a jeep, he could have seen for a hundred miles.

Despite the morning's tranquility, he couldn't get the P-38 crash out of his mind. Death could come so quickly and violently. And more than likely, it would hurt. If you died in combat, unless you were one of the lucky ones who got it quick, you had to pass through a portal of suffering to get to whatever awaited you in the afterlife.

Drew blinked. Shook his head as if trying to escape a swarm of gnats. The same fear had paralyzed him before.

"You all right?" Torres asked.

"Just thinking," Drew said. "I keep seeing that Lightning on fire."

"Yeah, me too. Awful thing."

Drew glanced over at his copilot. Torres came from a family of farmworkers. He'd grown up speaking both Spanish and English in the home. He'd started working in the fields before he started school. "They gave me a hoe before they gave me a pencil," Torres had said. First in his family to get any education beyond eighth grade. Now here he was: a pilot and a commissioned officer. Uncommon, but not unheard of. Drew knew of a handful of Hispanic pilots in the USAAF; he'd heard about one who'd become a fighter ace.

Torres gazed out to sea and held his hand in the wind as the jeep sped along. From time to time, he angled his palm as if changing a wing's angle of attack. He looked thoughtful, but not anxious. Like he took it all in stride. Chisholm, sitting in the backseat, leaned forward to take in the sights. "Brundisium," he said.

"Huh?" Torres said.

"That's what the Romans called this town," Chisholm said.

"Ah," Drew said. "Our navigator-philosopher."

In Brindisi, they found a bustle of activity. Horses pulled carts of vegetables and crates of fish. On the steps of a bakery, a little girl stroked a white cat. Women with kerchiefs over their heads strolled the streets, carrying baskets or buckets. Old men stood in doorways and smoked. Drew saw no young men at all, except those driving the military trucks that sputtered along the road to the port.

A few of the locals smiled or waved at Drew's jeep, with its white star on the hood. Others simply stared. Italy had only recently switched sides, and Drew wondered about the feelings of the townspeople he might encounter. The fighting had moved north, and life in Brindisi seemed almost . . . normal. Unlike England during Drew's previous tour, this region wasn't under bombardment by the Germans. Drew found himself surprised by the sense of calm in the town. But he knew he'd eventually have to fly into Nazi-occupied territory.

At the north end of the port, a causeway linked Brindisi to a pair of little islands. From the tip of one of the islands, a castle guarded the port. Drew had read about the Castello Alfonsino, which dated back to the 1400s. The stone ramparts rising above the water put him in mind of a stationary battleship. Drew parked the jeep and reached for the camera he'd brought with him. Snapped two shots with his Kodak Vigilant.

Drew and his crewmates spent the morning exploring the castle and the streets of town. From time to time, they encountered soldiers and sailors rushing about on whatever military errands had been assigned to them. The logistics that had brought the Allies this far boggled the mind, and Drew could only imagine the various roles these fellow servicemen might have played. He returned the salutes of enlisted men and offered salutes to superior officers.

At the corner of Via Pace Brindisina and Via Santa Maria Ausiliatrice, they found an open-air market. Vendors were selling fruit, vegetables, and even live chickens. It looked like this part of Italy, at least, was beginning to return to normal life. Drew had heard of terrible food shortages earlier in the war: Italian women prostituted themselves to feed their children. The columnist Ernie Pyle wrote of mobs fighting over crackers tossed by soldiers from the decks of LSTs. The black market drove up the price of staples by factors of ten or more. Drew felt glad to see things improving.

At the first booth, two mongrel dogs tussled and growled over a ham bone thrown away by a butcher. At another booth, an old man sold cappuccino—or at least a wartime approximation—made with milk heated over a wood-burning firepit. Aromas of woodsmoke and cinnamon wafted through the market.

Drew lacked Italian currency, but the old man seemed more than happy to get three American dimes. The man poured the cappuccino into three clay mugs; he had no paper cups to offer. He evidently expected his customers to drink the coffee there and return the mugs.

*"Grazie, grazie,"* the old man said. "America *molte bene."*

"Thank you, sir," Drew said. He spoke not a word of Italian. He took one of the mugs and passed the others to Torres and Chisholm.

Torres raised his cappuccino, took a sip, and said, "Looks like we're winning the war, at least from here."

"I just hope we live to see the end," Drew said. He tasted his cappuccino. It was weak, but better than the bitter coffee back in the San Pancrazio chow hall.

"'We'll see the end if we're meant to,'" Chisholm said.

"That's profound," Torres said.

"I wish I could say it's original," Chisholm said, "but it goes all the way back to the Stoics."

"The who?" Drew said.

"The Stoics. Like the Roman emperor Marcus Aurelius. We're in his old stomping grounds now."

The men strolled the marketplace. Drew snapped a few more photos with his Kodak, but he saw nothing he wanted to buy. One booth sold scarves that might have made a nice souvenir for a girlfriend. But Drew had no sweetheart back home. Ever since getting shipped home from England, he'd lacked the confidence to ask a woman out on a date. Occasionally he'd caught admiring glances from women; sometimes their eyes lingered on the silver wings on his uniform. *She thinks I'm some kind of war hero,* he often thought, *but she'll be gone as soon as she learns the truth.*

Around noon, Torres suggested lunch. In an alley off the marketplace, they found a sign that read: RISTORANTE. Drew pushed open the door and entered a dining room no bigger than the living room of a modest house. In fact, the decaying building appeared to have been a home at one time. Wine bottles lined a warped bookshelf. Worn timbers supported the ceiling. A fireplace dominated one corner, its stones now cold. Red-and-white-checkered cloths covered five tables. Something sizzled in the kitchen down the hall; Drew smelled onions and garlic.

Atop a small mahogany bar, a phonograph turned. To Drew's surprise, it played familiar music: The Andrews Sisters crooned

"Boogie Woogie Bugle Boy." *New music for a new clientele,* Drew supposed.

A middle-aged man greeted them. An apron covered his bulging paunch. Gray strands salted his black hair. He spoke passable English.

"Welcome, welcome," the man said. "Please have seat."

"Thank you," Torres said.

The fliers chose a table by the window. A crucifix and a vase of dried flowers lay on the sill.

"We have menus in English," the man said. He beamed as he spoke. He went to the bar and returned with three typewritten sheets.

Strikeovers and smudges marred the lettering. The pages had grown soft with grease stains. But Drew could still make out the simple offerings:

> *SasZZZ Sausages and Peppers*
> *Spaghetti*
> *MushrGGGoom Risotto*
> *Meats Pizza*
> *Bruschetta and Garlic on Bred*

Drew ordered the sausages and peppers. Torres and Chisholm went for the spaghetti.

"American cash okay?" Drew asked.

"We love American money," the man said. "Sometimes the Germans no pay. By the by, I am Antonio."

Antonio disappeared into the kitchen and barked orders in Italian. A few minutes later, he came back with two women behind him. One carried a tray of garlic bread. The other brought glasses of water.

"This is my daughter, Lucia," Antonio said, gesturing, "and my niece, Sienna."

Lucia flashed a broad smile as she placed the garlic bread on the table. Her brown curls stopped at her shoulders. Despite whatever privations the war had brought, she remained plump.

Sienna, on the other hand, was rail thin. She offered no expression as she set down the glasses. She wore a plain white cotton dress, buttoned to the throat. Her black hair hung to her waist. The angle of her nose and cheekbones gave her an almost chiseled look. Sienna regarded Drew with eyes black as ink. Something about her manner seemed familiar, and Drew made a strange connection: Those eyes reminded him of the thousand-yard stares of men who'd just climbed down from shot-up B-17s.

Drew tore a piece of garlic bread in half and nibbled on it while they waited for the main course. He watched Lucia and Sienna come and go as other customers entered the restaurant. Lucia chatted in rapid-fire Italian when locals came in, but Sienna never uttered a word. Her silent manner sent Drew's mind in a strange direction—thinking of beauty in bleakness. The way a gnarled tree on a cliff, a painting of a storm-tossed sea, or a swirl of autumn leaves could . . . calm you down. He shook his head, dismissed the thought.

Lucia returned to the kitchen and came back with three plates on a tray, the plates piled high and steaming. She placed spaghetti in front of Torres and Chisholm, and Drew slid the bread plate to make room for his sausages and peppers.

"Thanks," Drew said. For the sake of friendly relations with the locals, he asked, "Did you and Sienna grow up together here in Brindisi?"

Like her father, Lucia answered in accented but competent English. "No," she said. "I am from Brindisi. Sienna is from Ceccano."

"Sienna doesn't smile very much, does she?" Drew commented.

Lucia's demeanor changed in an instant. She sighed, wiped her hands on her apron. "Sienna is a sad girl," Lucia said. She turned and went back to the kitchen.

Drew forked a sausage link and took a bite. A blend of seasonings gave the meat a different taste from any breakfast sausage he'd eaten in the States. Torres picked up a knife and fork and began slicing through his spaghetti. He cut the noodles into short sections and mixed them with the sauce to form a kind of hash.

"What the hell are you doing?" Drew asked. "That's not how you eat spaghetti."

Torres grinned. "I could never get the hang of twirling it around a fork. My people don't eat a lot of spaghetti."

"You're going to cause an international incident."

When they finished eating, Sienna brought them their tab. She didn't look any of them in the face. She came close enough that Drew caught a whiff of soap scent from her hair. When he took the check from her, he noticed a jagged scar on her arm: The white scar tissue stood out from the downlike hair above her wrist. *Is that a war wound?* Drew wondered. *Flying glass from an air raid?*

"This one's on me," Drew said. The total came to three dollars. Drew opened his wallet and put five singles on the table.

"Thanks," Torres said.

"Too much," Sienna said, looking down at the table.

"For you and your cousin," he said. "The food was very good."

"Thank you."

Antonio waved when the aviators stood up. "Please come again, gentlemen," he said. "You pay, and you polite to my girls."

Drew left feeling he'd done his little share for relations with a new ally. If Antonio and his staff had been bullied by German troops, there was little wonder that a "please," a "thank you," and a two-dollar tip went a long way. And he realized he'd enjoyed this outing with his crew so much that at least for a couple of hours, he'd stopped worrying about the future and fretting about the past.

The afternoon grew hot during the drive back to San Pancrazio. Heat waves shimmered above the blacktop. The wind kicked up and whipped whitecaps across the harbor. As Drew drove through the main gate, he saw two C-47s in the traffic pattern. One glided along short final, and the other flew downwind.

Drew looked across the ramp, and a strange sight made him stop the jeep for a better look.

"What the hell?" Torres said.

Their engineer, Montreux, was driving a tug vehicle. A tow bar connected the tug to their C-47's tail wheel. Montreux was pulling the aircraft backward out of a hangar.

The whole airplane was painted black.

# CHAPTER 8
## Love of Country Leads Me

*F*INALLY BOGDONAVICH GOT A CHANCE TO SIT STILL AND REST. THE priest had found hiding places throughout his village for an ever-growing number of aviators. The men hid in cellars, haylofts, and attics. They seemed to come from all directions. Every day, Chetnik fighters brought them in twos and threes. One day, an intact crew of ten guys came in. The guerrillas seemed to be herding the fliers into whatever areas they judged safest. But to what end, Bogdonavich couldn't guess. More downed fliers meant more risk for the Chetniks and more mouths to feed for the villagers—who were poor enough already.

In a hayloft, Bogdonavich passed the time with Greenbaum and three enlisted men who'd just come in. Finding a crewmate alive and well stoked Bogdonavich's morale—for a while. But the navigator had no information about the rest of *Miss Caroline*'s crew. And after the joy of the initial reunion, Bogdonavich found his emotions crashing back to earth. He was still down in enemy territory, with no idea how he'd get home.

"I keep wishing I'd seen where the others came down," Greenbaum said.

"I wonder if HQ has any idea where we are," Bogdonavich said.

"Maybe they think we're all dead." From the hayloft floor, he picked up a length of straw. Regarded it for a moment, then crumpled it between his fingers.

One of the enlisted guys seemed to follow the conversation with interest. A young fellow, maybe twenty. He was a radio operator from the 459th Bomb Group. His jacket bore the group's official patch. It showed an armored fist clutching a red bomb, along with the motto *Ducit Amor Patriae*. Love of Country Leads Me. Bogdonavich liked that sentiment: to take motivation from what you love instead of what you hate.

"What's on your mind, Sergeant?" Bogdonavich asked.

"Oh, just thinking, sir," he said. Southern accent. "I know—dangerous habit."

Bogdonavich smiled. "Where are you from?"

"Birmingham, Alabama."

"You got a name?" Bogdonavich asked.

"Higgins. Carl Higgins."

Bogdonavich introduced himself and Greenbaum. Then he asked, "So, what were you thinking about? Anything in particular?"

"Well, sir, you said you were wondering if HQ knows we're here. So I was thinking maybe we can get a message to them."

"Sounds like you've got an idea."

"Those wild-looking dudes who found us had a first-aid kit and a fifty-cal they got out of a B-24. I think they scavenge stuff out of our wreckage all the time. If they can bring me a radio, or even parts of a radio, maybe I can rig something up."

Bogdonavich raised his eyebrows. The idea sounded far-fetched, at best. But it was the nearest thing to a plan he'd heard from anyone. Here was something they could *do*, an action they could take. Something other than just waiting to get rounded up by the enemy.

The fliers discussed the challenges involved in Sergeant Higgins's plan. They needed a transmitter, a receiver, a Morse key, and other components from a liaison radio set. A shorter-range command set would be useless. If they got lucky enough to find these things, or cobble them together from parts, they'd also need a power source. A battery from an airplane, or maybe a car battery, if they could find one. They'd need a way to recharge the battery, too. A liaison radio would run down a battery in no time.

Greenbaum shook his head. "We'd need about three miracles for this to work," he said. He lay back in the straw and stared up at the ceiling.

Higgins glared. "You got any better suggestions?"

"You talk to me," Greenbaum said, "you put a *sir* in there."

"Got any suggestions, *sir*?" The enlisted man's tone suggested anything but respect.

"Hey, hey," Bogdonavich said, "we can't afford this bickering. We got enough problems as it is."

After a long silence, Higgins talked about how he might wire up a radio set. Then the discussion turned to how the group might actually use it.

"We stay on the air too long," Higgins said, "and we give the Krauts a chance to home in on our location."

"Damn, we can't have that," Bogdonavich said. He imagined Stukas howling from the sky to blow away a barn turned radio shack. Or worse, SS or Gestapo goons torturing local Serbs for information.

"I guess we'd start with a short SOS," Higgins said.

That night, Bogdonavich and Higgins went to the church to find the priest. Incense hung in the air from the evening vespers, which had just ended. Kerosene lamps flickered along the walls and cast a yellow glow across the pews. The old clergyman stroked his beard and welcomed the Americans.

"Good evening, my sons," he said in Serbian. "I wish you had come earlier. Have you come to pray?"

"We have, Father," Bogdonavich said. "And we'd like to ask God for some specific things." He tried to explain the plan to assemble a radio set. Bogdonavich's Serbian was improving every day, but he still lacked the words for a technical explanation. He just said he needed "parts." And he asked if the priest could get word to Stefan and his men. "Maybe they know the location of some of our aeroplanes that have crash-landed," Bogdonavich added.

"*Vrlo dobar,*" the priest said. "Very good. Our heavenly Father helps those who help themselves. I will tell the men."

The next morning, Stefan and Gregor appeared—not on horseback this time, but in an old Opel truck. The vehicle wheezed its way to the barn where Bogdonavich and the other Americans had taken shelter. Bogdonavich was impressed that the Chetniks dedicated a motorized vehicle, however ancient, to the task. He knew they were hard up for resources.

"I didn't know if you would come," Bogdonavich said in Serbian. "We must ask for your help again." Bogdonavich wondered how much he could expect from his hosts. Everyone here had problems; everyone was in danger. Would the locals eventually decide to let the Americans fend for themselves?

"Father Milos sent for us," Stefan said. "If your radioman can make contact, that will be a very good thing." Stefan swept his hand toward the hills in the distance. "Here and in nearby villages," he said, "we are hiding at least one hundred fifty airmen that I know of."

Bogdonavich took a moment to let Stefan's words sink in. A rescue of that many men would require a major airlift operation. Multiple planes flying in and out, probably over days. The Germans could not possibly miss it. And in the unlikely event the aircraft made it this far, where would they land? Maybe Greenbaum was right; perhaps this was hopeless. Perhaps they were just going through the motions until the Nazis rolled in and mowed everybody down.

Finally Bogdonavich muttered, "A hundred fifty? That many?"

"Oh, yes. Some have been with us for many months. There may be even more. Some are hurt. Some are sick."

*And how would we gather up the sick and injured?* Bogdonavich thought. He almost changed his mind about trying to make a radio call. What was the point? Only because Stefan had made the effort to show up, Bogdonavich asked, "So, do you know where we might find a radio from one of our aeroplanes?"

"We believe so. We will take you there now. It is a long drive."

Bogdonavich climbed into the hayloft to rouse Higgins and the others.

"They think they have a radio," Bogdonavich explained. "Let's go."

Downstairs, Bogdonavich found Stefan speaking with three other guerrillas, who had just arrived on foot. Two carried Mausers, and one held an American M1 Garand.

"Are these men riding shotgun with us?" Bogdonavich asked. As soon as he said it, he wondered if the American slang made any sense in Serbian.

"I do not know this saying," Stefan said.

"Will they be guarding us on the road?"

Stefan nodded. "*Da.* In case we run into trouble."

The men piled into the vehicle. Gregor drove, and the man with the M1 rode in the passenger seat. Bogdonavich, Greenbaum, and Higgins climbed into the open truck bed with Stefan and the other two insurgents. Higgins's two crewmates stayed behind.

Gregor backed the Opel out of the barnyard. Black chickens squawked and flapped out of the way. The vehicle swayed across a ditch and sputtered onto the dirt road that constituted the village's one street. Bogdonavich clung to the wooden slats along the side of the truck bed. When the ride smoothed, he checked to make sure he had a round chambered in his .45.

"How far?" Bogdonavich asked.

"Three hours perhaps," Stefan answered. "A village called Pranjani."

The truck rumbled along dirt roads. Bogdonavich guessed the vehicle never got above thirty miles an hour. Fumes spewed from an exhaust pipe with holes rusted through it. Dust rose from the tires and irritated Bogdonavich's nose. But it felt good to be moving. At the same time, he knew a vehicle full of armed men became a target, and he felt exposed. A Messerschmitt could roll in at any moment and strafe them all to oblivion.

All during the drive, Stefan's men never spoke. They simply gazed across the hills and smoked. Their long silence reminded Bogdonavich of his father. Dad could go half a day without speaking, especially if he was angry. Bogdonavich wondered if his family had received a telegram saying he was missing in action. He wished he could let them know he was still alive. Alive and in the Old Country. Dad would certainly find that rich.

One of the Chetniks offered cigarettes to the Americans. Bogdonavich accepted. It was a short, hand-rolled cigarette, nothing like the Camels from back home. When he lit up, the rank fumes made him cough. Still, he nodded his thanks and smoked the cigarette down to his thumb and forefinger. Then he stubbed out the butt and flicked it away.

After about an hour, the truck slowed. Bogdonavich craned his neck to check out his surroundings. He saw not a living village— but the remains of one. Fire-stained stones marked the foundation of a home or barn, burned away. A charred chimney stood as a household's gravestone. The limbs of blackened, dead trees clawed the sky. A horse's skeleton lay dry and bleached by the roadside. The ribs reminded Bogdonavich of the timbers of a ship, run aground and long rotted. Bogdonavich smelled no smoke, no remnants of fire. Whatever happened here had taken place some time ago.

"Did the Germans bomb here?" he asked in Serbian.

"No," Stefan said. "Worse."

Stefan explained that about a year ago, in a village several miles from this one, a guerrilla team ambushed a German vehicle. The attack killed four *Wehrmacht* soldiers, including an officer. Bogdonavich thought immediately about Gregor's story of how the Nazis executed one hundred Serbs for every German killed.

"In that village," Stefan said, "there were not four hundred Serbs, so the Germans came here, too."

*No wonder these guys fight so hard,* Bogdonavich thought.

The truck rolled on for another hour. The next time it stopped, there was no village. Just a plank bridge across a stream, and a command post that amounted to little but an A-frame tent, open at both ends. To the left, a forest bordered the road. To the right, a barley field stretched to distant hills. The four Chetniks at the command post seemed to expect the truck. They called to Stefan by name.

"Stefan, you old sinner," one of the insurgents said. "I am surprised the Nazis haven't killed you by now."

Stefan climbed down from the truck and embraced the man in a bear hug. "Hah," he said, "so am I." Bogdonavich and the rest of the men dismounted.

"Your American friends must eat with us. We have little, but what is ours is theirs."

*"Hvala vam,"* Bogdonavich said, thanking them.

"And he speaks Serbian?" the command post leader said. To the extent that these men had ranks, Bogdonavich guessed him a senior NCO.

"Some," Bogdonavich said. "My father came from here."

"Then you are a son of these hills," the man said.

The travelers walked into the woods to relieve themselves, then sat down on the ground for lunch. The men at the checkpoint produced the usual fare of bread and cheese. One of the guerrillas offered dried pork strips that tasted vaguely like bacon. While Bogdonavich, Greenbaum, and Higgins ate, Stefan went inside the tent. In the tent, a field telephone—a model Bogdonavich did not recognize—rested on a table. Stefan lifted the handset with his left hand. With his right hand, minus the index finger, Stefan turned the crank.

"We are an hour away," Stefan said. "Is the road safe?" He listened for a moment and said, "Very good."

*So that's why we stopped,* Bogdonavich thought. *To make sure the Chetniks still hold the roads ahead. Everything these guys do amounts to a calculated risk.*

"Too bad we can't call HQ on that thing," Greenbaum said.

"I'm sure it doesn't connect to anything but another phone like in a tent somewhere," Higgins said.

The men passed around a canteen to wash down lunch, then climbed back into the truck. The sky remained clear, and Bogdonavich kept scanning for German fighters just as he would have done in a B-24. None appeared. He hoped an enemy pilot hunting for targets of opportunity would look for a column of trucks instead of a single vehicle.

Stefan's time estimate proved accurate. After another hour of rattling along dirt roads, the Opel pulled into a village square. The place looked like every other farming community Bogdonavich had seen in Serbia, only a little bigger. The same homes with thatch or tile roofs, the same barns and stables—just a few more of them. Ducks and chickens roamed free. Cattle lowed from a pasture downhill. A metallic banging sounded from one of the outbuildings. A burning scent drifted in the air. Bogdonavich glanced toward the noise and saw a blacksmith at his forge.

As the men dismounted, Stefan said, "This is Pranjani." It was the only village he'd bothered to name. Bogdonavich supposed the place served as some kind of hub for the Chetniks, especially if this was where they cached gear and supplies.

Stefan led Bogdonavich, Greenbaum, and Higgins to the blacksmith's shop. Gregor and the other guerrillas drifted into the village, perhaps to visit friends.

"I see you have brought us more Americans," the blacksmith said. He put down his hammer. Picked up a towel and wiped sweat from his face and beard. Coals glowed in the forge. A red-hot metal bar lay across an anvil. Bogdonavich couldn't tell what the man was working on. It sure as hell wasn't horseshoes.

"I have, indeed," Stefan said.

"Very good," the blacksmith said. "There are forty of them in our stables and cellars."

*Forty more?* Bogdonavich considered. *In this village alone?* The greater the numbers, the more impossible the rescue. Bogdonavich thought of a possible parallel to their situation—one that suggested little but despair. He had read the awful dispatches from the Pacific, of the men left to their fates on the Bataan Peninsula. Captivity by the Japanese. Rumors of a death march. Starvation and torture. No one had heard from those American and Filipino soldiers for more than two years. Would the Germans treat a large number of prisoners any differently?

Stefan made introductions. In the midst of dark thoughts, Bogdonavich had to force himself to listen, to pay attention. The blacksmith's name was Vlado.

"These fliers want to contact their bases," Stefan said. "I think I saw a radio back there a few weeks ago." Stefan pointed to a room at the rear of the blacksmith's shop.

"*Da,*" Vlado said. He motioned for the men to follow him.

Vlado pulled on a metal hasp bolted to a wooden door. He opened the door to reveal a supply room piled high with gear: ammunition boxes stacked to the ceiling, crates of field rations, boots and coats. Mausers, Enfields, and Springfields. And a radio marked: SIGNAL CORPS, U.S. ARMY. RADIO RECEIVER BC-348.

"Jackpot," Higgins said. He bent down to examine the receiver. Turned it over, inspected the tubes. "I don't see any obvious damage," he said. "This is great." But then he looked around and said, "Where's the rest of it?"

"What do you mean, 'Where's the rest of it?'" Greenbaum asked.

"The transmitter," Higgins said. "This is a receiver. I need a transmitter, too. And some other components that go with it."

Bogdonavich cursed under his breath. A cruel fortune to find a perfectly intact receiver—What were the chances of that?—and then to find it entirely useless without the rest of the gear. With effort, he tried to hide his disappointment.

"It was very good of you to save this radio," Bogdonavich said in Serbian. "But to reach our base, we also need . . ." He struggled for the Serbian word for "transmitter." Finally he said, "We need another part from an aeroplane."

Stefan folded his arms and nodded. He seemed to take the set-back in stride. *That's good,* Bogdonavich thought. *These guys are used to problems.*

Vlado and Stefan conferred in Serbian, some of it too quick for Bogdonavich to follow. Vlado shrugged. Stefan disappeared and came back with Gregor. Bogdonavich caught snatches of the conversations: "It was on Radovan's farm." "No, that one burned up." "Yes, the one that came down the year before." "Does he know where it is?"

Finally Stefan told Bogdonavich, "We know the location of a downed aeroplane that did not burn. But it is a long drive and walk from here. There is no guarantee this aeroplane will contain what you need."

Bogdonavich translated for Higgins and Greenbaum, then asked, "What do you think?"

"This ain't a Sunday drive," Greenbaum said. "If we keep roaming around, we're just begging to get captured."

The same thought had occurred to Bogdonavich. But he reminded himself to act like an officer, to try to keep up morale. Nothing better for morale than a project, a goal.

"I think we gotta try," Bogdonavich said.

"We've come this far," Higgins said. Greenbaum folded his arms and nodded.

Bogdonavich turned to the guerrillas. "We will take the risk," he said in Serbian, "and we appreciate your efforts. One of my men is a radio operator. He will know the gear he needs."

"I might need some tools to get the transmitter loose," Higgins said. He began looking around the supply shed. He found a USAAF mechanic's tool pouch made of canvas. Rust-colored stains covered much of the pouch. Old bloodstains, no doubt. Higgins opened the pouch and found a set of wrenches, an adjustable wrench, a roll of safety wire, a folding knife, a socket wrench set, and regular and Phillips screwdrivers.

"Is that what you need?" Bogdonavich asked.

"This oughtta do it," Higgins said.

Bogdonavich asked if they could take the tool pouch. "Anything we have is yours," Stefan answered.

*"Hvala vam."*

Just as Stefan warned, the trip to the crashed bomber took the rest of the day and continued into the night. The men made the last part of the journey on foot because the road ended. By the light of oil lanterns and flashlights, they crossed a wheat field and climbed a hillside forest. A guerrilla team walked point several hundred yards ahead of the Americans, just in case they flushed German troops. The men encountered no resistance.

Bogdonavich considered the absence of enemy forces: The Krauts couldn't be everywhere. If the Germans wanted to keep Yugoslavia under heel, it probably made sense for them to garrison most of their forces in the cities and larger towns. The very remoteness of Ravna Gora gave the downed fliers some protection and freedom of movement.

In a glade surrounded by evergreens, the team arrived at a place where a B-17 Flying Fortress had come to grief. In darkness broken only by flashlight beams and lantern light, Bogdonavich tried to assess the plane's condition. Half the left wing had either been shot off or had shorn away during the crash landing. The Fort lay on its belly with the landing gear retracted. The propellers on the right wing must have been turning when the aircraft touched down: The blades had bent backward into the shape of scythes. Cannon fire had blasted holes in the fuselage. The Plexiglas nose bubble had been smashed. Bogdonavich wondered whether it broke on landing or got blown away in flight. *If it got blasted away,* he thought, *what happened to the bombardier?*

"Fucking Krauts," Higgins whispered.

Bogdonavich exchanged glances with Higgins and Greenbaum. He felt as if they were violating a war grave, trespassing in a cemetery. But if there was a good radio in there, they needed it. The original crew sure as hell couldn't use it anymore.

"We found two men dead inside," Stefan said.

"I hate to see this," Greenbaum said.

"Yeah, me too," Bogdonavich said. "But the important thing is that some of it looks fairly intact. Maybe the comm gear still works."

"I'll go have a look at the radio room," Higgins said.

"Good man," Bogdonavich said.

Bogdonavich followed Higgins through the open waist door. They picked their way through torn wiring and expended shell casings. In the radio room, Higgins kneeled and played a flashlight across the knobs and switches of rack-mounted equipment.

"Looks like the shock mounts did their job," Higgins said. "Nothing looks busted up. Here's what I need." He shone his light on a unit labeled: RADIO TRANSMITTER BC-375. "Cabinet's still in one piece. I won't know if it works until we can power it up." Higgins moved the light to another part of the radio rack. "There's the dynamotor and the antenna tuning unit. We'll need all that, too."

"I'll go check the batteries," Bogdonavich said.

A few minutes later, Gregor held a lantern while Bogdonavich opened a compartment on top of the right wing. The batteries appeared undamaged, though there was no way to tell whether they still held power. With a wrench from Higgins's tool pouch, Bogdonavich loosened cables from the battery terminals. He pulled out two of the heavy batteries and handed them down to Gregor.

When Bogdonavich went back inside the aircraft, he found Higgins lying on his back with a screwdriver in his mouth. The radio operator was loosening connectors on the back of the transmitter unit. Greenbaum held a flashlight for him.

"Almost done," Higgins said. "This stuff's gonna get heavy as hell when we tote it back to the truck."

"Tell me about it," Bogdonavich said. Just the batteries weighed about twenty-five pounds apiece.

Higgins slid the transmitter out of the rack. Groaned as he set it on the floor. He looked around for a minute and collected a headset, a Morse key, and a spool of antenna wire from the radio compartment table.

Stefan and Gregor helped them place the gear into canvas sacks. Gregor slung a sack containing the batteries over his shoulder as easily as if it were full of cotton. When Bogdonavich tried to hoist the transmitter, he nearly yanked his arm out of joint. Steadied himself under his burden, and blew a droplet of sweat from the end of his nose.

"All right," Bogdonavich said. "Let's get out of here before the Krauts find us."

The men got back to Pranjani after midnight and immediately started working on the radio. Higgins put the system together in Vlado's blacksmith shop, and he wired it to one of the batteries. The Chetniks scrounged a gasoline-powered generator, which brought the battery back up to full charge.

When the tubes inside the receiver and transmitter began to glow, the men cheered.

With a smile spreading across his face, Higgins looked over at Bogdonavich. "What do you want me to send, sir?" he asked.

Bogdonavich had already prepared the short and simple message. Higgins could send it out by Morse code in just a few seconds. Less time, more than likely, than the Germans would need to get a fix on the source. Bogdonavich handed a slip of paper to the radio operator: *SOS . . . ONE HUNDRED FIFTY American crew waiting for rescue. Some sick and wounded. Call back. SOS . . . SOS . . .*

Higgins tapped out the message with his key. The men waited for an answer. Five minutes passed with no reply. Then ten minutes. Bogdonavich pointed and twirled his index finger, and Higgins tapped out the message again.

They waited another twenty minutes, and still they received no reply.

The men sat in silence, listening to the radio's unbroken hum. The electric odor of warm tubes joined the burned-metal smell of the blacksmith's shop. As the minutes passed without a callback, the mood darkened.

"Answer, you sons of bitches," Higgins hissed. He held a pencil stub, sharpened with a pocketknife, ready to write down the coded response. No response came. When he slammed the pencil down onto the table, the lead point broke off.

*Can anyone hear us?* Bogdonavich wondered. *Is anyone even looking for us?*

# CHAPTER 9
# Vasa the Wolf

*P*IOTRA CLASPED VASA'S HAND WITH A VISELIKE GRIP. VASA WALKED alongside the improvised stretcher that Nikolas and Miroslav were using to carry Piotra, and Vasa tried to comfort his wounded friend. During the firefight with the German patrol, a bullet had torn through Piotra's thigh. No one else had gotten hit; Nikolas said things could have gone much worse.

But to Vasa, they were bad enough. Piotra clenched his jaw in agony. Sweat beaded on his face. His skin had taken on an unhealthy paleness, like that of a cow's tongue. Blood kept soaking through the bandages on his leg. The team wanted to get him to Pranjani in hopes of finding a nurse or a medic—anyone who might help save him. On the stretcher, fashioned from a blanket and two tree limbs, Piotra called out.

"Tell my father I fought hard," he said. Piotra's voice trembled, and he shivered in the summer heat. Vasa knew little of medicine, but he suspected Piotra's wound was infected.

"You will tell him yourself, my friend," Vasa said.

Piotra appeared to shake his head. Or perhaps that was just his shivering. Seeing him suffer like that tore at Vasa's heart. He didn't want to see anyone in pain, but especially not Piotra, cousin to Aleksandra. Her heart would break, too, to see him like this. If he died, she'd be inconsolable.

Over and over, Vasa replayed the gun battle in his head. *Could I have done anything differently?* he wondered. *Is Piotra's wound my fault?* Nikolas had assured him he'd done nothing wrong.

"If anything, it is my fault," Nikolas had told him. "I chose to follow the Germans."

Still, Vasa kept reliving the moments of terror: During the firefight, he lay on the ground with his chest pounding, rounds scorching over his head. Nikolas crawled to take cover behind a boulder. When the enemy fire paused, Nikolas rose from behind the rock to unleash a torrent from his submachine gun. Empty brass rattled from the breech.

In that instant, Vasa shook off the fear that had frozen him. He scrabbled on his hands and knees. Peeked over a slight rise to see where Nikolas was aiming. Glimpsed a German helmet.

He aimed his Mauser and fired. Worked the bolt, fired again.

A round struck the boulder shielding Nikolas. The bullet fragmented. A shard of hot lead stung Vasa's cheek. This did not make him frightened. It enraged him. He fired once more. Racked the bolt. He fired until he emptied his rifle. Rolled behind the boulder. Reloaded and fired some more. In his fury, he uttered a wordless cry, more growl than speech.

Finally the Germans fled. Nikolas dropped one of them; Vasa saw the man fall. Vasa thought he hit one, too, but he couldn't be sure. Piotra's scream turned their attention away from the retreating Nazis.

They found Piotra bleeding. In his pain, he clawed at the earth. The wound pulsed gouts of blood, and the bullet appeared to have broken the bone. The team had only meager first-aid supplies—little but bandages and a tourniquet to control bleeding, and nothing to control pain.

Piotra bore the agony like a warrior. He stopped his screams by gritting his teeth.

Now, as the team carried him through the woods, Piotra breathed hard through his nose. Each step seemed to worsen his suffering. At this rate, they would never get him to help in time.

"If we can get him to a highway," Nikolas said, "maybe someone will come along with a truck or a horse cart."

Eventually they came to an unpaved road. The men shuffled along the graveled pathway. But nothing else moved along the road for an hour, and Vasa began to wonder if they must carry Piotra all the way to Pranjani.

"Leave me here, brothers," Piotra said. "Leave me here with a weapon, and I will finish this in my own way."

"No," Nikolas said. He looked down the road as if he could will a vehicle into existence. The sun beat down and sent heat waves shimmering up from the gravel.

At last, a gray mare clopped along the path. A boy a few years younger than Vasa led the animal, and she pulled a wagon of milk jugs. Nikolas stopped the boy and explained the situation. Without a word, the boy climbed into the cart and slid the jugs to make a place for Piotra. Late that afternoon, they arrived in Pranjani.

The village bustled with activity. Nikolas and Miroslav ran house to house, asking after help for Piotra. Vasa stayed with Piotra and watched the comings and goings. Three tall men in strange clothing came out of a barn. They talked in a language Vasa could not understand. Surely, these were some of the American aviators Vasa had heard so much about.

Nikolas and Miroslav came back with a young woman. She wore a peasant dress, and a kerchief covered her hair. The woman examined Piotra as he lay in the wagon. Placed a hand on his forehead.

"He is burning up," she said.

"Is she a nurse?" Vasa whispered to Nikolas.

"This is Katarina," Nikolas said. "She has not gone to nurse school, if that is what you mean. But she has worked for a doctor."

With a pair of scissors, Katarina sliced open the bandages on Piotra's wound. She grimaced as she worked. The skin around the wound was turning purple and black.

"He needs a surgeon," she said. "Help me get him inside. I need to change his dressing."

Nikolas and Miroslav lifted Piotra from the wagon. He groaned as they picked him up, and he left behind a smear of blood, half dried and sticky, on the slats of the wagon. They carried him to one of the houses. A dog ran alongside, barking. Hens scattered out of their way. Vasa started to follow them, but he paused when the Americans came over to him.

Two of the Yanks wore one-piece flying suits and heavy boots. The third wore trousers and a shirt with pocket flaps. Over one of the flaps was some sort of pin—a silver trinket that looked like a pair of wings. The man carried a leather jacket slung over his shoulder.

The fliers spoke among themselves in their language. English had some of the same hard edges as German, though the words sounded less brittle. To Vasa's wonderment, the man with the jacket spoke to him in Serbian.

"Is your friend hurt badly?" the man asked. He spoke with a funny accent, but Vasa had no trouble understanding him.

"He is shot in the leg," Vasa said. "A bad wound."

"I am sorry," the man said.

"How do you know my language?"

"My father came from here. I grew up in America, but he made me learn his native tongue."

This, Vasa could hardly process. An American flier speaking Serbian? He would have been less surprised if a *veela* had appeared before him and offered to grant wishes.

"I am—I am called Vasa," Vasa stammered.

"And I am called William," the man said. "William Bogdonavich."

The first name sounded strange, but Vasa knew the family name. A common one in Yugoslavia. He remembered his instructions regarding these aviators: You should extend every courtesy.

"We thank you for helping us, sir," Vasa said.

"It is I who must thank you," William Bogdonavich said. "Your people have protected me."

Nikolas and Miroslav emerged from the house and joined Vasa as he spoke with Bogdonavich. Nikolas furrowed his brow in confusion.

"This man speaks Serbian," Vasa said. "But he is American."

Nikolas continued to look puzzled for a moment, then snapped a salute.

"Salute him, Vasa," Nikolas said. "He is an officer."

Vasa saluted, then said, "Forgive me. I did not realize."

Bogdonavich's return salute looked more like a dismissive wave than a military greeting. "That's not necessary," he said. "We are all friends here. How is your wounded comrade?"

Nikolas shook his head. "Our nurse says he needs medicine, which she does not have."

"So you need medical supplies?" Bogdonavich asked.

"More than anything."

Nikolas introduced himself and Miroslav. Then he said, "I see you have already met young Vasa."

"I have," Bogdonavich said. He looked at Vasa and said, "How old are you?"

"Seventeen, sir."

"Though his name is Vasa," Nikolas said, "we should call him *vuk*. The wolf. When he fights the Germans, he does not cry like a baby. He growls like a wolf."

Bogdonavich laughed. "Very good, there, *vuk*," he said. "Vasa the Wolf."

Vasa beamed.

Nikolas decided the detachment would remain in Pranjani at least overnight. They would await further orders, replenish their ammunition, and see if Piotra improved. In a supply room behind a blacksmith's shop, Vasa collected several clips of 8mm rounds for his Mauser. He hoped also to find a new pair of boots. A hole had worn through the toe of his right boot, and his foot got soaked whenever he crossed a stream. But none of the five pairs of boots in the supply room fit his large feet.

In a corner of the room, William Bogdonavich and two other

Americans gathered around some sort of radio. They spoke in English, so Vasa understood none of their conversation. But they did not sound happy. One of the men tapped at a sending key. Vasa had never seen such gear, but he knew of radio, telephones, and telegraph. He knew commanders communicated with these things.

Bogdonavich waved his hands in the air in obvious frustration. Perhaps the Americans could not reach whomever they wanted to call. Or perhaps they had, and they did not like what they heard. Even if Vasa had understood English, he would not have understood the code of beeps they were sending on the radio.

In the evening, the Chetniks and the aviators feasted on mutton stew. Local women brought pots of it from their homes. They laid out a spread on tables set up outside. Vasa was surprised to see so many of the Americans; he counted forty. They came out of cellars and stables. They talked in that easy way of theirs, and they laughed often.

And some were so tall. A few stood a head higher than Vasa.

He could tell they were talking about him when Bogdonavich pointed in his direction. Amid a tumble of English words, Vasa recognized one in Serbian, *vuk*. Bogdonavich was telling his friends of Vasa's new nickname, Vasa the Wolf. One of the Americans grinned at him and made a growling noise. Another nodded approvingly and made a strange thumbs-up gesture. Vasa saw they were not mocking him. They were respecting him. He liked these men immediately.

At sunset, the horizon glowed red behind the hills. The sight reminded Vasa of the iron bars in the blacksmith's forge near the supply room. Nikolas brought Vasa a rare treat: a letter from home. In Chetnik camps, mail was infrequent at best. The letter was dated from weeks ago, before the Partisans took over Velika. Vasa wished he knew whether everyone was still safe, but this was better than nothing.

He tore open the letter. His heart leaped when he recognized Aleksandra's handwriting. But it shattered when he read the words:

*My dearest Vasa,*

*This must be my last letter to you. My father says I may not write to you anymore.*

*He says I must marry someone more suitable, someone who can give me a comfortable life. I tell him he does not know you as I do, but it is no use. And I cannot go against the wishes of my family.*

*I know this will hurt you, and I hope you can forgive me.*

*Above all, be careful. Someday you will make a fine husband for some lucky girl. I only wish it could be me. Come home safely to your family.*

*With all my love,*

*Aleksandra*

Vasa crumpled the page. He held it tight in his fist as the last rays of sunset purpled and died into darkness.

# CHAPTER 10
## Separation of Fears

*P*IGEONS FLUTTERED IN THE HANGAR'S RAFTERS. TIN SIDING POPPED under the heat of the afternoon sun. Airmen waited in rows of folding chairs for a classified briefing to begin. In the third row, Drew sat between his copilot, Torres, and his engineer, Montreux. Chisholm, his navigator, and Calvert, his radio operator, sat in the same row. Military police guarded closed doors. Everyone sweated in the stifling Italian air.

Next to the folding chairs, a Lightning sat unattended. Drip pans caught oil underneath its left engine. The right engine was missing. The mechanics had been shooed away for an hour. They had no need to know what Drew and the other fliers were about to hear.

At the back of the hangar, an MP opened a door. "Room, ten-hut!" he called.

Drew and the other fliers stood. A stocky, bearded man entered, carrying a manila folder. On his shoulders, the man wore the bars of an army captain. A silver parachutist's badge gleamed above his left breast pocket. Smoke curled from a pipe held between his teeth. Drew knew immediately this was no ordinary captain. *An army officer with a beard?*

The man removed the pipe from his mouth and said, "As you were, gentlemen." Drew and the others sat down. The strange, bearded captain dropped the folder on an empty chair in the front row. He took a puff from his pipe, then rolled right into his presentation without benefit of notes.

"This briefing is classified," the man said. "My name is Captain George Marich, and I am with the Office of Strategic Services. As you've probably gathered, our mission is to recover your fellow flyboys who are on the ground in Yugoslavia. We have done this before, in dribs and drabs. We brought out a group of fliers back in May. But we have reason to believe there are a lot more. The problem is finding out how many, and exactly where they are."

Marich explained how he'd been in contact with the leader of Yugoslavia's Chetnik guerrillas, General Draza Mihailovich. Drew had a vague memory of seeing that name in the news. Marich said Mihailovich knew of many downed fliers awaiting rescue, and guerrilla forces were working to locate them.

"We've had one unconfirmed report there are as many as one hundred fifty," Marich said. "That came from a source over the radio which has not yet been authenticated."

A murmur swept the room. When Marich called for questions, Drew raised his hand.

"Sir," Drew said, "what will it take to get things firmed up with actionable intelligence?"

Marich smiled, puffed from his pipe. He held the pipe in his hand for a moment before he spoke.

"Well, Lieutenant," Marich said. "You know that old saying 'If you want anything done right, you gotta do it yourself?' I'm going back into Yugoslavia to have a look for myself. Once we nail down a few more details, I'll drop into the area with a small team. One of you lucky crews will get to take me there."

Torres nudged Drew. "I think you just volunteered us," Torres whispered. He smiled as he spoke, apparently more intrigued than frightened.

Drew was interested, too. All along, he'd been told little except this was *not* a personnel drop mission. Or at least not a mass troop drop like the Normandy invasion. Of course, any operation to pick up downed fliers would involve an air-land mission to a clandestine field. But now it appeared the job would also involve inserting a commando team by parachute.

"Oh, yeah," Marich said, "that brings me to another point. Our sources tell us the German High Command has issued something they call the *Kommandobefehl.* The Commando Order. In a nutshell, it means any special operations teams, any saboteurs, any parachutists, are not to be treated as lawful prisoners of war. They are to be summarily executed. Or, worse, turned over to the Gestapo."

Marich paused to let his words sink in. This time, no whispers rose. The room remained dead silent.

"So, what does this mean?" the captain asked. "Well, it means if I'm caught, I've had it. I've made my peace with that. But it also means the Germans might consider anyone associated with this mission to be a commando. If you get forced down, don't expect the Krauts to make fine distinctions between your job and mine. If any man wants to back out, tell me now. You can go back to your old unit. Nothing will be held against you."

Suddenly Drew felt cold. In the heat, he'd sweated wet patches onto his gabardine shirt. Now the damp cloth chilled him. But he did not speak or put up his hand. No one else did, either.

Marich crossed his arms and nodded. "Very good," he said. "Any more questions?"

A pilot in the front row raised his hand, and Marich pointed to him.

"Given what you've just told us," the pilot said, "do you have any advice on what we should do if captured?"

Again Marich puffed on his pipe, considered his words. Finally he unbuttoned a pocket flap and pulled out a tiny object.

"I can't tell you what to do in that event," the captain said. "We all know the rules about name, rank, and serial number." He held up the object between his thumb and forefinger. "This is what we call an L-pill. *L* stands for lethal. It's cyanide. If you want to carry these, we can get them for you."

* * *

After the briefing, crews huddled together. They spoke in hushed tones about what they'd just heard. Drew fought to control his own anxieties. Reminded himself he was supposed to be an aircraft commander. The leader of his crew.

"Are you guys still okay with this?" he asked.

"Sir," Montreux said, "I been up to my ass in alligators since the day I was born. This ain't no different."

Drew nodded. "You're an inspiration, Jimmy."

"I just think about the boys on the ground in Yugoslavia," Torres said. "If our positions were switched, they'd do it for us. I don't think they'd care about some *Kommandosauerkrautmitbratwurst* order."

Drew laughed at Torres's pidgin German. "I suppose not," he said. But his laughter was forced, a matter of courtesy rather than mirth.

The prospect of combat was bad enough. Any man who said he wasn't afraid was a liar or a fool. Now, adding to all those fears, came talk of interrogation, torture, and suicide pills.

*Do I have the guts for this?* Drew asked himself. *Does anybody, really?*

Drew decided to take his crew out for dinner. He thought they needed a break from the events weighing on their shoulders. He needed a break, himself. This time, Montreux came with Drew and Torres. The navigator and radio operator stayed behind. Something about a special briefing on new navigational radios being installed in the airplane.

"Lieutenant Torres tells me y'all found a nice place," Montreux said as they rode in the jeep.

"We did," Drew said. "It ain't exactly the Ritz. But the food is good and we like the people who run it. Just remember—no talk about business when we're out in public."

"Got it," Montreux said.

Brindisi hummed with the usual activity. Military trucks shared the streets with horse carts. Troops strolled in groups of three and four. Children played on cobblestone walks. A pair of P-51 Mustangs knifed over the town and set up for final approach at San Pancrazio.

At the restaurant, Lucia invited the men to sit. Drew chose the same table by the window where he, Torres, and Chisholm had dined before. Three British officers sat at another table across the room. Sienna, unsmiling as usual, brought the typewritten menus. On the bar, the phonograph spun out "Praise the Lord and Pass the Ammunition" by Kay Kyser. The dining room smelled of sizzling sausages.

"Where's your uncle tonight?" Drew asked Sienna.

"Antonio is away. He will return tomorrow."

Drew ordered the spaghetti, and Torres and Montreux ordered the "Meats Pizza." Drew also asked for a bottle of Brunello. Sienna brought three glasses, and Lucia poured the wine.

While the aviators waited for their food, three men in civilian clothes entered the restaurant. Without waiting to be seated, they took a table between Drew's table and the British officers.

Lucia frowned, but brought them menus—not the typewritten English sheets, but larger menus printed in Italian on card stock. The men talked among themselves in Italian.

They ordered wine, a bottle apiece. Drew noticed that when Lucia and Sienna brought the bottles and glasses, they did not pour the wine, and they did not speak to the men. One of the men sloshed wine into his glass and spilled some on the table. He took a long drink that drained half the glass, then poured more. The other men began drinking as well. They kept up their conversation, louder now, and they cut cold glances at the Americans and at the Brits.

By the time the food arrived at Drew's table, the Italians were talking so loudly that any other conversation in the restaurant became impossible. Drew and his crewmates ate and sipped their wine. He had hoped for a relaxing dinner with his copilot and engineer, and he felt irritated that the noise made that impossible.

One of the Italians appeared drunker than his two friends. He spoke more loudly, and he began to gesture with his arms. From their conversation, Drew gathered that the man's name was Enzo. Enzo wore a flannel shirt and vest, with baggy trousers. He sported a thick, dark mustache, with beard stubble over the rest of his face. His hobnail boots could have been military-issued. His friends wore the same boots.

"Could you chaps please hold it down?" one of the Brits asked.

The Italians ignored him.

A few minutes later, another of the Brits said something to the Italians in their own language. Enzo made a dismissive gesture and spat words that sounded like a curse.

"What a bunch of *pendejos*," Torres said.

"Didn't their mamas teach them manners?" Montreux said.

Drew finished his spaghetti. He was almost ready to pay up and leave when Enzo shouted, *"Vino!"*

Sienna brought a bottle to the Italians' table. Enzo pulled the bottle from her hands and uttered rapid-fire words at her. She turned her back to him and escaped toward Drew's table.

"What's his problem?" Drew asked her.

"They were policemen under Mussolini," Sienna said, looking frightened. "Now they are nobody."

Enzo began shouting.

"What's eating that bastard?" Torres asked.

"He says we are whores and traitors to serve you," Sienna said.

Drew had never witnessed such an ugly scene in an American restaurant—or in any public place, for that matter. Apparently, neither had his crewmates. They looked at one another as if they couldn't quite believe what they were seeing.

Lucia rushed back from the kitchen. She spoke sharply to the men, which provoked more shouting. Sienna found a pad and scribbled out a bill. Tore off the bill and placed it on the Italians' table. Enzo brushed it to the floor. Stood up and grabbed Sienna by the arm. Shook her hard. She screamed and tried to pull away from him.

The scream jolted Drew from his frozen disbelief. As Enzo struggled with Sienna, Drew saw his opening. He sprang from his chair. Drove his right fist into Enzo's cheek. The blow knocked the Italian back a step and made him release Sienna, but it did not put him down.

Enzo lunged at Drew. Grabbed him by the shirt and shoved him against the wall.

Drew kneed him in the groin. Enzo doubled over. One of his buddies rushed toward Drew, but Torres blocked him. The man wrapped his arms around the copilot and tried to wrestle him to the floor. Torres brought both fists down on the back of the man's neck.

When Enzo raised himself again, he was brandishing a knife. The weapon had appeared so fast, Drew didn't see where it came from. Enzo set his feet apart in some kind of fighting stance. Slashed at the air with the blade.

In one smooth motion, Montreux got up from his chair, lifted it, and brought it down onto Enzo's head. The Italian crumpled to the floor. Drew kicked him in the gut. The man let go of the knife. Drew kicked the knife away.

The Brits joined the fight. One of them attacked the man grappling with Torres. Punched him in the small of the back. The man released Torres and turned toward his new opponent. For his trouble, he got another punch, this time to the face.

Lucia was shouting at the third Italian, the one who'd remained at his table. He slumped his shoulders and went to the door. Pulled it open and held it. The man who'd tackled Torres raised his arms in a gesture of surrender and staggered for the exit, but didn't leave.

"Get the hell out, you blighters!" one of the Brits said.

Enzo writhed on the floor. The blow from Drew's boot had knocked the breath out of him.

Drew grabbed him by the belt and shirt collar as if lifting a sack of potatoes. Dragged him to the door. Pitched him out onto the street. His two friends joined him outside.

Lucia slammed the door and locked it. Took Drew by the arm and kissed him on the cheek. Sienna, who had taken cover behind the bar, buried her face in her hands and disappeared into the kitchen.

"Hoo-ee," Montreux said. "Now I'm homesick. Reminds me of a juke joint in Slidell on a Saturday night."

"Capital work by you Yanks," one of the Brits said.

"Can't remember the last time I punched somebody," Drew said. In fact, it was the first time he had ever punched anybody.

Lucia brought them two open bottles of wine. She placed one on the Brits' table, and the other on the Americans'. Poured into all their glasses.

"This is—how do you say?—on the house," Lucia said. "Thank you so much."

"A shame you had to deal with those bums," Montreux said.

"Dead-enders, that lot," one of the Brits said.

"Have you had this kind of trouble in the restaurant before?" Drew asked.

"These men have made rude remarks before," Lucia said, "but never like this."

"Y'all let us know if they ever come back," Montreux said. "We'll kick their asses again."

The men finished their wine, and Drew let himself enjoy the little victory of prevailing in a fistfight. He looked around for Sienna but still didn't see her. Then she returned to the dining room, silently as a wraith. She stood by the bar, held back from the group. She looked at Drew for just a moment, and turned her face away.

Drew and his crewmates climbed into the jeep for the drive back to San Pancrazio. Torres and Montreux rehashed the fight, blow for blow.

"Did they think a bunch of Allied troops were gonna just sit there and let them act like that?" Torres asked.

"I imagine they'd gotten used to getting away with pretty much anything during Mussolini's time," Drew said.

"Damn," Montreux said, "we went and got all Louisiana on them *couillons*. Especially you, sir." From the backseat, the engineer reached forward and punched Drew's arm.

It had all happened so fast, Drew thought. He hadn't had time to think. When that guy grabbed Sienna, instinct just kicked in. Somehow Drew had separated his fears from his actions.

He rounded a curve that revealed the twilight Adriatic. A pewter sea stretched toward the night. Amid the emerging stars, red and green navigation lights glowed on the wingtips of a C-47 on final to San Pancrazio.

# CHAPTER 11
## Mudcat Driver

More fliers straggled into Pranjani. They crowded into haylofts, horse stalls, and cellars. They shared *rakija* with the locals. Some enjoyed happy reunions with crewmates, though Bogdonavich and Greenbaum found no one else from *Miss Caroline*. They began to fear they were the only survivors.

They also began to fear no one heard their radio calls—or at least that no one believed them. Three days went by without an answer. The signals intelligence guys may well have picked up the broadcasts and assumed it was Germans trying to lure rescuers into a trap.

"We gotta think of a way to authenticate ourselves without giving too much to the Krauts," Bogdonavich told Greenbaum after a breakfast of cheese and weak tea. They sat on the dirt floor of a root cellar. Baskets of potatoes and dried beans surrounded them. Above the aviators' heads, bundles of herbs hung by strings. The cellar smelled of earth and thyme.

"I wish we could just transmit our names and where we are," Greenbaum groused, "and get the hell out of here already."

"We have to keep our heads," Bogdonavich said. "If the Krauts heard our names, they could use them in a fake SOS to draw rescue planes into a trap."

Greenbaum drew a swastika in the dirt. Then he made an X across it.

Boot steps sounded at the top of the stairs. Someone was coming. Though the village seemed pretty secure, Bogdonavich placed his hand on his .45, just in case. Then someone called his name. It was the young fighter Vasa. The boy descended the steps. His feet were the first thing that came into view. Bogdonavich recognized the kid by the hole in one of his boots. Vasa looked downcast when he joined the aviators in the cellar.

"Hey, it's Vasa the Wolf," Bogdonavich said in English. Then he repeated the statement in Serbian. Vasa did not smile at the mention of his nickname. "Is something wrong?" Bogdonavich asked.

"My friend Piotra looks very bad," Vasa said. "His wound smells terrible. We tried to feed him this morning, and he threw everything up."

Bogdonavich translated for Greenbaum.

"That ain't good," Greenbaum said. "I'm not a medic, but that sounds like gangrene."

"What does the nurse say?" Bogdonavich asked Vasa in Serbian.

"He will die without medicine."

These Chetniks were fighting so hard, with so little. Why couldn't the army find a way to air-drop some things to them? *If we ever get out of here,* Bogdonavich thought, *we need to figure out how to get supplies to these people.* Again he translated for Greenbaum, and added his own thoughts about the supplies.

"If they manage to pick us up," Greenbaum said, "it'll probably be on C-47s. Maybe they can bring some stuff when they come to get us."

Bogdonavich nodded grimly. *"If they manage to pick us up." If . . . if . . . if we ever get rescued.*

Around noon, a group of guerrillas rode in on horseback with three more downed Americans. Bogdonavich, Higgins, and Stefan met them in the blacksmith's shop. The horsemen said a truck was on the way with a dozen more fliers.

"Where did you guys come from?" Bogdonavich asked the new

fliers. Sweat matted their hair, and dirt marred their faces. One of them, wearing pilot wings, had suffered a deep scratch on his cheek. *Probably parachuted into a tree,* Bogdonavich supposed, *just like I did.*

"Same as you, probably," the pilot answered. "We hit the refineries in Romania and got our asses chewed up."

Bogdonavich introduced himself.

The pilot shook Bogdonavich's hand. "Tom Oliver," he said, "with the four hundred fifty-ninth."

Bogdonavich explained the situation as best he could: He knew of 150 downed airmen, and Higgins was trying to get out a radio call. Bogdonavich also described the dilemma of authenticating themselves without bringing the *Luftwaffe* down on them.

Stefan spoke with the insurgents who'd brought in Oliver and his friends. Bogdonavich followed most of it. The biggest news was the numbers. This group of fighters had come from the other end of Ravna Gora, and they knew of a hundred more Americans.

"Now we have two hundred fifty?" Bogdonavich asked in Serbian. Every time that number rose, rescue seemed more impossible. Assuming they made radio contact, what would HQ do about it? He felt a hint of panic, then did his best to suppress it.

When Bogdonavich translated the news for Higgins, the radio operator gaped. Rolled his eyes and spread his arms in a gesture of capitulation. "Oh, that's just perfect," Higgins said. "They'll never believe we really have that many. They'll think it's a trap, for sure."

Irritation burned inside Bogdonavich's chest. He was not in the mood for complaints. "Stop it," he said. Held up his hand. "I don't want to hear it."

He didn't want to hear it because he was thinking the same thing. The situation put him in mind of a bomber crew trying to get back into a fogged-in base. You'd enter a holding pattern and hope the weather improved. With every minute that ticked by, those fuel gauges kept creeping lower and lower. You began to run out of time.

\* \* \*

Later that day, Bogdonavich asked Vasa if the Americans could visit his wounded friend.

Vasa led Bogdonavich, Greenbaum, Higgins, and Oliver to a thatched-roof home on the edge of the village. Nikolas and Katarina met them at the door. Vasa whispered a few words, and the nurse nodded. Nikolas held the door open and bade the Americans to enter.

The house looked like every other Serbian home Bogdonavich had seen on this journey. Meager furnishings, no indoor plumbing, certainly no electricity. The Chetnik insurgent Piotra lay on a bed stuffed with corn husks. The room smelled of urine from a bedpan and decay from a gangrenous wound. A blanket covered Piotra from the neck down. Sweat streaked his cheeks. His face had taken on a gray pallor, except for the skin around his eyes. Redness rimmed his eyes, now sunken back in their sockets. Piotra regarded the fliers in silence as they entered. An icon depicting Mary, Mother of Christ, hung above the headboard.

Bogdonavich stepped forward and kneeled beside Piotra's bed.

He looked worse than Bogdonavich had imagined. *He's done for*, Bogdonavich thought. *What can I possibly say to him?*

Bogdonavich decided to speak plainly and from the heart. That's how his dad had always spoken, and this dying man came from the same stock.

"Thank you for what you have done for us," Bogdonavich said in Serbian. "We owe you a great debt."

The blanket shifted. Piotra was trying to get his right arm out from under the covers.

"Just rest," Bogdonavich said.

Piotra ignored the command. His jaw muscles tightened as if in great strain. He brought out his hand in greeting, held it up with fingers spread.

Bogdonavich clasped Piotra's hand. The Chetnik fighter gripped so hard, it hurt.

"Fight on," Piotra hissed through gritted teeth. "Fight on, my brothers."

"We will, friend," Bogdonavich said.

When Piotra relaxed his grip, Bogdonavich eased the man's arm down to the blanket. Piotra closed his eyes and let out a long sigh.

The Americans filed out of the room, while Vasa, Nikolas, and Katarina kept vigil by their wounded comrade.

At the blacksmith's shop, Bogdonavich showed Tom Oliver the radio set the fliers had assembled. The transmitter and receiver cabinets rested on a wooden table. An antenna wire extended out a window and up to the roof. The Morse key lay in front of the transmitter, ready for the next message.

"Wow," Oliver said. "You guys all but re-created the radio room of a B-24."

"Yeah," Bogdonavich said. "Too bad this one doesn't fly."

"When is the next call? I might have an idea."

"Tonight. We've been transmitting at irregular times, so the Krauts don't catch on."

"To authenticate ourselves, we need to say something only we would know."

Bogdonavich nodded. "But it also needs to be something the Germans couldn't have tortured out of us. Something they wouldn't even know to ask."

"Just hear me out," Oliver said. "This is a little weird, so bear with me."

Oliver explained that the enemy probably wouldn't know the names of American airplanes. German spies might have recorded the tail numbers, but they probably wouldn't care about unofficial nicknames, such as *Miss Caroline, Bouncin' Betty,* or, in the case of Oliver's aircraft, *The Fighting Mudcat.*

"What the hell kind of name is *The Fighting Mudcat?*" Bogdonavich asked.

Oliver cackled. "That's a long story," he said. "But for this radio call, just to keep the Germans guessing, we don't even use the full name of the airplane."

"All right, but will that be enough for our guys back at base?"

"Maybe not."

Oliver and Bogdonavich hashed out how to improve on Oliver's idea. They couldn't just blurt out "Fifteenth Air Force" or "Four hundred fifty-ninth." While they talked, Oliver pulled a crumpled pack of Camels from his shirt pocket. He fingered the pack, withdrew two cigarettes.

"Damn, these are my last two," Oliver said. He offered one to Bogdonavich. Oliver dug into his pants pockets and found his lighter. Flicked open the Ronson and lit both Camels. Bogdonavich took a long drag, held the smoke in his lungs.

"I wish I could get my wife to mail me a package here," Oliver said. "I'd ask for a carton of cigarettes and some of her blackberry pie."

"Say that again," Bogdonavich said, frowning.

"Say what again? That I want my wife to mail me a package of cigarettes and blackberry pie? And some fried chicken, too, while she's at it."

"You just gave me an idea. The Krauts might know our units, but they don't know our mailing addresses."

Oliver raised his chin and regarded Bogdonavich. Placed the Camel between his lips. The fire on the end glowed as Oliver took in the smoke. He exhaled the smoke through his nose. Nodded for several seconds.

"You're right," Oliver said. "They don't know our Army Post Office numbers."

Bogdonavich could hardly wait for the sun to go down. The fliers had made their last attempted radio call during the afternoon of the day before. A night call would alter the time pattern. And, Bogdonavich hoped, the liaison radio would carry better at night.

At nine p.m., Higgins took his place at the makeshift radio shack in back of the blacksmith's shop. An oil lantern cast a yellow glow across the radio cabinets and the sending key. Bogdonavich, Greenbaum, Oliver, and several other Americans watched him work. Higgins flipped switches to power up his set, and they waited for the tubes to warm up.

While they waited, Bogdonavich leaned against the wall and folded his arms. He gazed out through an open window. Out here in the Yugoslav countryside, very little light from the ground competed with the stars. The Milky Way appeared as a band of shining dust across the heavens. For Bogdonavich, this night seemed an open book, filled with possibilities. He opened the flap of his shirt pocket and dug out a scrap of paper. He handed Higgins the message to send.

The radio operator read the short sentences. He gave the paper a questioning look, glanced up at Bogdonavich. Then he read the paper again, and he smiled. Higgins rolled up his sleeves and slid the Morse key in front of him. Placed his hand over the key and began to tap out the dots and dashes: *Mudcat driver to APO 520. 250 Yanks in Yugo. Send workhorses.*

"Workhorses" referred to C-47 Skytrains. The unglamorous, highly dependable workhorses of the USAAF. Big enough to carry a number of passengers, and rugged enough to land in an unpaved field.

If anyone heard the message, they'd need time to check with the 459th, the destination of mail sent to APO 520. They would need to ask what "Mudcat driver" meant. But somebody at the 459th would figure it out.

The aviators would keep the radio on and man it around the clock. Higgins had agreed to take the first shift—through the night until five in the morning.

As Bogdonavich and Greenbaum headed back toward the cellar where they would be sleeping, they passed the home where they'd visited the wounded guerrilla earlier in the day. Men stood around outside the door, whispering among themselves. Lantern light cast flickering shadows among them. Bogdonavich recognized Stefan, Nikolas, and young Vasa.

"Vasa the Wolf," Bogdonavich called. A silly greeting, but he was feeling optimistic.

The young Chetnik looked up at him. Even in the dim light, Bogdonavich could see the tears that slicked Vasa's cheeks.

"Piotra died tonight," Vasa said.

# CHAPTER 12
## Thinking Like a Man

$V$ ASA FELT AS IF HE'D TAKEN TWO ROUNDS TO THE HEART. FIRST Aleksandra's letter, and now the death of Piotra—his dear friend and Aleksandra's cousin. After reading Aleksandra's farewell letter, he'd moved about in a fog. He'd tried to keep up his duties as a proper Serbian fighter. He'd cleaned his weapons and those of Piotra. He'd helped look after Piotra as well as he could. He'd told no one of his anguish. What were such matters when people were dying?

But the weight of it all began to crush his spirit. Unable to sleep, he sat by himself outside the blacksmith's shop and watched sunrise bleed across the horizon. The morning came in silence, save for the lowing of cattle in a distant pasture. When Nikolas and Miroslav awoke and stepped outside, they nodded to Vasa. Nikolas carried his submachine gun, as usual, and Miroslav toted his Mauser. But they brought no packs with them. Wherever they were going, they expected to be back soon. They mounted the old Opel truck used by the guerrillas.

"We are going to fetch the priest," Nikolas said.

Vasa watched the Opel lurch along a dirt path until it disappeared over a hill. A short time later, Bogdonavich appeared.

"Good morning, Vasa the Wolf," the American said.

Vasa stood. "Good morning, sir."

Bogdonavich waved to him and entered the blacksmith's shop. He spoke in English with another Yank. Until they started talking, Vasa hadn't realized there was anyone inside the shop. Apparently, the Americans were manning their radio at all hours. The two men conversed for a long time. Vasa supposed they were trying to communicate with their headquarters and were having some sort of difficulty. After a while, Bogdonavich came outside and sat on the ground beside Vasa.

"It is hard to lose a comrade," he said. "I have lost friends, too. Other than Greenbaum, I don't know what happened to my crewmates. I would like to tell you that when you lose someone, you eventually get over it. But I don't know that you do. You just learn to live with the loss."

"Piotra is not the only person I have lost."

Vasa did not know why he chose to unburden himself to the American. Perhaps because Bogdonavich sounded sympathetic, like an older brother instead of a superior.

Vasa looked out across the hills. The sun's rays lit the fog rising above the fields.

He told Bogdonavich about the letter from Aleksandra, and about his worries for his hometown.

"I want to write her back," Vasa said. "I want to tell her to reconsider. But if the Partisans are in control of Velika, what if they are reading the mail and they see a letter from a Chetnik soldier?"

Bogdonavich regarded Vasa for a moment, then clapped him on the shoulder.

"You're not the first soldier to get a letter like that, and you sure won't be the last," the Yank said. "You're sad and angry, but you're not thinking about yourself. You're thinking like a man, and there are men twice your age who can't do that."

"Thank you, sir."

"Look, Vasa," Bogdonavich continued, "sometimes duty is hard. Sometimes just knowing you're doing the right thing has to be reward enough."

Vasa had heard such words before from his father and his priest back home. He'd always accepted the truth of them. But back then, the idea seemed so simple—and easy. Of course you always tried to do the right thing. If your neighbor's cow broke through the fence, you led the animal back to the pasture. If your cousin lost his garden to drought, you shared what food you had. If a farmer fell ill, you helped tend his crops until he recovered. Simple and easy.

But this life of soldiering presented harder challenges. Doing the right thing could mean a lot more than taking the time to bring a cow home. It could mean risking pain, crippling injury, or death. Weeks and months of fatigue and misery. And you had to push your feelings down into some small place inside yourself. You had to lock that small place away and forget it was there. Vasa wondered if he had the strength to keep this up.

Later in the day, Vasa helped some of the other Chetniks build a coffin for Piotra. One of the local farmers offered planks he'd stored in a barn. A guerrilla who'd worked as a carpenter in peacetime measured with a ruler and marked with a pencil. Whenever the carpenter finished marking a cut, he placed the pencil behind his ear. Vasa laid the boards across two sawhorses. With a handsaw, he cut where the carpenter had drawn lines.

At first, Vasa liked the manual labor. Working with his hands took his mind off his troubles. He liked the smell of sawdust that fell from the blade. Carpentry and woodwork had always appealed to him.

But the sawdust smell began to make him sad, and he realized why. That smell usually meant new beginnings: a new home for a family, a new stable for a farmer's growing herd, a new bed for a newlywed couple. But this time, it marked an end—one of terrible finality.

In the late afternoon, Nikolas and Miroslav returned with Father Milos. The privations of war prevented the ceremonies of a proper Orthodox funeral. But the guerrillas and their unofficial chaplain did the best they could. The men placed Piotra in his coffin in the front room of the largest home in Pranjani. Between

Piotra's hands, clasped over his chest, they placed a small wooden cross. On a table beside the coffin, they set a bowl of *koliva*, boiled wheat with honey. Father Milos explained that the wheat represented the brevity of mortal life, and the honey represented the sweetness of eternal life through Christ. Chetnik fighters and villagers crowded the room, and Bogdonavich stood in the back with a group of Americans.

As the mourners held lit candles, Father Milos said the *Panikhida*:

> *Grant rest eternal in blessed repose, O Lord,*
> *to Thy servant Piotra, who has fallen asleep,*
> *and make his memory be eternal.*

Following the service, Father Milos led a procession to Pranjani's cemetery. Vasa served as one of the pallbearers. He hoisted the coffin atop his shoulder, assisted by Nikolas, Miroslav, and three other Chetniks.

At the graveyard, the Serbian tetragrammic cross marked some of the weathered stones. Generations of villagers rested here, but none of Piotra's family. With Velika in Partisan hands, the body could not be sent back to his home. Vasa found that an especially cruel misfortune of war. But words from Father Milos gave him some comfort.

"Look at the crosses on the gravestones around you," Milos said. "Note the Cyrillics at each corner of our Serbian cross. Those letters stand for the motto 'Only Unity Saves the Serbs.' Our brother Piotra finds his final resting place far from his home village. But his mortal remains are surrounded by Serbs. Even now, in a place far better than this, they are welcoming our fallen warrior into their midst. Yes, Piotra has come home."

Vasa's eyes welled with tears as he helped lower the coffin into the freshly dug grave. Mounds of dark loam stood beside the grave. Each of the pallbearers took a handful of the soil and sprinkled it onto the coffin. Bogdonavich led the fliers in a slow salute, fingertips to their foreheads in the American style. This display of respect gave Vasa as much comfort as the words from the priest. He wished Aleksandra and the rest of Piotra's family could have seen it.

After the funeral, several of the Americans gathered in the blacksmith's shop around their radio. They spoke at length in English, and Vasa wondered what was going on. He sat on a stool in the shop and watched the aviators. Bogdonavich nodded to him, but the rest paid him no mind.

One of the Yanks handed a sheet of paper to the man sitting at the sending key. The radioman talked to Bogdonavich and pointed at something on the paper. They seemed to be debating something. Finally the radioman began to tap at his key. He tapped for several seconds; this was the longest Vasa had ever seen them transmit.

The radioman stopped tapping, and he placed his hand to his headset. Then he pumped his fist into the air and laughed. The men around him cheered. The radioman held up his hand for silence, and he listened for a moment. Then he tapped some more.

The group of men around the radio started to break up. They began to leave the blacksmith shop and return to their resting places in the barns and cellars. The radioman took off his headset and turned off the set. Bogdonavich shook his hand and patted his back.

When Bogdonavich prepared to leave, Vasa asked him what was happening.

"We made contact with our headquarters, and we found a way to convince them it's us—and not a trick by the Germans. Some of our people will coordinate with your General Mihailovich. I think we are about to get very busy, Vasa the Wolf."

At these words, Vasa found his dark mood easing. Something was happening, something in which he could participate. He might play some small role in getting these Americans home.

# CHAPTER 13
## Rebecca and Eureka

*I*N A FLIGHT PLANNING ROOM AT SAN PANCRAZIO, CAPTAIN MARICH spread a USAAF aeronautical chart across a table. Drew read a notation on the chart: *Prepared by the U.S. Coast and Geodetic Survey, from the best source material available, June 1944.*

Next to the map, Marich placed a black-and-white photograph. Taken from high altitude on a clear day, the picture showed a village surrounded by fields and woods. From what Drew could see, it could have been anywhere in Central Europe.

"A P-38 photoreconnaissance bird took this shot three days ago," Marich said. "Some of our boys on the ground there have made radio contact, and we've verified their identity."

Torres and Chisholm stood next to Drew, their arms folded. Marich briefed the pilots and navigator on their mission. They would take off at dusk. They would fly Marich and two other OSS operatives to a drop zone in a meadow near the village shown in the photo. The village was called Pranjani.

"How did the guys authenticate themselves?" Drew asked.

"Oh, it was ingenious," Marich said. "They made up a whole code based on things only they would know. Stuff like the name of an intel officer here at San Pancrazio, and the name of the bartender at the Officers' Club in Lecce. They transposed letters from those names to encode an alphabet."

"It must have taken a while to work that out," Torres said.

"Yeah, it did," Marich said. "And they took a chance by staying on the air that long. We just hope the Krauts never got a fix on them."

Drew considered the implications. He and his crew wouldn't be flying into a trap, at least. The radio calls really did come from downed Americans. But using that kind of code would have taken a hell of a lot of dots and dashes. Plenty of time for the Germans to home in with direction-finding equipment, if they happened to catch the right frequency. At any moment, the Stukas could dive in like a bunch of hawks.

Marich gave the crew the coordinates for the drop zone. Drew compared them against the aeronautical chart. He considered the information the chart provided—and the secrets it withheld. The mapmakers depicted the elevation of terrain, the courses of rivers, the frequencies of radio beacons. But they offered nothing on enemy positions, on emplacement of German weapons.

Somewhere on this chart could be Drew's future crash site, the point where his mortal existence would end. A smoking hole in the ground. A burned spot in the woods that might lie undiscovered for decades and vanish under regrowth of forest.

"Some of our contacts in Yugoslavia know how to use the Eureka beacon to home you into the drop zone," Marich continued. "We just installed a new Rebecca receiving set in your aircraft. I understand your navigator is qualified on the Eureka-Rebecca system."

"Yes, sir, I am," Chisholm said. "I've used it in training. This will be the first time I've used it operationally."

Drew had flown navigators on such training missions, and he had a basic idea of how the system worked. The Eureka unit on the ground transmitted a directional signal received by the Rebecca unit in the C-47. On the Rebecca, an oscilloscope provided a visual reference for the course to fly. During the run into the drop zone, the navigator stared into a hooded shroud over the scope. If the blip on the scope moved right or left of centerline, the navigator called out a course correction. As the plane flew over the drop zone, the Eureka operator on the ground signaled for the drop.

But the Eureka had only a fifteen-mile range. To get within that range of the drop zone, Drew and Chisholm would employ another type of radio navigation: They would use the Nazis' own propaganda against them. The Germans held Belgrade, and a radio station there spewed garbage about the invincibility of the Thousand-Year Reich. From that signal, Drew could take a bearing with the C-47's radio compass and cross-check his position.

Sunset found Drew in the cockpit. Sweat already soaked the back of his flight suit, so he slid open his side window. Any C-47 on the ground in a warm climate became a hotbox. But this one, painted black, felt like the pizza oven at Antonio's. A bead of sweat dripped from the end of Drew's nose and onto his clipboard. The droplet smeared ink on Form 1A. The form showed that Montreux had cleared all the minor maintenance write-ups on the aircraft, and she was ready to go. Right now, Montreux was in the back with Marich and the other OSS men. He was helping them get strapped into their fabric seats along the side of the cargo compartment. Above them hung a steel cable Montreux had installed earlier. The three OSS men would clip their static lines to the cable when it came time to parachute from the aircraft.

Next to Drew, in the right seat, Torres went through his preflight rituals. The copilot flipped two battery switches on the overhead panel. He moved the fuel gauge selector to check quantity in all four tanks, and he tapped the altimeter to remove any friction in the needles.

The process of waking up the aircraft settled Drew's mind a bit. The checklists, the procedures, brought focus and even comfort. Here was something familiar, something he knew, as he prepared to face the unknown. Behind him, he heard Chisholm and Calvert strapping into their seats at the navigator and radio operator positions.

The OSS team didn't seem nervous. Marich and his men laughed and joked as they hauled themselves aboard with their parachute rigs and packs. They'd done it all before. Maybe for these cloak-and-dagger spooks, jumping into enemy territory in the middle of the night was something familiar.

Drew heard the cargo door slam closed. Montreux came forward and sat in the folding jump seat behind the pilots. He put on his headset and buckled his throat mic. "All set in the back," Montreux said. *"Laissez les bon temps rouler."*

"Let the good times roll," Drew said. He tried to sound carefree for the benefit of his crew, though he hardly felt that way. "Start number one."

Torres worked the wobble pump to bring up the fuel pressure. He pushed the mixture levers to full rich and pressed the left starter switch. The big radial engine coughed, turned, belched smoke, and fired. The propeller spun up to idle RPM and sent dust flying across the ramp. Torres repeated the process with the number two engine.

When the oil temperature came up to 40 degrees Centigrade, Drew pushed up the throttles for engine run-up. He checked manifold pressures, watched RPM drop when he moved the prop levers, and also noted small RPM drops as he tested his magnetos. Everything checked good. Montreux had maintained the airplane well.

Drew flashed his landing light to signal the marshaller: We're ready to taxi. The marshaller raised his arms and waved the aircraft forward. Drew released the parking brake, set his boots on the toe brakes, then eased off the brakes. The C-47 rolled out of its hardstand as the sun's last burning crescent dropped beneath the horizon.

At the runway's hold-short line, Drew double-checked several items: carburetor heats off, trim tabs neutral, and props at full high RPM. The tower cleared him for takeoff. He lined up on the runway without stopping and pressed the throttles forward. Held the throttles to keep them from creeping backward due to vibration. The Twin Wasp engines thundered, and the aircraft accelerated toward whatever fate awaited. At rotation speed, Drew pulled back on the yoke, and the C-47 lifted into the dusk.

* * *

By the time the aircraft reached cruising altitude, the eastern sky had blackened to reveal the first silver pinpoints of starlight. Drew recognized Vega low on the horizon. Then he picked out Altair and Deneb, which together with Vega formed the Summer Triangle. He considered how this same sky hung over both allies and enemies, oppressed and oppressors. At this very moment, the gunner who might shoot him down could be looking up at these very stars. Drew pushed the thought from his mind, forced himself to concentrate on the task at hand. *You'll take counsel of your fears if you keep dwelling on them,* he told himself.

Besides, he had no practical use for these stars. Tonight he wasn't using celestial navigation. The pilots and the navigator would use plain old dead reckoning to head toward the general area of the drop zone. They'd narrow down their accuracy with a bearing from the Nazi radio station. Then Eureka would guide them the rest of the way.

Down below, moonlight bronzed the surface of the Adriatic. Torres was flying the plane now, and Drew pulled an aeronautical chart from the lower leg pocket of his flight suit.

"Coastline coming up," Drew called on the interphone.

Chisholm rose from the navigator's seat and peered out the windscreen. In his left hand, he held a stopwatch. When the C-47 crossed the Dalmatian Coast, he clicked the watch. Drew followed along on his chart. Working by a utility light's yellow beam, he double-checked the distance to the next landmark, the town of Mostar. Mostar was not much of a target for Allied bombers, and Drew hoped it wouldn't be under complete blackout. The darkened landscape scrolled past for several minutes. Eventually Drew spied a smattering of light on the horizon.

"That must be Mostar," Chisholm said.

Drew glanced at his chart again; sure enough, that was Mostar. Chisholm clicked the stopwatch again as the aircraft overflew the town.

Now that they'd flown a known distance at a known ground-speed, they could calculate what the wind was doing to them.

Chisholm sat down at the navigator's table and spun the wheel on his E6B flight computer.

"We got a twenty-knot tailwind," Chisholm announced. He recalculated the arrival time and gave Torres a new heading to steer. Then he tuned the automatic direction finder to the frequency of the Nazi radio station in the Yugoslav capital. On Drew's instrument panel, a dim glow lit the needle inside the radio compass. The needle came to life and swung toward Belgrade.

To confirm Chisholm had tuned correctly, Drew turned a knob on his audio panel and listened to the broadcast. The words sounded like Serbian, though he could understand none of it.

As the crew worked, Captain Marich appeared in the flight deck doorway. Marich steadied himself under the weight of his parachute rig, and he plugged a headset into an interphone jack.

"How's it going, boys?" he said. "Are we on course?"

"I think so, sir," Drew said. "We were just about to take a bearing on that Belgrade station."

"Very good."

Drew turned another knob so Marich could hear the station.

"I don't speak the language," Drew said. "What are they saying?"

Marich listened for a moment. Frowned.

"The Fatherland's unending generosity extends to all who accept the inevitable victory of the Third Reich," Marich translated. He listened for a moment, then continued: "Citizens who provide information on the positions and movement of terrorist forces, or the location of Allied personnel, shall be rewarded. But be warned: Anyone found harboring enemy elements shall be put to death."

"Well, that's inspiring," Torres said.

"Bastards," Drew added.

"That's all right," Marich said. "They keep broadcasting this bullshit, they get me where I need to go."

"Roger that, sir," Drew said.

A few minutes later, with Mostar several miles behind, Drew saw a spear of light in the corner of his eye. He looked down and to the left. He saw more flashes. Orange streams burst from a point somewhere in the black landscape below. They did not arc up-ward toward the C-47; they were aimed at a target on the ground. More tracers answered from an opposing angle. Drew realized he was witnessing a firefight.

"Looks like a battle down there," Drew said.

Marich leaned to look out Drew's side window.

"Get 'em," Marich said.

The captain sounded so casual in his bravado, like he took all this in stride. As an experienced OSS officer, he'd no doubt faced all manner of danger. Drew wished he shared that kind of élan. But he couldn't escape the thought that down below, *right there*, men were trying to kill one another. In some of the most violent circumstances imaginable.

*Try not to think about it,* Drew told himself. *Just press on.*

What was the alternative? Turn around and go back to San Pancrazio right now? Marich would lose his mind, and Drew would lose his soul. Drew knew he couldn't live with himself if he let his fears take control again. There was nothing for it but to steer the course. Follow the procedures. Make the drop.

Drew recalled once more the words from that GI in the Offi-cers' Club: *"Consider yourself already dead."* In a way, he was doing that. An L-pill, wrapped in foil, lay in his chest pocket. Drew fin-gered the deadly shape beneath the fabric of his flight suit. If cap-ture seemed imminent, he could crush the cyanide capsule between his molars and shuffle off this mortal coil. And deny in-formation to the enemy.

He didn't want to die young. And he certainly didn't want to die by poisoning. But the L-pill represented a measure of control. Drew took a perverse comfort in its presence. The pill meant *he* determined his fate and not the Germans.

The radio compass needle began to swing toward the bearing Drew had jotted on the notepad clipped to his kneeboard.

"It's almost showtime," Drew said.

The OSS officer disappeared aft. Montreux followed Marich into the cargo compartment. A few minutes later, he plugged his headset into a jack in the rear of the aircraft.

"Engineer's up in the back," he said.

"Got you loud and clear," Drew said.

Drew took the controls from Torres. He pulled back the throttles and began a gradual descent to one thousand feet above ground level. At this altitude, he flew within the threat range of practically every weapon the Krauts possessed: anything from antiaircraft artillery to a pistol, not to mention the Messerschmitts that could bounce him at any time. Drew and his crewmates were flying this mission unescorted, too. No fighter protection. Secret insertions of commandos relied on stealth rather than firepower.

This C-47's main protection was dull black paint that would blend in with the night and not reflect moonlight. The bad guys couldn't hit what they couldn't see. But the bad guys weren't deaf. Drew knew the enemy could hear his engines. He tried not to think about all that could go wrong.

"All right, let's get the airplane configured for the drop," Drew commanded. He called for Torres to lower the flaps, and Drew eased back the throttles to slow to a drop speed of 110 miles per hour. The slipstream's hiss changed tone as Montreux opened the cargo door. Torres flipped a switch that illuminated a red light on the panel. The light corresponded to a larger red light the jumpers could see in the cargo compartment. The red light meant: *We're near the drop zone. Stand up and hook up.*

"Navigator, pilot," Drew called. "Are you picking up anything on Rebecca?"

"Negative," Chisholm answered.

Drew scanned the landscape below. He saw nothing but a black void. Only Chisholm's calculations and the radio compass told him they were anywhere near the target.

"I don't see anything," Torres said. "Do you?"

"No, but you probably won't see anything," Drew said. "It's damned dark down there."

Drew began to wonder if the mission had been compromised. Had the Eureka operator been killed or captured? Had Germans overrun the whole area?

"Give me a left turn to three-zero-zero," Chisholm called.

"You got something?" Drew asked.

"Not yet."

Drew held the new heading for a minute. Behind him, Chisholm peered into the oscilloscope. Still, nothing. Maybe the mission *had* been compromised. And maybe there was a battalion of *Waffen-SS* down there, just waiting for a hapless C-47 with a valuable OSS team.

"Marich wants to know if you got anything," Montreux called from the back.

"Negative," Drew said.

*Should we get the hell out of here while the getting is good?* Drew wondered. Sweat from his palms slicked the yoke and the throttles.

But finding excuses to abort a mission had gotten him cashiered out of bombers. Excuses had marked him with a yellow streak.

*I came all this way to wash off that streak,* Drew considered. *Maybe I'll have to wash it off with blood.*

"Let's do another pass," Chisholm said. "Right turn to one-two-zero."

Drew banked, then rolled out on the new heading. The landscape below gave up nothing. Drew might as well have been flying over an ocean of ink.

"Anything?" Drew asked.

"Negative," Chisholm said. "Wait—I got it. Left turn to zero-one-zero."

"Zero-one-zero," Drew repeated. He banked the C-47 into the turn.

Outside, nothing looked different. Just an expanse of darkness.

"All right, there it is," Chisholm said. "There it is. Right five degrees."

Drew corrected to the right. At the same time, he tweaked the throttles to keep the speed at 110, and glanced at the vertical speed indicator to make sure he wasn't climbing or descending.

"Okay, we got some wind," Chisholm said. "Give me five more degrees right."

"Five degrees right," Drew said.

"Thirty seconds," Chisholm said.

"Thirty seconds," Drew told Montreux over the interphone. "Tell 'em we're thirty seconds out."

Even over the noise of the engines and slipstream, Drew heard Montreux bellow: "THIRTY SECONDS!"

Drew focused all his attention, all the core of his being, on holding course and speed.

"Twenty seconds," Chisholm said.

"TWENTY SECONDS!" Montreux shouted in the back.

"Three degrees left," Chisholm said.

"Three degrees left," Drew said. He moved the yoke ever so slightly for the fine-tuned course correction. Under other circumstances, three degrees would have made little difference. But Drew didn't know the size of the drop zone or surrounding obstacles. If the OSS men were jumping into a half-acre clearing surrounded by trees, a three-degree error at night could leave them hanging in branches. Or worse.

"Ten seconds," Chisholm called. Then he began a countdown: "Five, four, three, two, one. There's the signal. Green light."

"Green light," Drew said.

Torres flipped the toggle switch on the overhead panel to change the jump light from red to green. From the cargo compartment, three thumps sounded as Marich and his teammates leaped from the plane.

"Jumpers clear," Montreux said.

Drew held his wings level for a moment to give Montreux time to retrieve the static lines. He heard the cargo door slam shut.

"Drop complete," Montreux called.

Drew shoved the throttles forward. Pitched the nose up to climb, and called for Torres to raise the flaps. The C-47 clawed for altitude.

Montreux came forward and took his place in the flight deck's jump seat. Fastened his harness and plugged in his headset. Sweat streaked his face, and he looked flush with excitement.

"Navigator," Drew said, "gimme a course for home."

"Come to two-two-zero for now," Chisholm said. "I'll give you a better heading when we see what the wind's doing up at altitude."

"Two-two-zero," Drew said. After he rolled out on the south-westerly heading, he said, "Copilot's airplane."

"My airplane," Torres said.

Torres took the controls. When Drew let go of the yoke, he noticed pain in his knuckles. He'd been clutching the controls in a death grip—something he'd always taught students not to do. His heart pounded, too.

Drew turned to look into the companionway behind him. At the navigator's table, Chisholm had raised himself up from the scope. He spread a chart across his table. Clenched a pencil between his teeth. At the radio operator's seat, Calvert tweaked a dial on the liaison set to send a coded message: *mission complete.*

The night remained clear. A dome of stars arched over the Adriatic. Drew took in a long breath, then another. Closed his eyes for a moment and tried to calm his nerves by force of will. At least for now, Drew felt that whatever was left of his honor remained intact.

# CHAPTER 14
## Guerrilla Engineering

*E*ARLY MORNING MIST HUNG OVER THE HILLS OF RAVNA GORA. Bogdonavich had not slept well in his cellar, so he'd risen before first light. He longed for coffee or tea. Not wishing to disturb anyone inside the home, he'd stepped outside as quietly as possible.

Now, in the blacksmith's shop, he stoked the coals glowing in the forge. Added a stick of wood. Placed a kettle on an iron grate that lay across the fire. With a dipper made from a dried gourd, he transferred water from a wooden bucket to the kettle. From the supply room adjacent to the blacksmith's shop, he scrounged a tea bag. He dropped the tea bag into a clay cup. When the kettle began to steam, he poured hot water into the cup and waited for his tea to brew.

While he waited, he heard the sound of an engine laboring in the distance. He looked outside to see the Opel truck, used by the guerrillas, rolling along the path. This didn't worry him. The Chetniks came and went according to their own agenda, not all of which they shared with the Americans. Bogdonavich found more tea to offer the men, and he poured hot water into three more clay cups.

The Opel stopped in front of the blacksmith's shop. Bogdon-avich went outside to greet the fighters. Stefan and Gregor got out of the cab. They began talking with one of the three men sit-ting in the truck bed. Stefan gestured with his maimed right hand.

The man responded in Serbian so fluent and unaccented that Bogdonavich assumed he was another Chetnik. But when the stranger climbed down from the truck, Bogdonavich saw that he wore an assortment of U.S.-issued clothing. Mud spattered his leather paratrooper boots. His trousers, from an M42 jump uni-form, bulged with gear. Jump wings and captain's bars adorned his shirt. However, entirely out of accord with U.S. Army groom-ing standards, he wore a thick black beard. Atop his head, a Ser-bian *šajkača* completed his mixed ensemble. His hat, beard, and burly build let him fit right in with the Chetniks. In a leather hol-ster, he carried an M1911 handgun, just like Bogdonavich's. He called out to Bogdonavich in pure Yank English.

"Good morning, Lieutenant," the man said. "Who's in charge here?"

Bogdonavich gaped for a moment, unsure of what to make of this strange individual before him. Because they were technically in a combat zone, Bogdonavich did not salute. A salute could identify a valuable target for snipers. "Ah, I think you are now, sir," he said. "Captain?"

"That's right, Lieutenant. Captain George Marich. Let's just say I work for an agency other than the army."

"Yes, sir." The picture began to take shape in Bogdonavich's sleep-deprived mind. The radio calls. The codes. Finally the calls back, with vague answers. Clearly, this team had parachuted into Ravna Gora during the night. "It's very good to see you, sir," Bog-donavich said. "A lot of guys will be happy you're here."

Marich introduced the other two men: Sergeant Mike Racanin and radio operator Arthur Jezdich. The men had jumped with heavy packs. Bogdonavich helped them unload their gear from the truck, and he offered them tea. They sipped from their cups while Marich briefed Bogdonavich.

"We have three hundred of you boys here on the ground . . . ," Marich began.

"Three hundred?" Bogdonavich asked. "Every time I hear the number, it gets bigger."

"Yeah, same here. We keep getting intel from the field. And we think three hundred is on the low side. You guys said to send workhorses, so that's what we're going to do. We'll bring C-47s in here and fly you out," Marich said.

"Music to my ears, sir."

"First thing we gotta do is identify a landing site. Mike and Art and I are going to rest up a little. We've had a long night. But the locals will help us scout for a good field later today."

"What can we do to help?"

"Well, none of us are pilots. It'll help to have a pilot look at the landing ground."

"I'm a bombardier," Bogdonavich said. "But there are at least four pilots sleeping in that stable over there."

"Good. Let's take a little hike this afternoon."

Late in the day, Marich and his team, along with Bogdonavich and Tom Oliver, climbed into the back of the Opel. Stefan drove, with Gregor in the cab's passenger seat. After a couple of miles, Stefan turned off the dirt road onto a path barely wide enough for the truck. The vehicle churned across mud holes and the exposed roots of trees. A flock of mergansers burst from a streambed beside the path. Bogdonavich startled; his heart pounded. The ducks had taken flight so explosively that for an instant Bogdonavich thought the truck had hit a land mine.

Finally the vehicle stopped at the crest of a hill. Stefan turned off the engine and opened his door. Gregor exited from the other side. The Americans dismounted from the truck bed.

A green expanse of pasture sloped away from the crest. Pinewoods lined three sides of the pasture. A cornfield bordered one end. Oliver placed his hands on his hips and shook his head.

"Too short," he said.

"How much do we need?" Marich asked.

"I'm thinking at least three thousand feet."

Marich stroked his beard. Pulled a pipe and a pouch of to-bacco from his pockets and filled the bowl. To Bogdonavich, the gesture seemed so casual. Marich behaved more like a civil engi-neer surveying a job site than a special operator in a war zone.

"Didn't Doolittle's bombers have a whole lot less than that when they took off from the *Hornet?*" Marich asked. He packed the tobacco with his thumb, lit the pipe with a wooden match. The fragrance of burning pipe tobacco wafted through the air.

"Yeah," Oliver said, "but all they needed to do was take off, not land over obstacles like those trees. And they could turn that car-rier into the wind. We can't do that with a pasture."

In Serbian, Marich explained to Stefan why the pasture wouldn't do. Stefan nodded, made no argument. He conferred with Gregor, and the men piled back into the truck.

Stefan drove for twenty minutes. Never once did the wheels touch pavement; the entire route consisted of dirt roads and gravel paths. During the drive, Bogdonavich thanked Marich for his team's initiative.

"All in a day's work, Lieutenant," Marich said.

"Or a long night's work," Bogdonavich said.

"You got that right."

"Captain," Bogdonavich added, "you probably already know this, but our friends here are hurting for supplies." He told Marich about how Piotra died for want of antibiotics, and how Vasa was walking around with a hole in his boot.

"Yeah, we know," Marich said. "And I've been begging for months to get these guys some help."

"What's the holdup?"

"Some people in high places don't want to look like they're tak-ing sides between the Chetniks and the Partisans. Can't help one too much without helping the other. Wouldn't want our Soviet al-lies to get upset." Marich's voice dripped with sarcasm.

"I wish they could see what I've seen here," Bogdonavich said.

Marich smiled and looked away. Then he looked back at Bogdonavich and said, "In my agency, we have an unofficial slogan:
'Sometimes it's easier to ask forgiveness than permission.'"

Bogdonavich liked the sound of that. Maybe Marich had something in mind.

Finally Stefan stopped the truck. Here an open field stretched
for at least three thousand feet. It was not a pasture but a culti-
vated field left fallow for the season. Grass and weeds grew knee
high.

"I know the weeds are too high," Stefan said in his native
tongue. "Someone will have a horse-drawn mower. We will rake
up the weeds for hay and feed it to cattle."

"This might work," Oliver said. He scanned the field, swept at
the weeds with the toe of his boot. "Let's walk it and see if there's
any gullies or something under these weeds."

The men spread out line abreast and waded into the grass.
Weeds and vines tangled into Bogdonavich's bootlaces. He nearly
tripped twice. But he began to think they'd found their spot.

Then, in the middle of the field, they came to a slough. Grass
grew greener and thicker at the water's edge. In one of the larger
pools, minnows darted just beneath the surface. The presence of
the little fish suggested the slough was permanent, perhaps fed by
a spring. Not just a temporary wet spot after a rain.

From forty feet away, Bogdonavich heard Oliver muttering
curses.

"If a plane hits this wet spot," Bogdonavich told Marich, "she'll
cartwheel right over."

Once again, Stefan offered no argument when told why the
Americans were rejecting this field, too. He seemed to understand the considerations that went into choosing a landing
ground. He said, "I can think of another place, but it will require
some work."

"Why is that?" Marich asked.

"Rocks, mainly."

Stefan drove to a field that was closer to Pranjani than the other locations he'd shown the Americans. The field had been planted in grass for grazing cattle. Some of the grass had been cut for hay, and three haystacks stood at one end of the field. But when Bogdonavich jumped down from the truck bed, he saw immediately why Stefan hadn't chosen it first. The problem wasn't just rocks, which studded the entire field. There were also two granite boulders that rose up from the earth like the knees of a buried giant.

And the problem wasn't just rocks and boulders. The field dipped in the middle. The swale would have to be filled in.

With earthmoving equipment operated by combat engineers, the job would take days. With hand tools operated by flyboys and guerrillas, the job would take weeks.

Oliver stepped off the distance. He strode across the field, lips moving as he counted. When he came back, he said, "Well, it's long enough. And the obstacles aren't as bad as the other places— once we get rid of the boulders, anyway."

"Welcome to Pranjani International Airport," Marich said.

Bogdonavich eyed the field. Dandelions splashed bright yellow among the gray stones. He tried to imagine all the labor required to turn this into a safe airstrip.

"Can we get all this done before the Krauts catch on?" he wondered aloud.

"Not much choice," Marich said. "We'll need to post lookouts. If they see or hear a German plane, they'll blow a whistle or something."

"I get it," Oliver said. "The lookout blows the whistle, and the workers scatter into those trees." He pointed to woods on either side of the field.

"Exactly," Marich said. "If an enemy pilot sees a couple of guys working in a field, that's normal. But if he sees a hundred, he knows something's up."

"Well," Bogdonavich said, "if busting rocks like I'm on a chain gang is the quickest way home, then I'll bust rocks."

In Serbian, Marich told Stefan the fliers had decided this spot would answer their needs. He added that Stefan had been correct that the place would need a lot of improvement.

"We are used to work," Stefan said.

As if to prove his point, he picked up two stones that lay at his feet. Each looked nearly the size of a bowling ball. Stefan palmed them as if they were as light as pillows. His right hand, despite the missing finger, gripped as strongly as the left. He walked to the edge of the field and tossed the rocks into the woods.

# CHAPTER 15
# Why Are We So Poor?

V ASA SWUNG THE SLEDGEHAMMER AS IF HE COULD POUND AWAY ALL his worries and grief. The iron head rang each time it struck the boulder. Every blow reduced the granite stone. Sometimes large chunks cracked away. At other times, only chips flew. The fatigue in Vasa's muscles felt like a catharsis. Here, he could channel everything that vexed him. This boulder represented the enemy. This boulder represented the infection that killed Piotra. It represented the heartbreak of Aleksandra's letter and the awful uncertainty of Vasa's home under Partisan control.

Fifty meters away, Vasa's American friend Bogdonavich hammered on another boulder. Dozens of other men, Americans and Serbs, swarmed the field. They picked up stones, and they carried the larger ones into the woods. They placed smaller stones in wheelbarrows and dumped them along the low spot in the field. The plan called for filling the swale partly with small rocks, then smoothing it over with dirt.

"Welcome to the United States Army Air Forces," Bogdonavich said to Vasa. "You're building an air base, so now you're an honorary sergeant."

Vasa looked over at the Yank. He smiled and nodded, then

blew a drop of sweat from the tip of his nose. Raised the hammer and swung it again.

He could have had an easier job. At each corner of the field, a man stood with his arms folded in apparent idleness. But they were not shirkers. Each wore a whistle on a lanyard around his neck. If he saw or heard a German aircraft, he was to blow the whistle with all the breath his lungs could force. These men were to devote all their attention to scanning the skies. Vasa had declined an offer to post as a lookout today. He preferred this work with muscle and metal.

At midday, a truck pulled up beside the field—but not the old Opel that Vasa had seen coming and going from Pranjani. This was a newer model. When a man stepped down from the passenger side, Vasa recognized him as General Mihailovich. Though he'd never met the general, he'd seen pictures of him in newspapers. The commander with the scholarly bearing had become famous. Any Serb would have known that face with the thick black beard, the wire-rimmed glasses, the weathered brow, and atop his head, a *šajkača* bearing the royalist crest.

Other men dismounted from the truck bed. They began unloading crates. One of the men called out in a loud voice, "Brothers, our general has brought you lunch."

Across the field, cheers erupted. Men dropped their tools and gathered around the truck. The general's staff opened the crates to reveal apples, cheese, bread, and sausages. Metal canisters contained water. Workers lined up to receive the food. General Mihailovich gazed across the field, adjusted his eyeglasses, and lit a cigar.

"Splendid, my boys, splendid," Mihailovich called. "I see you are already changing the shape of the land."

Three Americans stood next to the general. Mihailovich spoke with them in Serbian. One of them looked like a Chetnik. He wore a *šajkača* and a thick beard. The man was thickset like a strong Serb, in contrast to his tall and skinny countrymen. The Yanks called him Marich.

Vasa joined the line to receive his lunch. He sat down in the grass with Bogdonavich, Nikolas, and Miroslav. Steadied his tin cup of water on a stone that would soon be removed. Broke a chunk of bread in half. Nikolas and Miroslav began devouring sausages with their hands. Bogdonavich crunched into an apple. While they ate, Mihailovich addressed the men.

"In the villages, in the hills around you," the general said, "we are harboring more than five hundred downed airmen."

Vasa's eyes widened. Bogdonavich stopped chewing on the apple. Miroslav and Nikolas looked at each other.

"Yes," Mihailovich continued, "that number surprises even me. It increases nearly every day, and it demonstrates the fierce commitment of our American friends."

Nikolas slapped Bogdonavich on the back. The Yanks who didn't speak Serbian—which was almost all of them—looked puzzled. But they seemed to gather from the cheers that the general had said something good about them.

Mihailovich introduced Marich; he called him "Captain George." "This man is coordinating between our forces and those of his country," Mihailovich said. "I have worked with him before. He is practically one of us. Captain George is so brave that he leaps from perfectly good aeroplanes—and that is merely how he travels to work."

Laughter rippled across the field. Vasa knew well how the Chetniks appreciated their leader's sense of humor. Several of them nodded and gave Marich respectful looks. Vasa also knew they admired courage above all.

"I cannot thank you enough for your efforts," Marich began, speaking in fluent Serbian. "I do not need to tell you time is critical, especially with five hundred downed fliers. You and your families have shown tremendous courage and initiative in hiding these men. But with numbers this large, our luck cannot hold out. The Germans will discover them. Not a question of *if*, but *when.* So every day counts. Every minute counts."

Marich paused and lit a pipe. Vasa sat close enough to smell the aroma of tobacco. Marich took a pull from his pipe, clenched the stem between his teeth, and shook out his match. Smoke curled around him as he continued.

"As soon as this airfield is ready," Marich said, "we will begin flying in transport aircraft to pick up our men. This will be the most dangerous phase of the operation, with the greatest risk of exposure. It will take place over several nights. Our challenge is to hold this area secure until the last plane leaves."

"Woe to any Nazi who trespasses here in Ravna Gora," Mihailovich said. The men cheered.

When the briefing ended, Marich conversed in English with the two Americans who had arrived with him in the truck. One of the Yanks began to set up radio gear in the back of the vehicle. The man connected wires to electric boxes, and he placed earphones over his head. The radioman fiddled with knobs and switches. He appeared to listen intently, and he spoke more words in English to Marich.

While the Americans worked, General Mihailovich filled his mess kit with food from the crates. This impressed Vasa: The general was the last man to eat. Mihailovich moved to join the little circle of men around Vasa. Vasa started to stand and salute, but the general motioned for him to stay seated.

"As you were, my boys," Mihailovich said.

Bogdonavich introduced himself. Mihailovich asked about the Yank's home and how he had come to be shot down. Bogdonavich described how he had bailed out of his stricken aeroplane—a story Vasa had not heard before.

"May you be reunited with all your friends soon," Mihailovich said.

"Thank you, sir," Bogdonavich said. "My American friends here are probably wondering what you and Captain Marich just briefed in Serbian. I'll go translate for them."

Men began returning to their work. As Vasa rose to go back to his sledgehammer, one of the Americans, Marich, came over to the general. He kneeled beside Mihailovich and whispered words in English. The general's face darkened. Mihailovich and Marich spoke for a few more minutes.

"Our mission keeps getting more complicated," the general said finally. "Our American friends have radioed some of their contacts. It seems Partisan squads are probing our region."

"We will meet them with fire and lead," Nikolas said.

"Indeed, we will," Mihailovich said. "We do not need their interference now."

Back at his boulder, Vasa lifted the hammer and swung it again. Tiny fragments of stone flew from the boulder and stung his face. But the blow knocked very little away from the main rock. Vasa swung again. This time, he broke off a piece the size of his fist.

While he worked, he considered the news he'd just overheard. *What is wrong with those Partisans?* Vasa wondered. *Why must they fight us when we should all be fighting the Germans? And why must those Communists trouble my own home village?*

The question had no answer, of course, but it reminded Vasa of a folk tale his father had told him. One evening by the fireplace, his father said, "Why are we Serbs so poor?" Then his father told the story of how the nations had divided among themselves the best things of life:

> *The Italians went first. "We wish for art," they said, and they were granted their wish.*
>
> *The British came next. "We want rule of the sea," they said, and they were granted their wish.*
>
> *Then came the Russians. "We would like vast forests and rich mines," they said, and they were granted their wish.*
>
> *Then came the Greeks. "We long for wisdom and philosophy," they said, and they were granted their wish.*
>
> *Then came the Serbs. "Wait for us to decide among ourselves," they said. And the world still waits.*

The general and his staff, along with Marich and the two Americans with him, mounted the truck. The engine clattered to life, and the vehicle pulled onto the gravel road and disappeared around a curve. Vasa had enjoyed Mihailovich's reassuring presence, and he wondered if he'd see the general again.

The shrill piercing of a whistle interrupted Vasa's thoughts. He looked up from the boulder. Men were running for the trees.

Three other whistles began blowing. In the corner of his eye, Vasa saw two specks above the horizon. He did not look closer. Instead, he dropped the hammer and sprinted.

Bogdonavich ran just ahead of him. The two took shelter beneath a spruce. The Yank bent over with his hands on his thighs, panting. All around them, workers dashed into the woods. Leaves and underbrush rustled with their footfalls. Bogdonavich wiped his forehead with his sleeve and squinted upward through the branches. Two aeroplanes growled overhead at a fairly low altitude. Each had two motors. Vasa noted bulblike noses. He could make out no markings.

"Are they German?" Vasa asked.

"Yes," Bogdonavich said. "They're Junkers Ju 88s. Sons of bitches."

"Did they see us?"

The American wiped sweat from his face again. Stared after the receding planes.

"No way to know."

# CHAPTER 16
# The Emperor and the Paratrooper

$O$N SHORT FINAL APPROACH DURING A TRAINING FLIGHT AT SAN
Pancrazio, Drew glanced down at his airspeed indicator. He
knuckled the throttles back slightly. The C-47 slowed to a little
above its power-off stall speed, about seventy miles per hour.
Drew eyed the touchdown zone marked on the runway. Though
no obstacles stood in his way, he imagined he was landing over a
line of fifty-foot trees at the edge of a dirt strip.

"Center line," Torres called.

The wind had blown the aircraft a bit to the left. Drew dipped his
right wing and corrected back toward the middle of the runway.

"Bird," Montreux called. He pointed to a seagull soaring at
about three hundred feet.

"I see him," Drew called.

When the gull saw the plane, it folded its wings and dived out
of the way.

"That was good of him," Montreux said.

"Birds usually do that," Drew said. "If they see you, they go
down, not up."

"You're looking good," Torres said.

The vertical speed indicator showed a five-hundred-foot-per-minute descent. Drew held his power setting and control inputs. The aircraft was crabbed a few degrees nose right. The crab angle held his course against the right crosswind. At fifty feet, he pressed the left rudder pedal to straighten the nose. Dropped the right wing a little to kill the resulting drift. He pulled back on the control column to begin his roundout. The C-47 touched down first on its right wheel, then on its left.

Drew chopped his power. He let the tail wheel settle to the ground, pressed hard on the toe brakes. He and his crewmates strained forward against their harnesses as the aircraft decelerated.

In the corner of his eye, he saw a runway distance marker go past.

"What do you think?" Drew asked. "Twenty-five hundred feet?"

"Yeah, about," Torres said.

Drew turned off the runway and taxied back toward the departure end. The big radial engines sputtered and belched smoke.

"All right," Drew told Torres. "Your turn. Let's see if we can cut that distance down."

Drew didn't know exactly how much distance they'd have when the time came to land for the rescue mission. But he knew it wouldn't be much. And they'd have to do it at night. Zero room for error. Both he and his copilot needed to be equally proficient. If the aircraft commander took a bullet from ground fire, the copilot would have to take over.

They practiced short-field landings for most of the morning. Drew offered Torres tips on easing out of the crab angle and flaring smoothly. The aircraft carried its full crew: Navigator Chisholm and radio operator Calvert suffered through the seemingly endless takeoffs and landings. They weren't there just for ballast; Drew wanted every man on board to get used to what a short landing should look like. At the navigator's table, Chisholm marked a check on a training form for every touchdown.

Finally Drew taxied back into the hardstand and pulled the mixture levers to cutoff. The propellers spun down, and a ground crewman placed chocks around the main wheels. In a hangar's shade, the crew debriefed.

"Could we cut the distance with a three-point touchdown?" Torres asked. He was referring to a technique that involved letting the tail wheel and both main wheels make contact at the same instant.

"The book says not to do that," Drew said. "If you happen to get too slow and drop her in, you could break something."

"Don't wanna do that," Montreux said.

Drew could well imagine what a disaster that would be: a broken airplane on the ground in hostile territory, injured crew members, and, worst of all, an airstrip blocked. Mission failure. The considerations brought to the front of his mind all the things that could go wrong. All his fears.

The crew discussed every landing from that morning—what had gone well, what could stand improvement. While they talked, Drew noticed activity on the other side of the hangar. A GMC deuce-and-a-half with army markings pulled up to the front of the building. Two men dismounted, and they began unloading boxes and cartons from the back. They sorted the cartons by size and laid them out on wooden pallets. Labeling on one box read: U.S. ARMY MEDICAL CORPS, DYED STERILIZED DRESSING. Another read: QUININE AND PHOSPHOROUS TABLETS. Yet another: IODINE SWABS.

Whatever the strangers were doing, Drew decided it didn't concern him. There was plenty besides Operation Halyard going on at San Pancrazio.

Drew wrapped up his debrief. He asked if anyone had any concerns, and no one spoke up. Drew decided now might be a good time to work on his own concerns—and to see if Chisholm's civilian studies offered any reassurance.

"Who was that guy you were telling me about the other day?" Drew asked his navigator. "The Roman emperor?"

"Marcus Aurelius," Chisholm said. "There's a book of his writings called *Meditations.*"

"So, what did he meditate about?"

"Stoic philosophy, mainly. He was big on understanding what you can control and what you can't. Your happiness isn't based on good fortune or wealth. It's based on knowing you've handled with virtue whatever came your way."

To Drew, it sounded like Marcus Aurelius would have made a good instructor pilot. Drew thanked his crew for their hard work that morning. Then he set off on his own for lunch. Though he always enjoyed the company of his crewmates, today he had another mission: He wanted to go back into town and check on Sienna.

At Antonio's, Drew found a bigger lunch crowd than he'd seen before. Diners filled every table. Soldiers and sailors, Tommies and Yanks, and even a couple of French officers—all babbled in at least two languages and a dozen accents. At first, Drew decided to fly a go-around, to give up and come back later. But Antonio saw him turn toward the door. Antonio waded through the busy tables and pulled him to the little wine bar. Drew took a seat on a wooden stool.

"Always a place for you, Lieutenant Drew," Antonio said.

"Thank you, sir."

Sienna emerged from the kitchen with a pitcher of water. Lucia followed her, carrying two plates of spaghetti. Lucia smiled at him. Sienna met his gaze, but offered no reaction.

Antonio brought a new menu. It featured the same misspellings and strikeovers, but included a few new dishes. Obviously, business was good. Drew decided on one of the new items: olives, onions, and sausages.

Lucia came to take Drew's order.

"I hope you like it," Lucia said. "I made it up myself."

"How is Sienna doing? I hope those men from the other night didn't come back?"

"No," Lucia said. "You and your friends did a fine job of putting them off this place. As for Sienna, I will send her over so she can tell you herself."

While Drew waited, he couldn't help but overhear the conversations around him. Three British officers at a nearby table seemed indignant about something.

"Nasty business, it was," one of them said. "Just a damned shame."

"Bloody disgrace," said another.

Drew wondered what sort of calamity they were talking about. They were British Army officers; none wore pilot's wings. Maybe they were discussing an infantry disaster. There had been a few: Earlier this year at Anzio, the Allies had nearly snatched defeat from the jaws of victory.

"The Frogs simply lost control of their men," one of the Brits said.

Drew changed his mind. That didn't sound like Anzio. What were they talking about?

"There are Italian women in Ceccano who'll have worse memories of the Allies than of the Germans," another said.

Drew looked up to see Sienna frozen outside the kitchen door, listening to the Brits. She seemed to understand whatever they were talking about, and it clearly wasn't good. She returned to the kitchen, then came back with Drew's plate of food.

Sienna set the dish down in front of him. She smelled of lavender and onions. Her modest cream-colored dress was buttoned to the neck, but it couldn't hide her figure. The long sleeves might have covered the scar on her arm, except that she'd pushed up the sleeves nearly to her elbows as she worked. Her dark hair flowed down her back in a ponytail.

"Lieutenant Drew," she said. "Can I get you anything else? More olives?" Her voice betrayed no emotion.

"No," Drew said. "I just . . . I know the other evening was a bad night for you, and I wanted to make sure you're okay."

Sienna did not answer. She did not smile. For what felt like an eternity—the eternity of the few seconds when a takeoff could go from normal to disaster—she spoke not a word. Some of the color drained from her face.

"It wasn't your fault," she said finally. "Things would have gone far worse, had you and your friends not been there."

Without another word, she turned and went back to the kitchen.

From the bar, Drew watched Sienna. She plunged her hands

into a sink filled with dishwater and began scrubbing. She paused her work and bowed her head. Looked like she was trying not to cry.

When she came back to the dining room, she had brought her emotions under control. She went about her work as if nothing had happened. She did not look at Drew.

He decided to stay just long enough to finish his meal without doing further damage. He pulled out dollar bills to pay for his meal. Sienna came to collect his tab.

She picked up the money and the paper slip. Crinkled them in her pocket.

"Lieutenant Drew," Sienna said, "truly, I am glad you were there."

As she spoke, she touched Drew's hand. He looked up, and he saw her eyes were brimming.

When Drew drove back to San Pancrazio, he found the usual afternoon activity at the base. A pair of P-51 Mustangs took off as he entered the gate. Their distinctive whistle-growl rose, then faded as they receded into the blue.

When he stopped by his tent, he found it empty. Tight blankets stretched over each cot. The air hung close and warm. On his own cot, he found a book.

Chisholm had left him a well-thumbed paperback copy of *The Meditations of Marcus Aurelius*. Drew sat on his cot and flipped through the pages. One particular line caught his eye: *Do not act as if you have ten thousand years to live. Death hangs over you. Be good for something while you live and it is in your power.*

That sounded so much like the paratrooper he'd met in an Officers' Club weeks ago. The guy had said, "Consider yourself already dead." At the time, the words sounded so resigned, so hopeless.

But Aurelius expressed the same idea with a different spin. Both the emperor and the paratrooper had found power in their own mortality. The prospect of death did not paralyze them; it emboldened them. Somehow a twentieth-century paratrooper and a second-century ruler had arrived at the same place.

Drew placed the book in his footlocker. He decided to stop by Operations and check the flying schedule. He expected more training flights in the coming week. That routine would probably hold until the OSS decided it was time for the main event.

But in Ops, he found the chalkboard for next week blank. Whatever the sergeant had written there, he'd scrubbed off with the white-powdered eraser. That was no surprise; schedules were always changing. Air force men had a joke about that: It's operational security. How can the enemy know what we're doing if *we* don't know what we're doing?

On the flight line, Drew found Montreux at their airplane. The engineer stood on a ladder by the right engine. He'd opened the cowl. Oily rags and a toolbox lay at the foot of the ladder.

"Afternoon, sir," Montreux said. "Just changing the oil."

"Need any help?"

"No, sir. I got it."

The Italian sun hammered the tarmac. Heat waves danced along the runway and taxiway. Drew sought shade in the open hangar where he'd debriefed his crew this morning.

The medical supplies unloaded by the strangers were still there. Other boxes also sat on pallets. Some were labeled: 1600 CARTRIDGES CAL. 30-06 M1. Others read: U.S. ARMY FIELD RATION K. One was stamped: U.S. ARMY SIGNAL CORPS. Drew supposed that contained radio equipment.

Everything was rigged for an airdrop.

# CHAPTER 17
## If This Rifle Could Talk

*B*OGDONAVICH EXAMINED THE RIFLE LOANED TO HIM BY HIS NEW Serbian friends. Scratches and gouges marred the wooden stock. He wondered which of the scars came during German service and which in service of the Serbs. A leather sling dangled from a swivel on the left side of the weapon. Age and use had cracked and faded the leather. Markings on the bolt read: Waffenfabrik Mauser A.G., Oberndorf, 1917.

*If only this thing could talk.* Bogdonavich wondered where it had been, what lives it had taken. And what journey it had traveled to become his for a time in the hills of Ravna Gora.

He opened the bolt and top-loaded a five-round clip of 8mm cartridges. Closed the bolt, which chambered a round. Thumbed the safety lever to the right, like Nikolas had shown him. Now the weapon was ready for action, but it wouldn't go off unless he moved the safety to the left. As always, Bogdonavich also carried his .45 in a holster on his belt, but the old rifle offered greater range.

With Vasa's help, Bogdonavich had talked Nikolas into letting him join them on patrol. He'd presented several arguments: With Piotra gone, the squad was down a man. Also, there were plenty of other men and boys to continue working on the airfield; Bogdonavich could let someone else pound rocks for a while. And why should the Serbs take all the risk while the Americans stayed behind in relative safety?

But he'd never voiced his main reason. He considered this mission a form of . . . atonement. All his life he'd felt a little embarrassed about his heritage. Some of his father's ways had appeared so old-fashioned and narrow. America was moving into the modern world of air travel, electricity, and radio. Indoor plumbing, for heaven's sake. Many of Bogdonavich's schoolmates came from families who'd lived in the United States for generations. Families that fit so naturally into the life of this century. But Dad, with his folk tales and stories of the Old Country, seemed a visitor. A tourist from another time, who'd never really wanted to leave that time.

Now, however, he saw his father in a new light. Dad came from people like Vasa, Nikolas, Piotra, and Miroslav. And General Mihailovich. They faced their world as it came, with little complaint. What did modern convenience and style matter with survival at stake? Yet they found time and resources to shelter hundreds of foreign airmen when it would have been easier to let the fliers fend for themselves.

Two squads coordinated for this mission—the one led by Nikolas and the one led by Stefan. Men climbed into the bed of the Opel truck, with Stefan and Gregor in the cab. Stefan steered along a dirt road that cut through a pine forest and opened into fields of corn and barley.

Bogdonavich rode in the back beside Vasa. They steadied themselves by clinging to wooden rails mounted along the sides of the truck. The balancing act took a bit of effort, because there wasn't much room for their feet. A Browning M2 .50-cal from an American airplane lay on the truck bed, along with a makeshift tripod and a metal ammo can. Evidently, the guerrillas had salvaged the weapon from a downed bomber. A hawk wheeled overhead. Bogdonavich squinted up at the bird, wished he could join it in the air. Then he lost the hawk in the glare of the sun.

From what he could gather, the overall mission plan, which included several other squads, was pretty simple. General Mihailovich was deploying detachments to watch the routes into sections of Ravna Gora where most of the airmen were hiding. The lockdown would remain in place until the Americans could fly in and take their men away. Any meddling Partisans or Germans would be dealt with.

At a seemingly random point in the forest, the truck stopped. Trees cast dappled shade over the road. The Opel's engine idled quietly enough for Bogdonavich to hear birds calling in the branches overhead.

"We walk from here," Nikolas said.

Without further instruction, what was left of Nikolas's squad dismounted. The other men moved out of the way while Miroslav dragged out the M2. He hefted the heavy-barreled weapon as if it were light as a hoe. On his web belt, Miroslav carried a hatchet and a long knife.

Vasa lifted the tripod. He carried his rifle across his back. Nikolas took the ammo can, along with a Thompson submachine gun slung over his shoulder. Bogdonavich felt almost guilty that he carried the lightest burden—just the Mauser and a knapsack of field rations. As soon as he hopped down from the vehicle, Stefan sped away with Gregor and the rest of his men. They were to take up an ambush site farther down the road.

Nikolas led through the trees. Vasa trotted close behind him, moving uphill over the leaf carpet as nimbly as a squirrel. Miroslav lagged just a few yards behind them. Bogdonavich found himself in the Tail-End Charlie position. He panted, took long strides in an effort to keep the others in sight. Morning dew clung to weeds and ferns and moistened his pants legs.

He caught up with the fighters at the top of a wooded ridge. From the ridge, the land pitched down at a steep angle into a gorge. A river surged through the gorge. Bogdonavich could not see the water, but he heard it rushing over rocks. He could, however, see a bridge that spanned the river. The bridge appeared to be part of the same road Stefan had taken in the Opel.

Now Bogdonavich understood the tactical situation a little better. He was an airman, not an infantryman, so these things didn't come naturally. But Nikolas had chosen an elevated firing position above the bridge. If he saw anything he didn't like, he could chew it to pieces with the .50-cal.

"We need to get closer," Nikolas said.

The squad shuffled downhill. Vasa nearly slipped under the weight of the tripod, but he shifted to a one-handed grip and crooked his free arm around a sapling. They stopped at a rock shelf a few hundred yards above the bridge. A fairly long shot for the Mauser, but within its lethal range. And well within the range of the .50. Pine boughs sheltered the rock shelf. The branches provided natural camouflage.

From this closer position, Bogdonavich spotted a mill beneath the bridge. Water flowed clear and fast through the raceway, but the waterwheel stood motionless. The mill appeared to be abandoned. Bogdonavich could not tell whether it was still operational at all.

Miroslav bolted the M2 to its tripod. Lifted the breech cover, opened the ammo can, and loaded the cartridge belt into the feedway. Cycled the slide handle. He swiveled the barrel toward the bridge. Aimed left and right. Twisted the tripod to adjust his field of fire. Aimed again. When he was satisfied with his setup, he sat on the ground behind the .50 and took a pack of cigarettes from his shirt pocket. Shook out a cigarette and placed it in his mouth. Wordlessly offered one to Bogdonavich.

"No, thank you," Bogdonavich said.

Miroslav lit the cigarette, exhaled the smoke. A bitter tang wafted through the air; this was one of those harsh smokes of local manufacture. Nikolas crouched with the Thompson gun cradled under his arm. Vasa leaned against a tree and placed his rifle—a Mauser, like the one loaned to Bogdonavich—across his lap.

At first glance, the guerrillas would have seemed in repose, like factory workers outside on a smoke break. But Bogdonavich noticed their eyes. They scanned constantly. The men didn't talk much, because they were listening. They seemed to fall into a familiar pattern of watching and waiting. This duty had become second nature. Even Vasa looked like a veteran.

An hour passed without a word between them. Eventually Vasa pointed, silently. His teammates raised up for a better look.

A man led a mule pulling a cart. Some sort of equipment lay in the cart.

Bogdonavich opened the knapsack. In addition to rations, he'd also brought a pair of binoculars. He raised the binoculars to his eyes, twisted the adjustment ring. The effort brought the mule and cart into focus. The equipment in the cart was a mule-drawn plow. Bogdonavich passed the field glasses to Nikolas. The team leader looked, shrugged, and passed the field glasses back. The mule clopped across the bridge, its owner oblivious to the weaponry locked and loaded above him.

Two hours later, firing echoed from the next ridge. The fighters rose into ready positions, fingers across trigger guards. More shots crackled in the distance.

"That is one of our posts," Nikolas said.

The shooting paused. For a moment, Bogdonavich thought it was over. Then it started up again. From across the valley, the fusillade sounded like popcorn.

Nikolas and his men watched the bridge, scanned the road. Nothing came into view. Bogdonavich and the guerrillas could only wait and wonder.

When trouble did come their way, it came not by road.

Bogdonavich heard the engines first. He looked up. Didn't sound like B-24s or B-17s. In fact, it didn't sound like an American formation at all. The buzz filled the valley; the noise emanated from something flying low.

A cruciform shape appeared just over the horizon. Bogdonavich reached for the binoculars again. When he raised them to his eyes, he lost sight of the aircraft. He had to search for a moment, then readjust the focus ring. When the view sharpened, he recognized a twin-engine aircraft with a bulbous cockpit. A greenhouse-like canopy shielded two crew members. A swastika had been painted across the vertical stabilizer.

"Is it German?" Nikolas asked.

"Yeah," Bogdonavich said in English. Then in Serbian: "It's a Messerschmitt 410. They call it the Hornet."

From aircraft recognition charts, Bogdonavich remembered it as a fighter-bomber. But the Krauts could use it for reconnaissance as well. That appeared to be this aircraft's mission, given that it flew alone. And if it were reconning for guerrilla forces, it wouldn't fly high like an American P-38 taking pictures of German factories. It would get down in the weeds, just like this. If the aircraft came a bit closer, Bogdonavich could hit it with his borrowed Mauser.

From behind the Browning, Miroslav gave Nikolas a questioning look. Nikolas shook his head.

"Are you sure?" Miroslav asked. He slid the tripod. Repositioned the weapon for a firing position aimed upward instead of down toward the bridge. Tree branches remained in his way, but not as many as before.

"Fire only if they try to strafe us," Nikolas said. "They do not need to know we are here."

"It would be a fine thing to take down one of their aeroplanes," Miroslav said.

"Yes, it would," Nikolas said. "But not today." He spoke the last three words slowly, for emphasis.

"It's still out of range," Bogdonavich offered. He understood Miroslav's temptation; part of him wanted to raise the Mauser to his shoulder and start shooting at the German plane.

The Hornet banked over the valley and came around for another pass. Bogdonavich wondered if it mounted a camera like the photorecon versions of the P-38, or if the crew was simply scanning visually. Miroslav began to track the aircraft with the Browning. The barrel swung in an arc.

"These trees provide us cover," Nikolas said. "The pilot probably will not see us."

"And what if he does?" Miroslav said. His eyes—and his hands and the gun barrel—still followed the Hornet. "He will go back and report our position, but I could take him down now."

"And if he doesn't get back to his base," Nikolas said, "the Germans will find the crash site and find the Americans. You follow my orders!"

Nikolas rested his right hand on the receiver of his Thompson gun, still hanging from his shoulder by its sling. *Would he shoot Miroslav?* Bogdonavich wondered.

The plane drew nearer. Inside the bubble canopy, figures of two crewmen became clearer. Bogdonavich could discern their leather helmets. Miroslav kept both hands on the spade handle grips of the M2. Nikolas raised his submachine gun. His face remained expressionless, impassive. In that moment, Bogdonavich knew without doubt that Nikolas would gun down his friend if necessary to protect the mission. These guerrillas could not afford an ounce of sentimentality. Or indiscipline.

Underneath the buzz of engine noise, Bogdonavich heard a distinct click. It was Nikolas, thumbing the safety on his Thompson gun.

Bogdonavich raised the field glasses again. Now he could make out the antenna on the underside of the fuselage. The wings stayed level; the plane was not turning.

"I don't think they see us," Bogdonavich said. He hoped his remark would help defuse the situation.

Neither man fired. Nor did the Hornet crew.

The aircraft whooshed over the ridgeline and disappeared behind the trees. When the plane came back into view, it was climbing.

"I think it's leaving," Bogdonavich said.

The aircraft shrank to a speck in the distance. The engine noise lowered from a roar to a whine, and then to silence broken only by the rustle of leaves.

Bogdonavich looked at the rifle in his hands. Considered the strangeness of what had just happened. Here he was, a downed airman seeking rescue, and with a team that had almost opened fire on an enemy plane. If they had, he would have fired this rifle at it, too—and the rifle would have had another story to tell.

He thought of a saying he kept hearing. He'd heard it when a short in a fuel pump blew up a B-24 sitting safely on the ground. He'd heard it when a stricken German fighter fell through a formation and cut the wing off a bomber. He'd heard it when a radio operator's oxygen mask failed and the man nearly died of hypoxia: *"Funny kind of war."*

Miroslav took his hands off the M2. He eyed Nikolas, who still gripped the Thompson gun.

"Would you have shot me?" Miroslav asked. He smiled as he spoke.

Nikolas made no response. He only stared at Miroslav as if he'd asked an unbelievably stupid question.

# CHAPTER 18
## If You Set Out for Revenge

V ASA PONDERED THE SCENE HE'D JUST WITNESSED. TRIED TO THINK through whatever lessons it offered. Everyone is expendable, he concluded. And the mission reigns supreme. Surely, Miroslav, like any guerrilla, would have loved to bag a Nazi aeroplane. But as Nikolas had said, today was not the day. One must be guided by judgment and not emotion. Nor bloodlust.

No other vehicles, German or Partisan, passed by road or air for the rest of the day. At sundown, the men heard footsteps coming up the timbered hillside. They readied their weapons, but relaxed when they heard the whistled sign. Nikolas whistled the countersign. Four men came to relieve them. They carried the usual assortment of Mausers, Springfields, and Enfields. Their web belts sagged with canteens, knives, and ammunition pouches. Vasa had seen them before, but did not know them well.

"What have you spotted?" one of them asked.

"We saw a German aeroplane," Nikolas said. "It was searching, but it did not find us."

"Very good. By the by, your friends have a guest."

Nikolas cocked his head in a questioning manner, but the other guerrilla offered no explanation. The new team took over the position on the rock shelf above the bridge. Nikolas left the

Browning in place for them. He briefed them on its operation, how to use the trigger lever, how to clear a jam.

Vasa was curious about this "guest," but he didn't ask. He, Miroslav, and Bogdonavich followed Nikolas downhill to the road. In the earlier excitement, Vasa hadn't noticed how tired he had become. But now, the rifle across his shoulder and the British pistol on his belt hung heavy. The day's last light still revealed the tops of the trees, but the ground lay in near darkness. They found the Opel idling. The men with whom they'd ridden that morning waited in the truck bed. But with them rode an additional passenger.

A boy no older than Vasa sat with his back to the rear of the cab. His hands were tied behind him. Even in the dim light, Vasa saw bruises and scrapes on the boy's face. The captive kept his eyes fixed on the wooden slats of the truck bed. Dirt and scraps of leaves mingled in his hair. Over black civilian trousers, he wore a military tunic in the Russian style.

Vasa put together the day's events: Before the German aeroplane, he and his team had heard a firefight in the distance. The skirmish must have involved the squad led by Stefan. And they had captured a Partisan.

Grief and anger welled up inside Vasa as if a great illness had seized him. This . . . this *thing* in front of him kept him from writing home. This damnable Communist and his like had taken over Velika. This satanic son of a whore forced the Serbs to divide their resources, to fight Soviet godlessness and German evil at the same time.

Vasa sprang like a cat.

He lunged forward. Drove his left fist into the boy's chest. Ignored the rifle clattering from the sling around his shoulder. Pounded with his right fist. The boy grunted as Vasa's blows forced air from his chest. Vasa dropped his hand to the rifle.

Before he could do more damage, Nikolas and Bogdonavich pulled him back.

"STOP IT!" Nikolas shouted. Nikolas shoved him against the side rails. "What is wrong with you?"

Vasa breathed hard, glared back at Nikolas.

"Let him beat the Partisan to death," a man from Stefan's detachment said. "It would make good sport."

"He is under my command," Nikolas said. "Tend to your business."

"What difference does it make if we kill him now or later?" the man asked.

Nikolas turned on the man, fists clenched. "I said tend to your business," he said.

From the driver's seat, Stefan opened his door. He twisted toward the truck bed and asked, "What is going on back there?"

"Nothing," Nikolas called. "Drive on."

Vasa's rage began to subside. He picked up his rifle and placed it across his knees. Bogdonavich took the weapon.

"I'll hold that for you," the American said.

A needless gesture. Vasa wasn't going to shoot the boy, at least not now. He steadied his breaths, tried to collect his thoughts. The truck jolted into gear and began rolling through the twilight.

In Pranjani, the men climbed down from the vehicle. Stefan ordered two of his fighters to take the prisoner. They grabbed him by the arms, slid him to the back of the truck bed, and dropped him to the ground. The boy tumbled onto his side. He rose up on his knees, then stood. Kept his eyes on the ground.

"Put him in the stable," Stefan said. "Keep two guards on him. Do not kill him."

"What will happen to him?" Bogdonavich asked.

"I do not know," Stefan said. "We will tell the staff we have him."

Stefan's men marched the boy away into the darkness. Vasa watched him go.

Vasa's squad took their evening meal by lantern light in the blacksmith's shop. Bogdonavich joined them. The village wives had made *gibanica*, a pastrylike dish of phyllo crust, white cheese, and eggs. Vasa had seen *gibanica* served at festivals and passed out to workers at the end of a big job, such as building a barn. Maybe the women had baked to celebrate the work on the airfield. If so, they were a little early. There was still much work to do. The men ate cold slices with their fingers as they discussed the day's events.

"How did they come to capture the prisoner?" Miroslav asked.

Nikolas wiped his hands on his sleeves and sipped from a canteen. "They said the Partisans did not come by road," Nikolas said. "They just encountered them in the forest. There was a gun battle. The boy was the only survivor."

"He probably knows little of use to us."

"True."

Vasa wondered how much to say. He was beginning to feel ashamed he had lost his temper. But would it be better simply not to mention it? Finally he said, "I am sorry I got so mad."

Several seconds passed before Nikolas responded. After what felt like a long time, he said, "I understand your anger. They hold your home village. But we must be better than they are, just like we must be better than the Nazis."

Vasa knew his team leader was right. But he also knew not every Chetnik felt that way. He'd heard stories of Partisan captives lined up against a wall and shot. "They shoot us, so we shoot them," the logic went. But Vasa had also heard his priest say that if a man sets out for revenge, he should dig two graves.

"It's not my place to tell people here what to do," Bogdonavich said, "but I worry about the prisoner. My army has rules about such things."

"Stefan's men will follow his orders," Nikolas said. "Beyond that, I do not know what will happen."

Morning brought a rush of activity to Pranjani. After breakfast, guerrillas and aviators began heading out to work on the airfield. A few caught rides in a truck. Most walked. Vasa laced on his boots to get ready for work. The hole in his right boot had grown larger. His socks had holes in them, too. He wiggled his right toes, visible through what remained of his footwear.

Vasa wasn't the only one lacking proper boots. He watched Miroslav getting dressed. The sole was separating from his left boot. And Miroslav and Vasa were the lucky ones. A few of the men had begun to work in bare feet. Tolerable for now in the summer, but what would they do in winter?

In front of the blacksmith's shop, Vasa and Miroslav waited for Nikolas. While they waited, a truck Vasa had never seen before pitched and weaved along the path toward the village. When the vehicle parked in the middle of the village, Vasa saw it carried men he didn't know. The truck's sides were lower than the Opel, and its cab had a different shape.

"What is that vehicle?" Vasa asked Miroslav.

"It's a Fiat 626. How we came to possess an Italian truck is beyond me."

Two men rode in the cab, and two rode in the bed. They were clearly Chetniks. Their hats bore the royalist crest. Bandoleers of ammunition crossed their chests. Knives and grenades dangled from their belts. The driver's door swung open.

Stefan emerged from a nearby house. He conferred with the driver, though Vasa could not hear what they said. Stefan pointed to the stable, gestured with his disfigured right hand. The driver barked orders, and the two fighters in the back of the truck leaped to the ground. They entered the stable. After a few moments, they came out with the prisoner.

The boy's hands were still tied behind his back. His hair flew wild and unkempt, littered with straw. In the daylight, Vasa could better see the scrapes on the prisoner's face. They oozed red. As before, the boy kept his eyes on the ground. The men marched him to the Fiat. They lifted him by the arms and shoved him into the back.

*That could be me if I were captured by the Partisans,* Vasa thought. He still hated the boy and what he represented. He did not think he could ever forgive the Partisans for their takeover of Velika and his inability to write home. But the boy was out of action now. There was no need to harm him further. Vasa felt ashamed of how he'd reacted the day before. He thought about what Nikolas had said last night.

*We must be better than our enemies,* Vasa realized.

The airfield showed progress since Vasa had last worked on it. The boulder he'd been pounding stood smaller now, though it still jutted up from the ground. Soil and small rocks lay in the swale. With more work, the field could be brought to near level. An ox grazed at the edge of the field. The ox was harnessed to a cart. Men were already filling the cart with stones.

Beside the boulder, Vasa found the sledgehammer where the last worker had left it. He picked up the hammer. Checked the little metal wedge at the top end of the handle, which had been driven into the wood to make a tight fit with the head. The iron head still held fast. Vasa gripped the handle with both hands. Swung hard. The first blow echoed across the field and cracked away a section that must have weighed thirty kilos. Vasa carried the broken piece to the oxcart, then took up his hammer again. He spent the rest of the day breaking down the big rock.

Near suppertime, the American by the name of Marich came by to check progress on the airfield. Bogdonavich hurried over to him. The two Yanks discussed something in hushed tones, in English. Neither looked happy. Then Bogdonavich sat down in the grass. He picked up a stone. Threw it like he was angry.

Vasa sat down beside him. Vasa wanted to know what was wrong, but he did not know if he should ask. He did not have to wait long, however. Bogdonavich told him.

"I told Captain Marich about the prisoner," Bogdonavich said. "He knew about it. He tried to take custody of him. But he was too late."

"What happened?"

"They shot him."

# CHAPTER 19
# Maestro Winds

*I*N THE OLD SECTION OF BRINDISI, DREW STROLLED ALONG THE WALLS of the Castello Alfonsino. He had come into town alone, to gather his thoughts, to settle his mind. He had another mission to fly tonight. Not Operation Halyard's main event—that was still days away. But a risky flight nonetheless.

A tern lifted off from the causeway and glided inches above the harbor. For several seconds, the bird flew without effort, not flapping a wing. Taking advantage of ground effect, Drew noted. Then the tern zoomed for altitude, circled, and plunged into the water. The bird snatched a fish and took off again.

Scattered cumulus floated overhead and speckled the sea with their shadows. A light breeze pushed the clouds toward the west. Good flying weather. Drew hoped the conditions held through the night.

But this morning, he could take a break from the war. Drew had begun his day with a mug of cappuccino from the old man in the marketplace. The old man's product had improved. Somehow he'd gotten his hands on real cinnamon. The taste remained with Drew even after he'd returned his mug.

His mind kept returning to Sienna—wondering how she was

doing and what was troubling her. And he kept telling himself to forget about her. Yes, he and his crew had done her a good turn by stopping the ugly incident in the restaurant. But that was that, and that was enough. It made no sense to get involved with a foreign woman—just imagine the complications. Besides, given the risks of Operation Halyard, Drew was in no position to get involved with anyone. Hell, he was flying into hostile airspace tonight; for all he knew, this could be his last morning.

Drew didn't let himself dwell too long on that thought. Conquering his fears was the reason he'd volunteered for this operation in the first place. And that was *another* reason to forget about Sienna. Women wanted a hero—not someone barely hanging on by his fingernails to what little remained of his honor.

For an hour, Drew watched boats traverse the harbor and people pass on the sidewalks. Late morning brought a bustle of activity to Brindisi. Horses pulling carts clopped along cobblestones. Jeeps and trucks bearing white stars rumbled through the streets. Pedestrians came out of their homes. Drew joined the foot traffic.

Near Antonio's, on the cobblestone ahead of him, he noticed a woman who walked with a familiar gait. He thought it might be Sienna, but he wasn't sure until she stopped on a corner and joined Lucia. Each carried a pair of bulging cloth sacks. Drew trotted to catch up with them, and he waved when Lucia recognized him.

"*Buongiorno*, Lieutenant Drew," Lucia called.

Sienna turned to face him. Instead of her work clothes, she wore a blue dress that fluttered around her calves. The dress wasn't especially revealing; it buttoned to her collarbone. But the sea breeze pressed the fabric against her hips in a way that flattered her figure. Her hair cascaded free over her shoulders. She brushed strands from her eyes in a gesture that Drew found endearing.

For the first time, he saw her smile, ever so slightly. She raised her cloth bags.

"We have been shopping for Uncle Antonio," Sienna said. "Onions and peppers and the like for the restaurant."

"Those bags look heavy," Drew said. "Let me help you carry them."

He took two of the bags of produce. Each sack weighed about twenty pounds.

"You are not working today?" Sienna said.

"Off duty until tonight," Drew said.

The women led him down a side street to the rear entrance of Antonio's. A stray cat dashed from the doorstep, climbed a stone fence, and vanished.

"That is Lorenzo," Lucia said. "We feed him, but he does not want to be petted. He was starving when we found him."

"I'm sure he appreciates your kindness," Drew said.

Lucia opened the door. Drew entered to find himself at the back of the kitchen. With the ovens cold, the room smelled musty, with a hint of garlic. Pots hung from hooks in the ceiling. He placed his bags on a wooden table, and Sienna and Lucia did the same.

"I will wash and cut the tomatoes," Lucia said. "Sienna, maybe you can show Lieutenant Drew our town today."

Sienna said nothing. She looked at Lucia, then at Drew.

"I think it will be good for you," Lucia whispered.

Sienna looked unconvinced, and Drew wasn't sure it was a good idea, either. Finally Sienna said, "Perhaps a short walk. It is a beautiful morning."

Drew followed her outside. Lorenzo the cat sat atop the stone fence now. This time, he didn't run away. He simply flicked his tail and watched them leave.

As they strolled through town, Drew felt more than a little awkward. To speak with Sienna beyond pleasantries, he needed to cross a gulf of culture and experience. Neither he nor anyone he knew had suffered the kind of deprivations Europeans had seen during the war. So Drew chose his words with care, tried to stay on safe ground.

"Tell me about your family," he said. "Do you have brothers and sisters?"

"I have two brothers. Massimo is a priest in Rome. Riccardo is in the army. He is missing."

"I'm very sorry to hear that." After a moment, he asked about her parents.

"They died when I was still in school. Uncle Antonio raised me for a time here in Brindisi. When I grew up, I went back home to Ceccano to teach English and Italian."

"No wonder your English is so good."

There was that hint of a smile again. "Thank you."

Sienna asked about Drew's family, and he told her the basics: His father was a banker in Columbus. His mother was a home-maker. He had no siblings. His uncle's stories had inspired him to join the military and learn to fly. Uncle Frank had flown SPADs with the Lafayette Escadrille during the Great War. The escadrille consisted of pilots who'd volunteered to fight for France before the U.S. came into the conflict. Brave almost to a fault, they flew hard, drank hard, and took heavy casualties. And they did it with style: The unit's mascots were two lions named Whiskey and Soda.

But Drew did not tell her how he envied his uncle's dauntless nature. Drew had Frank's aptitude for flying, but he couldn't muster the same kind of courage. At least not so easily. He had to work on it.

"Any sights you can show me?" Drew asked. "I don't know the town well."

They decided that Sienna would show him the Roman column, which marked the end of the Appian Way. Drew had heard of the famous road built by the Romans, but he didn't know much else. Sienna led him to the oldest part of town, where they climbed a set of stone steps that led up from the harbor. At the top of the steps, an ancient column rose about fifty feet into the sky. Figures at the top depicted Roman gods. Beside it stood the base of what had been a second column.

"The second column fell during the 1500s," Sienna said. "The road connected this port to Rome."

Her manner changed entirely as she explained the history. She didn't sound like the shy woman waiting tables at Antonio's. Now she sounded more like a teacher.

Drew imagined Roman merchant ships filled with amphoras of wine and olive oil docking in the harbor below. The sea breeze rose and lifted locks of Sienna's hair. Drew recalled that the meteorologists had a name for this summer wind across the Adriatic: the maestro. Lesser known than the mistral and the sirocco, the maestro blew as pressure changed across the Balkan Peninsula. *Fitting,* he thought. The wind hinted of trouble from the direction of Yugoslavia.

Drew took a seat on the top of the stone stairway. Sienna gathered the folds of her dress and sat beside him. She wrapped her arms around her knees and gazed out across the water.

"Lucia and I used to come here when we were little girls," Sienna said. "We loved this spot."

"I see why," Drew said.

Somewhere in the town behind them, a clock tower chimed.

"I should get back to the restaurant," Sienna said.

"Yes, don't let me make you late."

But she didn't get up immediately. She sat with him for a while longer, as if reluctant to leave. He admired the way the sun lit the black waves of her hair, and she caught him looking. She smiled, then turned to watch the harbor again. At the terminus of a two-thousand-year-old road, Drew felt the maestro flowing over both of them.

At one thousand feet above the ridgelines, Drew watched the darkened terrain of Yugoslavia flowing beneath his wings. He held course and speed as best he could. Two other C-47s flew with him in close formation, though he could not see them from his seat. Drew was flying the Pathfinder ship; the other aircraft depended on him to get to the drop zone. Chisholm, at the navigator's station, had picked up the Eureka signal. He began providing Drew with heading corrections.

"Five degrees left," Chisholm called.

"Five left," Drew repeated.

With the slightest turn of his wrist, he pressed the yoke to the left. Eyed the compass and rolled the wings level on the new heading.

The sound of the slipstream deepened, like a violin section that had suddenly changed keys. That was Montreux in the back, opening the cargo door. He and Calvert, the radio operator, were standing by for the green light. When it came, they'd begin kicking airdrop-rigged boxes out the door.

"Manifold pressure," Torres said. The right engine's power had dropped a bit. Cylinder head temp had risen, too. Drew thought little of it; he could do nothing about it now. At present, he functioned purely as the mind of the C-47. In this moment, he lived only to lock on course, speed, and altitude. Steady flying made the math easier for the navigator, which made the drop more accurate. You didn't do much good if you delivered supplies into the wrong hands—and it had happened before. Drew eased the right throttle forward and checked his airspeed. Still zipping along at 110 miles per hour.

"Twenty seconds," Chisholm called. He transmitted on the radio and the interphone at the same time, so everyone in all three aircraft could hear him. Then, on the interphone only, he said, "Three degrees left."

"Three degrees," Drew said. He made another barely perceptible turn. Held course and speed. Held his breath.

"Ten seconds," Chisholm called.

Then came the countdown to green light. At zero, Torres reached up and flipped the switch. Immediately thumps sounded from the cargo compartment as the enlisted men pushed out the bundles. Drew imagined the parachutes streaming into the night from all three planes.

The thumps ceased.

"Load clear," Montreux said.

"Red light," Chisholm called on the radio and the interphone.

Torres flipped another switch. "Red light," he called. The drop zone was behind them now.

As briefed, Drew pressed the throttles forward, pulled the nose up ten degrees, and began a ninety-degree turn to the left. A double crescendo rose from the engines. Drew glanced down at the engine instruments. The right engine's manifold pressure still lagged. Drew pressed up the right throttle. The slipstream changed keys again as Montreux closed the door.

"Flaps up," Drew called.

"Flaps up," Torres repeated.

Climbing through three thousand feet, Drew transferred the controls to Torres.

"Able Lead to Able Flight," Drew called on the radio. "Goalpost." The code word for "drop complete."

"Able Two, Goalpost," came the response.

"Able Three, Goalpost."

"Well done, boss," Torres said.

"Thanks," Drew said. He felt relieved to hear the other aircraft call "drop complete." Otherwise, they'd have had to racetrack for another pass and spend that much more time in enemy airspace. Now, they could fly the egress route and head for home.

The mission had gone well. Three successful drops, no ground fire, no serious malfunctions. Drew's right engine still ran hot, but those big radial engines did that sometimes. He'd write it up and let Montreux look at it tomorrow.

The formation climbed through a cloud layer that bounced the aircraft with turbulence. But when the C-47s rose above the stratus, the ride smoothed out and the view opened to reveal a night sky filled with stardust. Moonlight painted the tops of the clouds. Drew doubted any artist could capture this scene, and he wished Sienna could see it. The memory of their time together gave him a warm turn in the pit of his stomach.

"Can you give me the autopilot, please?" Torres asked.

"Sure thing."

Drew switched the autopilot servo valve to ON. The crew flew in silence over the Adriatic. The water turned to quicksilver in the starshine and moonglow. When Calvert tuned the tower frequency for San Pancrazio, Drew heard the controllers give landing clearance to a pair of night fighters. Apart from that, the radios gave little indication a war was on. The cloud deck beneath them tapered away, and the coastline of Italy became visible in the distance. A few lights gleamed along the shoreline. Now that the Allies had established air superiority over Italy, blackout was no longer strictly enforced.

"You led the mission," Torres said. "Do you want the landing?"

"Yeah," Drew said. "I'll take it. Pilot's controls."

Drew disengaged the autopilot. A short time later, he eased the throttles back to begin the descent. The altimeter began to unwind at a comfortable rate of one thousand feet per minute. At five thousand feet, Drew shoved the throttles forward to level off for a few minutes. He looked down at Brindisi. Somewhere down there, Sienna was sleeping.

A bang sounded from out on the right wing.

The C-47 yawed to the right. Instinctively Drew kicked left rudder to straighten the aircraft. Torres turned to look out his window. Montreux unstrapped from his seat to scan from the cargo compartment.

"Right engine's on fire," Torres said. He glanced at the engine instruments. "It's failed, too."

The copilot's statement confirmed what Drew already felt in the controls. The plane yawed toward the right because only the left engine was producing power. The right propeller windmilled uselessly, creating drag.

Drew tried to remember what to do next. Fear interrupted the flow of his thoughts like a short in an electrical circuit.

"The whole nacelle's wrapped up in fire," Montreux called from the back.

Inside Drew's head, his gyroscopes tumbled. In an instant, he'd gone from pleasant thoughts of Sienna to an in-flight emergency. Somehow he could not work his mind toward emergency procedures. He froze.

"Ah, right engine," Drew said. "Um . . ."

Where were the correct words? He'd gone through this in training. He'd *taught* this in training.

"Able Lead, Able Two," a pilot radioed from the second C-47. "Your right engine's burning."

"We're working on it," Torres answered. Then on the interphone, he asked, "Do you want me to blow the fire bottle?"

"Ah, yeah," Drew said. "Hit it."

The copilot reached for the fire extinguisher control on the floor between the seats. Flipped the selector valve to RIGHT. Pulled the red handle. Then he appeared to wait a moment for instructions.

"Want me to secure the right engine?" Torres asked.

"Ah, yeah. Yeah. Feather it."

Torres placed his hand on the right throttle. "Confirm right engine," he said.

"Yeah, uh, confirm."

Torres pulled the throttle to idle. Then he pulled the mixture control for the bad engine to IDLE CUTOFF. He reached to the overhead panel and put two fingers against the feathering button. "Confirm?" he said.

"Ah, confirm."

Torres pressed the feathering button. Drew felt the yawing ease as the right propeller spun down to a stop.

"Right prop's standing tall," Montreux said. "Fire's out."

Checklist in hand, Torres flipped a fuel valve and closed the bad engine's oil shutter. "All right," he said, "I think we got her secured." He leaned back in his seat and scanned the instruments. "Watch your airspeed," he said.

Drew glanced at the airspeed indicator. He'd let speed bleed off with the loss of power. Now he was dangerously slow. A twin-engine plane flying on one engine would roll over on her back if she got below minimum control speed.

He pressed the yoke forward to drop the nose. Added power on the good engine. The airspeed needle began to creep higher.

"You okay, boss?" Torres asked.

"Ah, yeah, I got it," Drew said. His thoughts came clearer now. And it was clear he'd just let his crew down. Locked up. Checked out. AWOL, for all intents. Thank God, a good copilot had backed him up. *How did I let this happen?* he wondered.

Drew turned a hand crank to adjust his rudder trim. Checked his speed again. Better now—120 miles per hour.

"Tell the tower we're an emergency aircraft," Drew said.

Torres made the call, and the tower cleared the formation to land. Drew descended to pattern altitude. On the downwind leg, he could tell those winds that felt so good this morning were going to make this a tough landing.

By the time Drew rolled out on final approach, the crosswind had only grown stronger. It was gusty, too. Drew goosed the good throttle to speed up ten miles per hour. The extra speed would give him a safety pad in case a gust suddenly died away and left his airspeed low. To hold course on final, Drew found he needed to crab the airplane into the wind nearly ten degrees. Tired, rattled, coming in fast with a dead engine at night in a crosswind, he faced all he could handle. To make matters worse, he crossed the threshold too high.

With the rudder pedals, Drew straightened the nose. Dipped a wing into the wind to stop the crosswind drift. Pulled back on the yoke to begin his flare.

The C-47 thunked down on its left wheel. Bounced back into the air. Yawed into the wind. Bounced on its right wheel. Drew fought for control. Kicked the rudder pedals to straighten the plane.

Finally the aircraft landed hard, this time on all three wheels at once. Veered off the side of the runway into the grass. Spun to the left. Came to rest perpendicular to the runway, smoking, one prop still spinning, but in one piece.

Drew closed his eyes. A sense of failure came over him like nausea. He released the yoke and collapsed in his seat, defeated. He looked over at his copilot.

"Shut her down for me, will you?" Drew said. "I got nothing left."

# CHAPTER 20
# Deadly in Your Hands

*B*UNDLES AND PACKAGES, BOXES AND CARTONS, LAY ACROSS THE pasture. Beside them or across them rested the deflated parachutes that had brought them safely to earth. At first, Bogdonavich wondered why the planes hadn't dropped the packages at the airfield the men were building. This pasture was miles farther from Pranjani. But then he saw the logic: This way, even if the resupply mission had been compromised, the Germans still might not know the location of the airfield.

But, thank goodness, the mission hadn't been compromised. The OSS team, or guerrillas working with them, had guided in the airdrop—probably with a Eureka set. From the looks of it, they'd guided in more than one plane. A single C-47 couldn't have carried all this stuff. Chetniks broke open bundles to find medical supplies, K rations, ammunition, and even weapons and communications gear. One of the largest crates contained M1 Garand rifles, still packed in Cosmoline to preserve them during their ocean journey from U.S. factories.

Vasa came up to Bogdonavich with a broad grin across his face. He carried an M1, his hands smeared in Cosmoline.

"This is the most beautiful rifle I have ever seen," Vasa said. "But why did they cover it in grease?"

Bogdonavich explained about protecting weapons shipments from salt spray. "The rifle came to Ravna Gora by air," Bogdonavich said, "but it came to Europe by sea."

"Very good," Vasa said. "Please tell all of America we said thank you."

"We should thank *you* for all you're doing, Vasa the Wolf. This is just a down payment."

Vasa laughed. Bogdonavich had seldom seen the boy laugh.

"Did your army teach you to fire this rifle?" Vasa asked.

"Yes, but because I'm a flier, the pistol is my primary duty weapon." Bogdonavich patted the .45 holstered on his belt. "I remember how to load it, though. When you get it cleaned up, I will show you."

"Thank you, sir," Vasa said. "I am sure Nikolas and Miroslav would like to see that, too."

Bogdonavich and Vasa joined other fliers and guerrillas in unpacking and sorting the gear. Weapons went under a fir tree beside the pasture. Ammunition went under another, separated by caliber. Bandages and medicines got stacked by the dirt path. Field rations, which made up the bulk of the supplies, were collected in four different piles. The Chetniks wasted nothing. They saved the crates for lumber, or perhaps winter firewood. They even saved the nails.

Bogdonavich searched, however, and did not find any boots. He looked through every package, hoping to find footwear for Vasa. That hole in Vasa's boots got bigger every day. Most of the Chetniks and villagers needed new footwear.

"Damn, Vasa," Bogdonavich said. "When I first saw all these packages, I would have bet a year's pay there were boots for you."

"That is all right," Vasa said. "Your aeroplanes have brought so much else." He pointed to the path where the medical supplies were stacked. Katarina kneeled beside a crate filled with tubes, ampules, and bottles. Within the crate, each box had been wrapped in cotton. From time to time, she picked out a broken bottle and dropped it on the ground, but most of the containers had survived impact. General Mihailovich himself sat on the ground next to her. He adjusted his glasses, read labels, then translated the contents into Serbian. Bogdonavich overheard him say, "This is an antibiotic. This one is morphine, for pain."

"Wonderful, my general," Katarina said. "This is wonderful."

Three trucks arrived at the pasture. One was the familiar Opel. Bogdonavich hadn't seen the others before, and he guessed they belonged to some of the more far-flung Chetnik detachments. The Serbs began loading the supplies into the vehicles. They also brought oxcarts and even a wagon pulled by a tractor.

The detachments led by Nikolas and Stefan received a share of the rifles, ammunition, and medical supplies. In Pranjani, they stacked goods in the blacksmith's storeroom. Katarina took charge of the medicines and bandages. In one of the homes, she set up a makeshift two-bed hospital.

By midday, the initial excitement of the airdrop had passed, at least for Bogdonavich. His mind kept returning to the young Partisan fighter who had been executed. The boy probably had no more knowledge of politics than of brain surgery. More than likely, he'd joined Tito's forces because they were the first to recruit in his village.

He didn't even know who had shot him. A group of strangers had come and picked up the boy. Nikolas and Stefan had not taken part. Bogdonavich didn't see how he might have prevented the shooting. But a black cloud of guilt came over him, anyway.

Late in the afternoon, Bogdonavich found Vasa sitting outside the blacksmith's shop. With an oily rag, he was wiping down his new M1. He wore a new ammunition belt marked U.S. The belt carried pouches for clips of .30-06 rounds.

"Got it all cleaned up?" Bogdonavich asked.

"Yes, sir," Vasa said. "The woodwork of this weapon is beautiful."

"May I see it?"

Vasa handed over the M1. Bogdonavich pulled back the bolt, checked to make sure the chamber was empty.

"When you load this thing," Bogdonavich said, "it will bite your thumb if you're not careful." He looked the weapon over. It bore no scratches, no powder residue, no sign of use. "Wow," he added, "it's brand-spanking-new."

Vasa rounded up Nikolas and Miroslav. They brought an empty K ration box to use as a target, and they walked with Bogdonavich down the road from Pranjani to a bean field. They chose the grassy border between the field and the woods as a shooting range. A wooded rise at the end of the field provided a natural backstop for bullets. Vasa placed the empty wooden box on the ground. He stepped off distance from the box. At roughly a hundred yards from the target, he marked a line in the dirt with his heel. Bogdonavich handed the M1 back to Vasa.

"Let me see your ammunition belt," Bogdonavich said.

Vasa removed the belt and passed it to Bogdonavich. Bogdonavich sat cross-legged on the ground and opened one of the pouches. He withdrew a clip loaded with eight cartridges.

"First," Bogdonavich said, "you need to know how to load these clips. There's a little bit of a trick to it."

Bogdonavich thumbed the rounds out of the metal clip. The eight cartridges lay scattered in the grass in front of him. Then he took one of them and placed it back into the clip. He held it in place with his forefinger.

"Guide the round into a corner like this," he said. "Then place the next one on top and to the side of it. You have to hold it with your finger, or they'll tumble back out." He filled the clip and showed them how the eighth round snapped into place and held the other rounds tight.

Conducting the training session improved Bogdonavich's mood, at least for the moment. He felt like an officer again instead of a victim on the run. But he hoped these men would always use this powerful weapon for the right reasons.

"Once you have a clip loaded," he said, "you're ready to load the rifle."

Vasa passed the M1 to Bogdonavich. The bolt remained locked open.

"You load the clip from the top of the breech," Bogdonavich

said. "But don't just stick it in with your thumb. The bolt slams quick and hard."

Bogdonavich demonstrated how to guard the bolt with the heel of the right hand and insert the clip with the left. He used his right hand to control the bolt's closure.

"Now it's ready to go," he said.

Bogdonavich brought the rifle to his shoulder, placed his cheek against the stock. Clicked off the safety. Aimed at the box. Fired.

Empty brass flipped from the rifle as the report echoed across the field. The bullet flew high. The round kicked up a little fountain of dirt behind the box. Bogdonavich pointed out the windage and elevation knobs on the rear sight. He turned the elevation knob two clicks. Fired again.

The bullet punched a hole through the box. At this distance, Bogdonavich couldn't see the hole, but he saw the splinters fly. Nikolas raised his field glasses and said, "Very good. Right in the middle."

Bogdonavich aimed again. This time, he demonstrated the semiautomatic weapon's rapid-fire capability. He pulled the trigger six times as fast as he could. The box danced as six high-velocity rounds went through it. The six shots emptied the weapon, and the empty clip pinged from the breech. Vasa and his teammates cheered.

"It's not as fast as your Thompson gun," Bogdonavich told Nikolas, "but it hits harder and it has longer range."

The guerrillas took turns loading and firing the M1. By the time they finished, they'd reduced the box to kindling. Bogdonavich showed them how to take apart the weapon, clean it, and put it back together.

"This is the best rifle training we have had," Miroslav said. "Usually we must figure it out for ourselves."

"You do a pretty good job from what I've seen," Bogdonavich said. "I just thought I could speed things up for you."

"You have," Nikolas said. "We thank you."

Before heading back to Pranjani, the men rested at the edge of the field for a few minutes. Vasa gathered up the expended clip and the empty brass. Bogdonavich doubted the guerrillas had the equipment to make their own ammunition from used cartridges. But, as he'd observed before, these guys saved *everything*.

Above them stretched a dome of blue sky marked only by horsetail cirrus, thin clouds way up high. The land lay quiet. A pair of sparrows twittered over the rows of beans. In the stillness, Bogdonavich became aware of a low buzz. He scanned the horizon until he saw the formation.

It was distant. So distant that the aircraft appeared as specks. Bogdonavich couldn't tell if they were B-24s, B-17s, or some combination. But he knew they were American, because the *Luftwaffe* couldn't mass a formation of heavies like that, at least not anymore.

"There go your friends," Miroslav said.

"Yes," Bogdonavich said. "But I am with friends now, too."

The bombers faded from view, never coming close enough to identify.

Vasa picked up the M1. He practiced the technique of guarding the bolt with the heel of his hand while loading.

"That thing suits you," Bogdonavich said.

"Yes, sir," Vasa said. "It does."

"This makes me think of *The Mountain Wreath*," Nikolas said.

"The what?" Bogdonavich asked.

"It's a Serbian epic play. Prince-Bishop Petrovi -Njegoš wrote it a hundred years ago."

Bogdonavich recalled that Nikolas had talked about wanting to attend a university after the war. The scholar among guerrillas.

"It's about the struggle against the Ottomans," Nikolas continued.

He told how at the end of the play, one of the characters, Vuk Manduŝic, has lost his rifle in battle. A Turkish bullet has struck and ruined his *jeferdar*, a finely crafted muzzleloader. A *jeferdar* was more than a weapon, Nikolas explained. Often inlaid with jewels and mother-of-pearl, *jeferdars* were given to warriors as a good-luck symbol. The richer the family, the more elaborate the inlays.

The very presence of a *jeferdar* in the home could bring good fortune.

"Vuk Mandušic," Bogdonavich said. "So his name was Wolf, like our Vasa the Wolf."

"Exactly," Nikolas said. "Anyway, Vuk Mandušic tells the bishop of his sadness that he has lost his lucky rifle. But the bishop assures him he can find another good weapon—and that in his brave hands, any weapon is deadly."

"Well, Springfield Armory doesn't put jewels on its rifles," Bogdonavich said. "But they're sure as hell deadly."

"I can see that already," Vasa said, admiring the M1.

"May it bring you luck," Bogdonavich said. He looked into the distance, where the bomber formation had faded from view. He thought of the immense firepower it represented, of the lethal force he'd wielded with his own hands. "May they bring luck to all of you. Use them well and wisely."

*Because whatever you do with a weapon will stay with you for all of your days,* he thought.

# CHAPTER 21
# No Happily Ever After

$V$ ASA LAY PRONE ON A CARPET OF PINE NEEDLES. PINE BOUGHS shaded him from the midday sun. He cradled his new M1 Garand and peered downhill through the trees. His previous rifle, the Mauser captured from Germans, had been sent to another detachment in need of weapons. But Vasa still wore his Webley pistol on his side.

On overwatch duty again, this time he guarded a dirt crossroads five miles from Pranjani. The shipment of M1s, with the greater firepower they provided, allowed the guerrillas to man more checkpoints with fewer shooters. Only Vasa and Miroslav waited at this crossroads. Miroslav lay hidden on the other side of the intersection, still armed with the mighty Browning. Nikolas and Bogdonavich guarded another spot miles away.

The guerrillas hoped they had the area sealed off entirely now, with gunmen at every possible approach to the new airfield. They even covered the streams where Germans might seek water. The timing could not have been better. The fliers said the field was nearly ready for the aeroplanes to come in.

Alone in the quiet forest, Vasa recalled the story from *The Mountain Wreath* of Vuk Mandušic and his lucky *jeferdar*. Observing the crossroads from over the M1's sights, Vasa believed he possessed his own mystical weapon. More than ever, he felt part of the tradition of Serbian warriors fighting epic battles for their people and land.

At the same time, he considered Bogdonavich's words about the new rifles: *"Use them well and wisely."* The American had been upset when he learned of the Partisan boy's death. Vasa still felt shame when he recalled how he'd beaten the prisoner. *Yes,* Vasa thought, *one must be wise, as well as brave.*

The day passed without anyone traveling through the crossroads. Not a truck, not an oxcart, not a man on foot. In the late afternoon, two fighters Vasa had not met before came to relieve him and Miroslav. They rode on horseback, and they arrived with instructions: Vasa and Miroslav were to ride the horses back to Pranjani and return them to the farmer who had loaned them to the war effort. One was a gray mare of long years, and the other was a young stallion with a hide the color of gunmetal. The mare looked reasonably strong, and the stallion was calm and friendly. Perhaps by now, they had become used to being ridden by strangers.

Vasa and Miroslav left the Browning in place. They mounted the horses and clopped along the dusty path, their M1s slung across their shoulders. A light wind blew, and the breeze felt good on Vasa's face. Overhead, the clouds that had scudded along all day began to assemble themselves.

All in all, Vasa felt encouraged about his role among the guerrillas. His superiors seemed to think he carried his load, and today had brought another sign: They'd trusted him enough to let him man one side of an ambush point without supervision. His shift had passed without violence; in fact, the day had almost seemed restful. Vasa's duties were done for the moment. This was, he believed, the closest thing to a good day one might experience in wartime.

In Pranjani, they found much activity. General Mihailovich was there; they saw his personal vehicle parked in the square. Chetnik officers and American airmen who were strangers to Vasa came and went. This did not surprise him. Soon the aeroplanes would come to pick up the Yanks. If there were hundreds of downed fliers, as the general had said, more of them would be arriving to prepare to fly out.

What did surprise him was the demeanor of the Chetnik officers and detachment leaders. They looked grave. They gathered in groups of three and four, speaking in hushed tones. On the other side of the square, across from the blacksmith's, two of them conferred with General Mihailovich. The general did not seem like himself, either. He was not telling stories and roaring with laughter. He was not smiling. He was not smoking a cigar. He did not look happy at all. He glanced at Vasa, then looked away.

Vasa and Miroslav returned the horses to their stable, then searched for Nikolas, but did not find him. While they waited to find out what was happening, some of the village women served an early supper. From an outdoor table laden with cold foods, Vasa chose a slice of pork loin and a chunk of black bread. He knifed off a section from a wheel of cheese, and cut a wedge from a red onion the size of a horse's hoof. Vasa sat outside the blacksmith's shop, leaned his M1 against the wall. He rolled the meat and cheese into the bread and ate it all together. He ate the onion wedge by itself, as if it were a section of sweet melon.

Finally Nikolas appeared. He emerged from one of the homes and joined the group with General Mihailovich. They whispered for a few moments, and they kept glancing at Vasa. *What is happening?* Vasa wondered. *Have I done something wrong?*

Nikolas and the general walked over to Vasa. Vasa put down his plate of food and stood up.

"Please be seated, my son," General Mihailovich said.

What was this? They would not treat him with such courtesy if he'd done something wrong. Puzzled, Vasa sat beside what was left of his supper, now forgotten. Nikolas and the general sat beside him.

"We have some bad news," the general said. "There is no good way to tell you this, so we will just tell you what we know."

"Vasa," Nikolas said, "the Nazis have committed a great crime in your village. They have killed many people. They have burned many homes."

Vasa stared at the two men. He slumped against the wall of the blacksmith's shop.

"In Velika?" Vasa asked. "Are you sure?"

"Yes, my son," General Mihailovich said.

"Is my papa all right? My brothers?"

"We do not know," the general said. "We have no list of names. But the intelligence section informs us that a great many civilians have been killed."

The earth seemed to tumble and spin. Vasa felt dizzy. He felt sick. He felt cold. Blood drained from his face.

"No," Vasa said. "This cannot be. They were just farmers. They would not . . . Why?"

"The Partisans were operating in that area," Nikolas said. "Perhaps this was some sort of reprisal."

"I, I have to get home," Vasa cried. "I have to see if my papa is alive. Please let me go right now. Please take me in the truck."

"We cannot, Vasa," Nikolas said. "The Germans are all over that area now."

"I can only imagine how difficult this is for you," General Mihailovich said. "You may have as much leave as you need. We will send for Father Milos to help you during this time. But you must not try to go home. The enemy will only kill you, too."

"But I must know. Papa and my brothers? And Aleksandra?"

"Vasa, we just do not know," Nikolas said. "We know only that the enemy has killed hundreds in Velika."

Vasa began breathing hard. Grief came down on him like a great weight, as if something crushed his bones. Tears did not come; he was too shocked even to mourn.

"Son, all of Serbia weeps with you," the general said. "And all of Serbia honors you for your brave service."

Vasa leaped to his feet and grabbed his M1. "Oh, I will take revenge!" he shouted. "I will kill every German I see. For the rest of my life, I will kill every German I see."

Nikolas stood and placed his hand around the barrel of the

weapon. With his other hand, he patted Vasa's shoulder. With great gentleness, he pressed Vasa back to a sitting position.

"The enemy will pay for this, I can promise you that," the general said. "You have fought well. But we do not want you to become foolhardy in battle. Take the time you need, and when you are sure you are ready, you may return to the fight."

General Mihailovich and Nikolas sat with Vasa for a short time. They let the minutes pass in silence. Vasa simply stared into the distance at nothing. Finally Nikolas said, "We have arranged a room where you can sleep by yourself and have some privacy. Do you want me to take you there?"

The words sounded like they were coming from far away, but Vasa managed to understand them. He nodded. Nikolas led him to the home of an old couple.

The couple reminded Vasa of his paternal grandparents, who were now likely dead. The wife wore a gray kerchief and a white apron. The old man looked as if work and weather had worn him down to the frame. A homemade leather belt cinched his pants to a waist so thin, Vasa might have placed his hands around it.

"May God comfort you," the woman said.

"Thank you," Vasa answered. In a daze, he followed them through the house.

They ushered him to a small room with a bed, a nightstand, and an oil lamp. The furnishings were meager and roughshod, but the blankets were clean. Perhaps this had been the room of a daughter married away or a son off to war. The old man closed the door and left Vasa alone in the room.

He propped his M1 in a corner. He removed his ammunition belt and his gun belt with the pistol holster. Took off his boots and sat on the bed.

Finally, with no eyes on him, he began to weep. He shook with racking sobs. His tears fell on the wooden floor and soaked into the grain.

To the extent that he could gather his thoughts at all, he thought most of the cruel uncertainty. The report sounded as if the Germans had murdered everybody in Velika. Not the first village they'd wiped out. There was no way to know if anyone escaped. And no way to find out anytime soon.

Vasa had experienced sadness before. He had lost his mother and his maternal grandparents. Friends and cousins in Velika had died of typhus and tuberculosis, or in farm accidents. But in each case, Vasa had known what happened. Not knowing, perhaps *never* knowing, brought a whole new order of grief.

He wished he'd been at home. Not to prevent what had happened; he knew he could not have done that by himself. But he would have shared the fate of his family and friends. Wherever they were, he would have been with them now. He would have been with Aleksandra—in this world or the next.

The big Webley pistol lay in its holster on top of the pile of Vasa's gear. He eyed the weapon. He gave a thought to placing its barrel against the roof of his mouth. The press of a trigger could take him away from this existence of war and grief and loss. Then he dismissed the idea, if only to spare the old couple the horror of finding him. To return their generosity with a room full of blood and brains would have been . . . disrespectful.

Vasa stretched out on the bed and gazed at the ceiling. The room spun as he realized the entire course of his life had tumbled off in some unforeseen direction. There would be no happily ever after, no joyous homecoming.

He faced a future as unknown as life on a distant planet. And in all likelihood, he faced it entirely alone.

# CHAPTER 22
# The Glories of Liberation

*I*N HIS PINKS-AND-GREENS DRESS UNIFORM, IN SHINED SHOES AND A tightly knotted USAAF tie, Drew sat outside the base commander's office at San Pancrazio. Behind the closed door, a flight review board was deciding his fate. The commander and four instructor pilots comprised the board.

A sergeant opened the door and said, "Lieutenant Carlton, please come in." Drew entered, and the sergeant closed the door behind him.

In the middle of the room sat a wooden office chair on swivels, the kind one might find in a bank's loan office. The chair faced a government-issued metal table where the review board sat. Drew came to attention and saluted, then took his seat.

Breeze from an oscillating table fan ruffled the board members' papers. Even at the edge of the fan's arc, the breeze did not reach Drew's chair. Base commander Jason Frey, a colonel in his forties, adjusted his wire-rimmed glasses. The other four board members ranged in rank from captain to lieutenant colonel. They glanced up at Drew. None of them smiled.

"Lieutenant Carlton," Colonel Frey said, "we have heard testimony from your crew and from the tower controllers on duty at the time of your incident."

"Yes, sir," Drew said. He was trying to appear courteous. But the commander looked annoyed and held up his hand for Drew to remain quiet.

"Frankly," Frey continued, "I have seen better flying. I have seen *much* better flying. Captain Geiser, please summarize the board's findings."

The captain to Frey's left opened a manila folder. He glared at Drew for a moment, then looked down at his papers.

"Even in a single-engine scenario," the captain said, "the C-47 provides good control characteristics. We recognize that fatigue and crosswind were factors in your departure from the runway. But the crosswind was well within the demonstrated capability of your aircraft. It is difficult to understand why an experienced pilot such as yourself, an instructor, no less, could lose control under these conditions."

To Drew's surprise, the board was talking about his botched landing. Not his botched handling of the fire, which to his mind was even worse.

"We have reached the following conclusions," the captain continued. As he spoke, he held up a typed document. "You will remain on duty as a rated pilot. You will remain on duty with Operation Halyard. But you will be downgraded from instructor to line pilot until further notice. Your training folder will also reflect that you are no longer qualified as a formation lead pilot."

The captain put down the sheet of paper and closed his manila folder.

"Thank you, Captain Geiser," the commander said. "Lieutenant Carlton, do you have any questions?"

"No, sir," Drew answered.

"You are dismissed."

Drew stood up and saluted. He waited for the return salute. Then he executed an about-face with all the crispness he could muster. The sergeant opened the door, and Drew marched from the room.

The review board had cut him a break. A big break. Drew had fully expected to leave his wings on the board's table. The only reason he kept his wings, he suspected, was that his crew had gone to bat for him. He did not know this for certain; he had not been allowed to hear their testimony.

Drew had not coached them in any way. He hadn't asked them to cover for him, to forget to mention how he'd frozen in a critical moment. He didn't ask for their help because he didn't think he deserved it. He had let them down. He had placed them at risk.

The board could have come to its decision based entirely on the tower controllers' observations. Anybody could have seen that by the time Drew landed, the fire was out and the airplane was controllable. But still, he'd bounced hard and ground-looped. Apparently, the board didn't even know that while the fire was burning, panic had paralyzed him. Torres had filled in the leadership gap.

In the chow tent at lunchtime, Drew's crewmates asked him about the inquiry. He told them the board's decision. In his second surprise of the day, they smiled when he told them he was still their aircraft commander.

"You guys must have sugarcoated what happened," Drew said.

"We all make mistakes," Torres said. "I ground-looped a Stearman one time."

"Yeah, but you were in training," Drew said. "And a Stearman is practically made to ground-loop."

"You were tired," Chisholm said. "Sometimes it's hard to get out the right words when you're that tired."

Drew had frozen at a critical moment, and he knew they had all seen it.

He did not know why they had come through for him. But, for whatever reason, they had given him another chance.

Sunday was Sienna's day off, and he had invited her to go for another walk with him. Given recent events, Drew was hardly in the mood to play tourist, but he didn't want to let Sienna down. He kept on his pinks-and-greens, and he signed out a jeep.

Sienna lived in a cold-water apartment above a butcher shop.

Drew found it down a side street off the main market square. The wooden steps creaked as he climbed; the building looked to be at least a century old. At the top of the stairs, he knocked at the door. The door bore no number, no mail slot, no decoration of any kind.

When Sienna opened the door, she was wearing a flower-print dress. Black made up the predominant color, but red and pink roses highlighted the fabric. Less severe than her usual clothing, the dress revealed just a hint of the rise of her breasts. Locks of her hair fell across the hollow at the base of her throat. Drew caught the barest whiff of perfume.

"You look better every time I see you," Drew said.

"And so do you." She eyed his uniform. "I have never seen you dressed this way."

"It doesn't happen often." *And if she knew why I put this uniform on, to begin with,* Drew thought, *she wouldn't want to go out with me.*

Sienna was carrying a wicker basket. A checkered cloth covered most of the contents. The neck of a wine bottle stuck out from under the cloth.

"I made us a—what is your word for it? For eating outside?"

"A picnic," Drew said with a smile.


Drew turned the jeep wherever Sienna said to turn. After a few minutes, they were speeding down a seaside lane south of Brindisi. The wind tousled Sienna's hair; Drew kept looking over at her. She noticed his glances and smiled, but said nothing. Sunlight sparkled across the water. Not a single cloud cast a shadow. Drew guessed the clear weather stretched at least as far south as the North African coast. A solitary silver dot traversed the sky— perhaps a transport or bomber high up, heading for Cairo on some military task.

"The spot is up ahead, I think," Sienna said. "Look for a path on your left."

The jeep rounded a curve that revealed a bluff overlooking a rock-strewn beach. Waves crashed white among the stones. Seagulls flapped and circled above the surf. Sienna pointed.

"Yes," she said. "Here."

Drew slowed and spun the wheel to the left. The jeep swayed into a graveled turnoff beside the road. Grass and wildflowers grew between the turnoff and the bluff. The sea air smelled good, and the breeze offered relief from the afternoon's heat.

After Drew shut down the jeep, Sienna unfolded her cloth and spread out a picnic of olives, cheese, bread, and wine. They spoke little during their meal; Drew enjoyed the company and the food so much that for an hour, he almost forgot his upcoming mission and the things that might be waiting for him on the other side of that sea.

When Sienna tore a piece of bread in half, Drew again noticed the scar on her arm. "If you don't mind my asking," he said, "were you injured during the war?"

Sienna told a story Drew had never heard, and it horrified him. As the Allies fought their way up the boot of Italy, they were accompanied by irregular forces from French colonies in North Africa. These *goumiers* brought with them a reputation for ruthlessness. And their ruthlessness extended to conquered civilians. Women were a spoil of war. Sienna and several other women in her hometown of Ceccano were raped. One of her attackers slashed her arm with a bayonet.

Sienna's story broke Drew's heart—for her, mainly, but also for her country, his country, and all the Allies. There was nothing anyone could say to the women of Ceccano about the glories of liberation. The crimes of a small number of small men had inflicted irreparable damage. The Stoics had one thing right: Everything came down to individual actions and individual responsibility.

"I don't know what kind of future I have now," Sienna said. "No man will want me, at least not as a wife and the mother of his children. I am sullied. Dirtied."

"No, you're not, Sienna," Drew said. "You did nothing to cause what happened to you, so it doesn't say anything about what you are."

Sienna made no reply. But as she let Drew's words sink in, she did not look away. She tilted her head slightly, as if he'd made a point she'd not considered.

"You said you liked me in this dress uniform," Drew said. "Let me tell you the real reason I put it on today."

He told her about the flight review board, about how he'd frozen in an emergency and botched a landing. He didn't go into detail about his abbreviated tour in bombers, but he did say he'd made more than one mistake. He had let people down repeatedly.

"I'm not comparing my situation to yours," Drew said. "Just the opposite. In my case, I did it to myself. I own it, and I have to live with it. It *is* who I am. But you getting attacked is not who you are."

Sienna let a minute go by before she responded. Then she leaned forward so she could look into his eyes.

"Your mistakes are not all there is of you, either," Sienna said. "You haven't given up. You haven't run away. You are still here, trying to do the right thing. I believe there is more to you than your mistakes," she said. "Much more."

# CHAPTER 23
## The Most Dangerous Thing in the World

$A$T THE EDGE OF THE NEW AIRSTRIP, BOGDONAVICH LOWERED HIM-
self to one knee and peered across the field. Greenbaum, the navigator from Bogdonavich's crew, and Tom Oliver, the pilot from
the 459th, wandered across the newly cleared ground. The weeks
of hard manual labor had paid off. The fliers, villagers, and guerrillas had filled in the swale. They had leveled the boulders. They
had removed all the rocks that looked big enough to damage
landing gear. The OSS officer, George Marich, had asked for the
aviators' judgment on whether the field was ready for flight operations.

The field smelled of freshly turned earth. A light breeze blew
from the far end of the strip. If aircraft were landing today, they'd
benefit from a quartering headwind. A hawk lifted off from a tree
to the right and flapped across the airfield. Two crows launched
from the woods and followed the hawk. The crows cawed, swooped,
and dived around the raptor. They pestered the hawk until all
three birds disappeared into the trees to Bogdonavich's left. The
crows' mission seemed to mirror the Chetniks' effort to keep the
Krauts away from the airfield. That made him think of Vasa. He'd

heard what had happened in Vasa's home village, and his heart ached over it. To lose a parent or a sibling at that age was awful enough. But to lose your whole family—and your home village at the same time—was unimaginable. To add to the cruelty, Vasa couldn't know for sure what had happened or if anyone had survived. If no witnesses were left, he might never know.

Oliver and Greenbaum began heading back in Bogdonavich's direction. Along the way, they stopped now and then to pick up a stone. *You can always find a few more,* Bogdonavich mused. But C-47s had landed in worse places than this.

"What do you boys think?" Bogdonavich asked.

By now, Oliver cradled several rocks in both hands, like a farmer who'd just gathered a bunch of eggs. He dropped them in the weeds at the end of the airstrip. Greenbaum threw two larger stones into the woods. One ricocheted off a pine.

"The C-47 is pretty tough," Oliver said. "I think the field's okay."

Greenbaum pointed to the far end. "The only real obstacles left are those haystacks down there," he said. But they're so close to the end, I don't think they're a factor."

"And if the Germans fly over," Oliver said, "the haystacks will make the place look more like a working farm."

"We might as well give Marich the green light then," Bogdonavich said. "Every day we hang around here is another day for the Germans to catch on."

"Yeah, and it's getting crowded, too," Oliver said.

Bogdonavich had seen the evidence of that. As the guerrilla leaders brought more downed fliers into the vicinity of Pranjani, villagers ran out of places to put them. The stables and cellars were packed, and some of the airmen were camping out in the woods. The Germans couldn't miss a concentration like this for long.

The three men walked back toward the village to wait for Marich to show up. Along the way, they passed one of the new encampments for fliers. Inside a woodlot, lean-to shelters and makeshift tents clustered around cooking fires. The aviators and guerrillas had crafted the tents from old tarps and feed bags sewn together.

Someone in the camp was cooking lunch. Bogdonavich caught a whiff of what smelled like ham or bacon frying. The people of Pranjani seemed always to share the best of what food they had.

Bogdonavich had yet to find anyone from his crew except Greenbaum. He kept hoping someone would turn up.

"Let's see if we know anybody," Bogdonavich said. Greenbaum and Oliver followed him into the camp.

Through open tent flaps, Bogdonavich saw men working at little tasks of daily survival. One scraped a knife against a stone to hone the edge. He wore his USAAF crush cap at a jaunty angle. Another guy sorted through a pan of mushrooms and morels gathered from the forest. A third cut firewood. He placed a wedge of pine atop a stump. Lifted an ax over his head and brought down the blade. The wedge cleaved in two.

Here the distinction between officers and enlisted men disappeared, at least in terms of quarters. Everyone shared the same rough accommodations. At a firepit, a technical sergeant poked at slabs of pork sizzling on a grate over a bed of coals. Beside him, a lieutenant sliced an onion with a government-issued Case pocketknife. Both wore the arm patch of the Fifteenth Air Force.

"Hi, Sarge," Bogdonavich said to the cook. "What unit are you guys from?"

"Ninety-ninth Bomb Group, sir," the man said. "B-17s."

"Sorry to meet you here, but glad you made it."

"Ain't that the truth!" The tech sergeant forked a slice of pork onto a plate. "You guys hungry?"

"We're good, thanks. How long have you been here?"

"Got shot down a week ago. Everybody got out but the aircraft commander. He kept the plane stable as he could while we bailed. I don't think he ever got out of his seat."

"I'm afraid our AC did the same thing. Have you run into anybody from a B-24 named *Miss Caroline?*"

"No, sir. Can't say that I have."

Bogdonavich and Greenbaum exchanged a glance. Green-

baum folded his arms and sighed. The uncertainty about the fate
of their crewmates hurt more every day. Bogdonavich supposed
that amounted to a fraction of what Vasa was feeling right now.
He looked up toward the sky. Through a break in the leaf canopy,
Bogdonavich watched a bomber formation etch condensation
trails across a blue canvas. The war went on, regardless of what
happened to individuals or how they felt.

In Pranjani, Bogdonavich, Greenbaum, and Oliver found
Marich waiting for them. He looked like he'd just returned from
the field. Sleep deprivation hollowed his eyes, and his clothing
appeared dirty and slept-in. Heaven only knew what tasks had
kept him and his team out all night as he coordinated among Mihailovich's forces, the OSS, and the USAAF.

"So you guys think the field is ready?" Marich said.

"Yes, sir," Oliver said. "It's tight, especially for night ops, but the
C-47 drivers are used to that."

"All right. Showtime, then," Marich said. "I'll tell Mihailovich
and the ACRU boys we're ready."

Bogdonavich could hardly believe the time had come. He'd
worked hard on the airfield, and he'd tried to help the Chetniks
with their security efforts. But part of him suspected this was
merely a token attempt. They had to try, but was it really possible?
To evacuate hundreds of downed airmen from hostile territory
without the Germans finding out?

Sneaking even one airplane in and out would be an accom-
plishment. But the plan required multiple shuttles over a period
of days. Bogdonavich could well imagine the Germans getting
wise and launching their Messerschmitts. Kraut fighters versus
C-47s would amount to a turkey shoot. And once the German pilots blew away the transport planes, they'd strafe the men on the
ground.

"Are we going to have any top cover?" Bogdonavich asked.
"Maybe get some P-51s to escort the Skytrains?"

"Unknown," Marich said. "I've asked, and I'd love to have it.
But I haven't gotten an answer."

Down in the pit of Bogdonavich's stomach, a hollow sensation began to form. He imagined *Luftwaffe* fighters low on the horizon, slashing in at treetop level. Wings blazing with cannon fire.

*Just put it out of your mind,* he told himself. *There's no way out of here without risk.*

As he weighed the odds, he felt a surge of gratitude for his Serbian hosts. The sensation came on almost physically, as if he'd taken a shot of *rakija.* If this far-fetched rescue operation actually came off, it would be because of them. There was a chance that the shuttle flights would *not* get interrupted by a *Luftwaffe* squadron or a *Waffen-SS* patrol. Why? Because the Germans were terrified of the Chetniks. By now, there were probably a lot of guerrillas like Vasa, who had lost everything to Nazi occupation. The most dangerous thing was not a superweapon like a V-1 rocket or a strategic bomber. The most dangerous thing on this bloody, fire-blasted earth was a man with nothing to lose.

Another advantage, if one could call it that, involved plain old military logistics. That, too, came thanks to the Serbs. The Germans couldn't be everywhere in Serbia, but the Serbs sure as hell could. They kept the Krauts spread thin. If the Nazis stayed tied down keeping Belgrade and Novi Sad under control, they couldn't spare divisions for Ravna Gora.

Bogdonavich imagined telling his father about all he had experienced. What would Dad say? He'd probably say none of it surprised him. And he'd want to hear every detail. *It'll be an awful shame if he never gets to hear them,* Bogdonavich thought. He recalled the way his father would tap the end of his cigarette on the kitchen table before lighting up. That usually meant he was in a relaxed mood and felt like talking. Bogdonavich longed to talk to him now. Their relationship had always been fraught, but this story would change things between them—if he lived to tell it.

In the early evening, Bogdonavich found Vasa sitting on the ground, with his back against the wall of the blacksmith's shop. The sunset cast scarlet rays through a layer of high cirrus. The colors reminded Bogdonavich of the fires of Ploesti during his last mission, and the way the sky had burned with flak.

He didn't know what to say to Vasa, but he felt he should say something. The boy needed all the moral support he could get.

"Red sky at night, sailor's delight," Bogdonavich said. He doubted he'd translated the expression well into Serbian. The words didn't rhyme.

"I do not know this saying," Vasa said. He spoke without looking at Bogdonavich.

"It means good weather is on the way."

"That is a fine thing, if your aeroplanes are coming to get you."

Vasa was dressed for combat. He wore his new U.S.-marked ammo belt across his chest, bandoleer style. The leather belt around his trousers supported a holster that contained an enormous revolver. His M1 stood propped against the wall.

"I'm so sorry to hear about what happened in Velika," Bogdonavich said. "I know there is nothing anyone can say now that will help. But know that your friends are thinking about you, praying for you."

For the first time, Vasa looked up at Bogdonavich. "Thank you, sir," he said. "I . . . I am lost. In one moment, I want to put a gun to my head and join my family. In the next, I want only vengeance. But Father Milos tells me the best revenge is to be unlike him who performed the injury."

"Father Milos is a wise man."

Vasa rested the back of his head against the wall. Stared into the sunset. "I keep remembering the last time I saw most of my family and neighbors together," he said. "It was the *Slava* feast for Aleksandra's family."

The boy described a grand celebration honoring a family and venerating its patron saint. In this case, Saint Demetrius of Thessaloniki, whose feast day came in the fall. Demetrius had died, run through with lances, during a Roman persecution of Christians.

"Not unlike what happened in Velika," Vasa said. "Anyway, everyone was there. The priest lit the *Slava* candle. We ate *koljivo* and desserts. We knew war had come, but we did not think it would find our village."

Vasa shook his head. He stopped for a long moment to compose himself. His eyes brimmed, but he did not cry.

"They wanted only to live in peace," he said. "They wanted only to be left alone. The Germans will pay for what they did to Velika."

"That is fine, Vasa, but be careful. It may be hard to see now, but you have your whole life ahead of you."

"It is hard to see anything ahead of me but the next patrol."

"I understand," Bogdonavich said. "I always told myself not to look beyond my next bombing mission. It keeps you focused, and that's a good thing. But if you survive the war—if I survive the war, for that matter—life may hold futures for us we can't even imagine now."

The guerrillas' Opel truck pulled into the village. The vehicle stopped with a diesel clatter and a screech of brakes. Gunmen hopped out of the back, bearing old Springfields, worn Mausers, and new Garands. All looked tired and unshaven. They shuffled away to find resting places throughout the village.

Other fighters came out of homes and barns, equally well armed. Nikolas and Miroslav appeared and waved to Vasa. Vasa rose to his feet to join them. Miroslav carried a field radio on his back—part of the comm gear the Chetniks had received in the supply drop.

Nikolas, Miroslav, and Vasa climbed into the truck bed. *Shift change at the overwatches,* Bogdonavich surmised. He wanted to go with them, but he needed to stay behind to help Marich organize the airlifts.

He and the OSS team had already discussed how many men to put aboard each shuttle. Although the C-47 could carry twenty or more, the shuttles would haul only a dozen at a time. The aircraft needed to remain light enough to take off from the short field. There were so many trade-offs to consider: If they loaded more men on each plane, they'd need to fly fewer shuttles. The fewer flights, the less risk of detection. But if one failed to clear the trees and spun flaming cartwheels through the forest, many would die. And the Germans couldn't miss the explosion.

The Opel's engine rattled to life. Its bed filled with fresh fighters, the vehicle groaned forward, turned, and headed for the main road. Nikolas handed Vasa a cigarette, then lit it for him. It was the first time Bogdonavich had seen Vasa smoke. Vasa leaned against the side of the truck bed, took the cigarette from his mouth, and exhaled the smoke through his nose.

The truck rounded a curve and disappeared behind a screen of trees. And the war went on.

# CHAPTER 24
## Archangel

*B*Y THE TIME THE TRUCK STOPPED, THE SUNSET HAD FADED TO A purple sky. Stars began to wink, and a half-moon sailed above the hills, bright enough to throw shadows. Nikolas had briefed Vasa and Miroslav on the way. They would not conduct overwatch at a crossroads tonight; other squads drew that duty. This was another reconnaissance mission.

Dangerous stuff, like the operation that killed Piotra. But necessary, since the flights to evacuate the Yank airmen would begin any day now. General Mihailovich needed to seal off the area, and he needed to know what sort of enemy forces lurked anywhere nearby.

The instructions were simple, really: They were to prowl the woods and fields like wolves searching for prey. Detachments all over Ravna Gora would go on the hunt. They would communicate by field telephone, radio, or runner. That was the purpose of the backpack radio carried by Miroslav. Enemy forces, depending on their size, would be eliminated, bogged down, or at least delayed. Anything to keep them away from the new airfield.

The Opel left Vasa, Nikolas, and Miroslav at a point where the road bordered a meadow. Beyond the meadow, a forest dominated. According to a topographical map, the woods went on for many hectares. During the ride, Vasa had studied the map by flashlight. Contour lines indicated elevation. The closer the lines, the steeper the grade.

The lines and colors suggested that if the team hiked northeast, they would climb a wooded hill. The land would flatten and open up into fields, then rise again in timber. The second ridge loomed higher and steeper, and it would overlook a valley.

"We can make that valley before dawn," Vasa whispered.

"Very good," Nikolas said. "That is my hope. You will become a detachment commander yourself one day, Vasa the Wolf."

Days ago, such a remark would have flattered Vasa. He appreciated his leader's attempt to encourage him. But right now, he could not think about the future. He could think only about the present. Not even the entire night ahead of him—just the next hour or so. If he survived that hour—and he almost didn't care—then he would think about the hour after that.

The guerrillas waded into the overgrown meadow, line abreast. They had taken extra precautions to keep their gear from clanking. Noise discipline, Nikolas called it. Their canteens were full to the cap, to prevent sloshing. When they stopped to drink, they would drink every drop. All three men carried M1 Garands now, and they brought no loose ammunition. Every round was loaded into a full clip, and each pouch in their ammo belts held only a single clip. Vasa wore his pistol at his side, as usual. But a leather lanyard tied the end of the holster tight to his thigh. That way, the holster would not flop against his leg. The fighters had taped over every buckle or zipper that might rattle. The only sound came from their footfalls, and they stepped with care to keep the noise faint.

In their own silence, Vasa could hear every noise across the countryside. Somewhere to his left, a barn owl screeched. To his right, an engine surged. Sounded like a vehicle traversing a distant road. Behind him, a wolf howled.

To Vasa, the night became filled with ghosts. He imagined spirits of his family and friends around him. *Is Aleksandra here,* he wondered, *right by my side? Are they protecting me? Do they spur me to vengeance? Or do they simply send their love?*

The darkness offered endless questions and no answers. Vasa's squad reached the end of the meadow and entered the tree line. As they stepped, from time to time a twig snapped or a leaf crunched. But for the most part, they moved noiselessly. At a low place in the forest, frogs trilled in a bog.

Vasa carried his rifle in a ready position now. He held the weapon across his chest with his finger on the safety. But thus far, he saw nothing threatening in the gloom.

A few months ago, he realized, he would have seen a storm trooper in every moon shadow. A sniper behind every trunk. But his eyes and his mind had adapted to war. The present task focused him, settled him. He felt more possessed of himself than at any time since he'd learned the horrible news from Velika. Part of him wished this patrol could go on forever.

He went over in his mind some of the things Father Milos had said to him. "Dwell on the beauty of life," the priest had said. "Watch the stars. Note the flowers of the field."

A full canopy of stars now wheeled overhead. Through breaks in the leaf cover, Vasa spied galaxies that glittered like diamonds on black velvet. Perhaps his loved ones were there as well. Next to him, yes, with him always in their influence on his life. But among the heavens as well. Gone to whatever infinity awaits.

The team hiked on. As the map had indicated, eventually they came to another opening. When a night-blue horizon materialized through the trees, Vasa knew they'd reached the edge of the timber. Nikolas held up his fist for a halt. He crept forward. Crouched at the edge of a field. Motioned for Vasa and Miroslav to join him.

Beside Nikolas, Vasa rested on one knee. He placed the butt of his M1 on the ground and cradled the rifle against his collarbone. Scanned the opening before him.

Fields of some sort of grain stretched for at least a kilometer. In the darkness, Vasa could not tell if it was barley, wheat, or rye. Not that it mattered; what mattered was that he saw no evidence of a

German encampment. On the other side of the fields, yellow light gleamed from the windows of two farmhouses. Perhaps the homes were the outskirts of a larger village. Nothing seemed amiss.

Nikolas made a circling motion with his hand. Vasa understood. Though the way ahead seemed clear, the team would take no chances. Rather than marching across the open fields, they would keep to the woods and continue toward the ridgeline.

The detour cost them nearly an hour. They stole around the farmland, remaining in the cover of timber. When they reached the other side of the fields, Nikolas set down his rifle and took off his pack. From his pack, he selected a flashlight and a small tarp of waxed cotton. He took his map and compass from the cargo pocket of his trousers. Motioned for Vasa and Miroslav to approach.

They kneeled beside the map, and Nikolas spread the tarp over their heads. He had briefed them on this technique: They could use the flashlight to take a compass bearing without being seen.

Even under the tarp, Nikolas still shaded the flashlight beam with his palm. He placed the compass on the map and oriented the map to north. Pointed to the clustered contour lines of the ridge. He lifted the compass, let the needle float freely. Glanced at Vasa, then at Miroslav. Both nodded. They would continue their northeasterly course.

Nikolas switched off the light and stowed his gear. For a moment, blackness enveloped Vasa so completely that he saw nothing. Then his eyes began to adjust. His night vision returned, and the trees and the stars and his comrades came back into view.

The team found their way to the base of the ridge. At first, the slope rose gently, and the walking came easy. But the land grew steeper, just as the map had shown. Eventually Vasa slung his rifle across his shoulder so he could use his hands. He grabbed branches and saplings to help pull himself upward. Nikolas and Miroslav did the same. The effort made their progress slower and louder. They tried hard to move quietly, but the occasional crunch and snap became unavoidable. Every few minutes, they stopped to listen. Vasa heard nothing to suggest enemy presence.

Two hours of hard climbing brought them to the top. The ridge offered a good view of the land below. Vasa surveyed the valley. Despite the night's warmth, he felt goose bumps form up and down his arms.

"*Jebem,*" Nikolas hissed. Vasa had never before heard him curse.

Campfires flickered all along the valley. Vasa counted five, six; no, seven. Men walked around with flashlights, making no effort to conceal themselves. Moonlight backdropped the silhouettes of tents. Two trucks were parked at the campsite.

Chetniks would never operate this way, so brazen and out in the open. Neither would Partisans, for that matter. This was a German encampment. In the strength of a company, at least.

Vasa slid the M1 off his shoulder. Opened a pouch on his ammunition belt and took out a spare clip. He lay on the ground in the prone position, and he took out a second spare clip. He assumed his squad would fight—and against these numbers, it would become a last stand. Somehow his mind turned a gear, clicked into a position where he accepted imminent death. He would begin firing as soon as he could identify targets. He would fire and reload, fire and reload, until mortal injury stopped him. *So this is how it ends for me,* he thought. *Very well.*

"No," Nikolas whispered.

"What?" Vasa asked.

"There are too many. They will wipe us out, and then maybe find the airfield."

"Then what do we do?"

"We wait. We observe. We report what we see."

"With that radio Miroslav is carrying?"

"Yes."

"How did you learn to use it?"

"That crazy American, Marich, showed us."

The team kept vigil on the ridgeline. After what felt like an eternity to Vasa, the first wash of dawn cast a milky light into the valley. Without orders from Nikolas, Vasa and Miroslav moved into underbrush, to make sure they remained concealed. Morning dew formed. Cold droplets fell on Vasa's sleeves and hands.

Through the vines and branches, he watched the German encampment wake up. They lit cooking fires. They heated water for
coffee or tea. They bantered in that hard-edged language of
theirs. In the stillness, their laughter carried all the way to the
ridge.

To the east, petals of red light unfolded over the hills, and Vasa
could observe the enemy more clearly. They wore grayish green
field tunics and their distinctive coal scuttle helmets. Two of them
sat by a fire and laced up their ankle boots. Nearly all carried
Mausers. Some wore pistol holsters. Officers with Lugers, Vasa
supposed. He began to count. There were fifty of them, and those
were just the ones he could see. Vasa guessed that many more
were inside the tents.

Outside one of the tents, three of them worked on some sort of
weapon. It consisted of a tube, supported by a bipod. The weapon
caught Nikolas's attention, too. He raised his binoculars for a better look.

"Damn them to hell," Nikolas whispered. "A mortar. That's a
mortar company."

Vasa had not experienced mortar fire, but he knew the damage
it could do. Rounds as big as the head of a sledgehammer, arcing
in to flay victims with shrapnel. One shot might take out a dozen
men. One tube could keep firing and firing. And this unit probably had several. They could turn the airstrip into a killing field.

Nikolas motioned for Miroslav and Vasa to withdraw into the
forest, back the way they had come. They collected their gear and
slid downhill several steps. Miroslav carried the radio on his back.
When they were just below the top of the ridge, Nikolas halted
them.

"This ridge is a good place to do the radio call," he said. "I just
wanted to make sure we were out of sight."

Miroslav kneeled on the ground with his back to Nikolas. Nikolas sat, and he began turning knobs on the radio. The set warmed
up and hummed with life.

Vasa watched while Nikolas prepared to make his call. An antenna, a little less than a meter long, extended from the top of

the set. The antenna danced anytime Miroslav moved. Two cords connected a handset to the radio. Vasa could make no sense of the controls because all the labeling was in English, but Nikolas seemed to know what he was doing. Nikolas lifted the handset and thumbed a switch.

"Archangel, Archangel," he said. "This is Jeferdar Three."

At first, no answer interrupted the radio's hiss.

"Archangel," Nikolas repeated, "This is Jeferdar Three. Come in, please."

Vasa had no idea who or where Archangel was, but apparently some sort of radio net had been set up. He understood the main thing: Important people, perhaps General Mihailovich himself, could know in minutes what the team had discovered.

A tinny voice finally responded to Nikolas's second call:

"Jeferdar Three, Archangel. Go ahead."

Nikolas reported the size and location of the mortar company. As he spoke, he consulted his map and called in the coordinates. When he finished, a long silence transpired before Archangel answered back. Vasa wondered if the person on the other end was scribbling notes—or if he was simply having a hard time believing what he'd heard. When the response finally came, it was simple and matter-of-fact.

"Archangel copies all," the voice said. "Remain in position until relieved. Do not engage enemy forces."

"Understood," Nikolas said. "Jeferdar Three will hold position and not engage. Do you have further instructions for us?"

"Negative, Jeferdar Three."

"Jeferdar Three out," Nikolas said.

Nikolas replaced the handset and turned off the radio. Patted Miroslav's shoulder to let him know the call was finished. Miroslav stood up and stretched.

"Who is Archangel?" Vasa asked.

"Merely a base station," Nikolas said. "This radio carries only five kilometers at best. Archangel will relay our information to General Mihailovich and the American commandos."

"Are the Americans going to bomb those Germans?"

Nikolas smiled and shook his head. "No, I am afraid not," he said. "I would give everything I own to call in an air strike like that. But we are lucky to have a radio at all. We Chetniks will have to deal with this ourselves."

"What will we do?"

"I honestly don't know. But some of the general's other detachments have specialists who might help us."

The three men climbed back to the top of the ridge. Once more, they peered through the underbrush. Vasa dug into a pocket and found a little notepad and a pencil stub sharpened with a knife. He counted the Germans again and wrote down the number. He counted their rifles and mortars and wrote down the number. When a vehicle came or went, he made a note. Nikolas nodded in approval.

As the sun climbed, the breeze picked up. Treetops whispered and swayed. Though Vasa had been up all night, he did not feel tired. The morning wore into midday, and Vasa kept watch.

# CHAPTER 25
## Throw Me to the Wolves

*T*HE C-47'S PROPELLERS SPUN DOWN TO A STOP AS DREW AND HIS crewmates completed another training flight. The flight had gone well. Drew and Torres flew a dozen approaches, all with a stiff crosswind, and some with a throttle pulled to idle to simulate an engine failure. They touched down right on centerline every time. No bounces and no ground loops. The results confirmed what Drew already knew: His botched landing the other night had everything to do with nerves and nothing to do with proficiency.

As Drew climbed down from the aircraft, he noticed an unfamiliar plane in the traffic pattern. He shaded his eyes with his palm for a better look.

The plane was a little thing—a light twin-engine ship. No camouflage paint; its burnished aluminum reflected the morning sun. Twin tail fins. Drew recognized it as a Beechcraft C-45 Expeditor. The army used it for aircrew training, light transport, and VIP movement. Drew had never seen one before at San Pancrazio.

The Expeditor banked onto final approach and dropped its landing gear. The aircraft shone spotless. Red and white stripes adorned its rudders, and the fuselage boasted the white star roundel of the USAAF. When the plane flared and settled to the runway, Drew saw a blue placard in one of the windows. The placard bore two white stars. A major general was on board.

"That's some high-priced help," Torres said.

"You got that right," Drew said. "I wonder who it is."

Two hours later, they found out. In a hangar locked up for a classified briefing, Drew and the men of Operation Halyard came to attention for Major General Nathan F. Twining, Commander, Fifteenth Air Force.

"At ease," the general said. "Please take your seats."

To Drew and his fellow aviators, Twining was already a legend. He had worked his way up from the rank of private in the Oregon National Guard. During a previous command, only a year and a half ago, his B-17 was forced down in the Coral Sea. At night. The bomber sank in less than a minute, but Twining and the other fourteen men made it into two life rafts. They survived on the open ocean for six days with nothing but one half-full canteen, a chocolate bar, and a can of sardines. They collected rainwater. They shot two albatrosses and ate them raw. They used paddles to beat off a shark attack. A navy PBY finally rescued them. For this man, saving downed aviators was personal.

"Tomorrow night, gentlemen," Twining said, "you will launch Operation Halyard. If you succeed, you will make history in one of the most magnificent rescues in the annals of war. More than five hundred of your brethren on the ground in Yugoslavia have awaited this deliverance for weeks, and in some cases, months."

Twining described the mission's particulars: The C-47s would launch in a six-ship formation. They would take off from Brindisi initially, but on return to Italy, they would deliver the rescued aviators to Bari. If everything went according to plan, the operation would go on for several nights. In Yugoslavia, they would land on an unpaved strip that had been cleared with hand tools. For that reason, pilots should use techniques for a short-field landing on soft ground.

The general also shared a threat assessment: The planned

route avoided all known antiaircraft gun emplacements, but the possibility of small-arms fire existed everywhere. Friendly guerrilla forces had been scouting in the vicinity of the landing zone. According to their reports, the nearest enemy unit was a mortar company encamped ten miles from the airfield.

"It goes without saying that this mission is classified Secret," Twining said. "After thirteen hundred tomorrow, you will be restricted to base. After you land in Bari, you will be restricted to base there for the duration of the flights."

Twining finished his briefing and invited questions.

"Will we have fighter escort, sir?" a pilot asked.

"That will depend on the situation," Twining said. "Ideally, we'd like to go in with as small a footprint as possible to avoid detection. But if we suspect the enemy is getting wise, we'll send fighters with you."

Another flier raised his hand. The general pointed to him.

"Sir," he said, "after we complete this operation, will we stay here with the Air Crew Rescue Unit?"

"I'm sure we'll keep some rescue assets on hand here in Italy," Twining said. "But some of you may go back to your old units or to other assignments."

Drew couldn't think that far ahead; he was learning to focus on the task at hand, to concentrate on the good he could do here and now. No time to worry about where he might go next. A German bullet or flak shell might make that determination for him.

Twining dismissed the crews, and they spent the afternoon collecting personal equipment for the mission. Drew picked up a flak vest and helmet, a silk evasion map of Yugoslavia, and an E-17 survival kit. The survival kit included all kinds of things he hoped not to need, such as first-aid items, fishing line, and emergency rations. Aviators didn't normally carry long guns, but Montreux strapped down five M1 rifles in the back of the C-47.

"I reckon they issued us these in case things *really* go to hell," Montreux said.

"Sure hope we don't need those," Drew said. For a moment, his imagination ran wild with nightmare scenarios of mission failure and firefights on the ground. He shut his eyes tight and forced himself to stop thinking.

That evening, Drew took his crew to dinner at Antonio's.

He was happy to see Sienna's smile when he walked through the door. She and Lucia pulled two tables together for the fliers. Antonio placed a pair of candlesticks on the tables. He struck a kitchen match and lit both candles. Drew started the festivities by ordering three bottles of Chianti.

Antonio's menu had expanded further. Drew ordered pork *rotolini*. Chisholm chose *tortelli* stuffed with Parmesan. The other men stuck with the more familiar pizza and spaghetti.

When the wine came, Drew raised his glass and said, "To you guys. Best crew I could ask for."

Torres proposed the next toast: "And to our, uh, passengers."

Another group of servicemen entered the restaurant. When they opened the door, the breeze caused the candle flames to sputter. One nearly went out. Smoke rose from the wick. But then the fire caught again.

*Life is as fragile as the flame on those guttering candles,* Drew thought. He excused himself and stole into the kitchen. He found Sienna stirring a pot of boiling pasta.

"Listen," he said, "I'm going to be away for a few days."

"Where are you going?" Sienna asked.

"I can't say. I shouldn't have told you even this much. But I'll see you when I get back . . . ?"

Sienna smiled; this time, it seemed quick and natural, perhaps the most unguarded reaction he'd seen from her. After a moment, the smile faded. "But what if you don't . . ."

Drew didn't speak for a moment. "Someone will let you know," he said, finally.

Back at his table, Drew poured another round. The men talked of home and their plans for after the war. Sienna and Lucia brought their plates of food, and the conversation continued over dinner. But no one spoke about the mission ahead, and no one said anything about the screwup on the last one.

Drew thought back to his time in bombers. On his first mission, the group launched from their base in East Anglia to hit the German submarine pens at Brest. The ball turret gunner's turret wouldn't rotate. The gunner couldn't swivel to engage enemy fighters. Drew turned back. On his second mission, the B-17s rose to hit a railroad yard at Rouen. Oil temperature ran high on the number four engine. Drew turned back. On his third mission, the bombers formed up to strike another U-boat base, this one at Lorient. The bombardier reported a problem with his Norden. He offered simply to toggle his bombs when he saw the plane in front of them unload. But Drew turned back.

The group commander decided the war effort needed Drew in Training Command.

Each of his aborts in the B-17 had been a judgment call. No one of them was damning, but the combination marked him.

Drew clung to the hope that courage was a virtue or a skill you could develop like any other. Like a child's repeated efforts to ride a bicycle: The child falls and skins a knee. He gets back up and tries again. He falls and skins the heel of his hand. He gets back up and tries again. He falls over and over, and eventually he rides.

But in a war for national survival, with an airplane that cost six figures, the government would give you only so many tries.

At the end of the evening, after Drew paid the tab, Sienna followed him outside. In full view of his crew, not caring who saw, she held him close. To Drew's surprise, the men didn't hoot or make teasing comments. They just waited at the jeep in respectful silence. After a long embrace, Sienna placed her hand against Drew's cheek.

"Be safe," she said. "Come back to me." From around her neck, she removed a gold chain with a tiny crucifix. She pressed it into his hand. "For good luck," she added.

A misting rain began falling by the time Drew and his crew-mates returned to San Pancrazio. The diminished *Luftwaffe* no longer threatened the base, so blackout orders had been lifted. Portable floodlights cast glare across a wet and gleaming ramp. Six C-47s stood wingtip to wingtip. Beside one of them, a hose snaked from a fuel truck. Two ground personnel were topping off the tanks with one-hundred-octane aviation fuel.

"Almost showtime," Torres said.

Drew parked under a canvas shelter and shut down the engine. The men trudged through the mist to their tents. At the entrance to the officers' tent, Chisholm stopped to admire the row of air-craft prepped for the mission.

"'Throw me to the wolves, and I will return leading the pack,'" Chisholm said.

"I guess that's why we came here," Drew said. "Did you just think of that?"

"No, that's Seneca the Younger. But I bet it was a day like today when he said it."

In his tent, Drew opened his footlocker and found a box of military stationery, each sheet of paper adorned at the top with a blue circle that contained a white star and a set of golden wings. Beneath the circle, lettering read: U.S. ARMY AIR FORCES. Drew took a pen from his pocket and began to write:

> *Dear Sienna,*
>
> *You told me to come back safe. But if you are reading this letter, then I failed to do that. I am sorry I won't get to see you again.*
>
> *During these few weeks, your courage has inspired me. I have struggled to find the courage to carry out what my country asked of me. There were times when I considered giving up.*
>
> *Your example helped me find my way. You face an awful past and an uncertain future with a beautiful bravery. I ask you to use that same bravery now. Make a future worthy of you.*
>
> *Love,*
> *Drew*

Drew sealed the letter in an envelope. Across the envelope, in large block letters, he wrote: *IN THE EVENT OF MY DEATH, PLEASE DELIVER TO SIENNA ROSSI, ANTONIO'S RESTAURANT, BRINDISI, ITALY. 1ST LT. DREW CARLTON.*

He placed the letter on top of the clothing and other personal items in his footlocker. Drew closed the locker, and he left the padlock unlatched.

# CHAPTER 26
## The Key to Airpower

Norman Rockwell could have painted the scene unfolding before Bogdonavich. A mule pulled a flatbed wagon piled with hay bales. At one end of the field, four cattle grazed in an enclosure built of wooden posts and two strands of barbed wire. The fresh aroma of hay joined with the scent of evergreens.

A pointy-eared dog of mixed ancestry bounded and barked alongside the mule. The mule's black fur shone in the sunlight, and she flicked her tail at flies buzzing around her. Atop the wagon, a boy steadied the bales. Another boy, leading the mule, waved for the dog to get out of the way. Bogdonavich had witnessed moments like this many times during drives through Pennsylvania's dairy country.

But none of this had anything to do with farming.

The boys were not picking up hay from the field; they were dropping it off. And the hay would not feed livestock. At some point after dark, men would douse the bales with kerosene and set them afire. These primitive flares would guide C-47s to land at the makeshift airfield.

Bogdonavich pointed wherever he wanted the boys to drop a hay bale. He needed to set up two parallel lines of bales on either side of the field. The burning hay would mark the sides of the airstrip. *A hell of a way to create runway edge lighting,* Bogdonavich thought.

Marich, the OSS officer, walked the airstrip with his teammates, Racanin and Jezdich, along with General Mihailovich. Jezdich, the radio operator, had pitched a tent in the woods just off the field. On folding tables underneath the canvas, he'd wired up his voice radio and a Eureka set. After surveying the airstrip, Mihailovich and the OSS men returned to the tent. Jezdich sat at his radios and put on a headset. He made calls, scribbled notes, made more calls.

Behind the radio tent, other tents sheltered the men who would take the first flights out. They were the sick and injured. Greenbaum, Oliver, and other officers moved among them. Greenbaum carried a clipboard he'd scrounged from somewhere. He'd been assigned the task of putting names to flights.

Bogdonavich watched as the boys finished building the two lines of hay bales. Like pretty much everyone else around Pranjani, they seemed eager to help. They'd brought more hay than Bogdonavich needed. When they finished, they had eight bales left on their wagon.

"Can we get anything else for you, sir?" one of the boys asked in Serbian.

"No, thank you," Bogdonavich said. He felt one of the bales. "The hay is nice and dry," he added. "It will burn well. You fellows did a good job."

The boy leading the mule gave a wide grin. He patted the animal's side and led her away. Bogdonavich joined the men in the radio tent and watched Jezdich work. The radio operator signed off with someone, then made more notes. He conferred with Marich and Mihailovich. The general uncapped a pen and scratched marks on a topographical map.

"Anything new, sir?" Bogdonavich asked Marich.

"The Krauts don't plan on making this easy for us," Marich said.

"How's that?"

"They got a mortar unit camped out just a couple ridges away. And the *Luftwaffe* has a squadron bedded down at Kraljevo."

"Damn. How do we know all this, if you don't mind my asking?"

Marich gestured with his thumb toward Mihailovich. "The hills have eyes," Marich said.

The general looked up from his map. "Yes, they do," he said, "but I don't like what they're seeing."

"Are we still on for the flights?"

"Yeah, barring anything unforeseen," Marich said. "I don't think things are going to get any better. If we wait for the Germans just to go away, we'll be waiting a long time."

Bogdonavich looked deeper into the forest where the wounded waited. A woman kneeled next to a man lying on a blanket. She carried a U.S.-issued medic's pouch. Bogdonavich realized it was Katarina, the guerrillas' nurse. She wore work boots and a peasant dress. She had tied her hair back, and dirt streaked her face. She looked like she'd been working all night.

Katarina spoke softly to the man on the ground, who shrugged. Language barrier, evidently. Bogdonavich went over to translate.

"It is good of you to help us," he said in Serbian.

"It is the least I can do," she said. "Please tell him I need to change his dressings. It will hurt when I take off the old ones, but I will be as gentle as I can be."

Bogdonavich nodded, then addressed the wounded man. He was a sergeant barely out of his teens. Stains splotched bandages that covered his hands and forearms. A burn on his cheek oozed pink fluid. Katarina found a tube of burn salve in her kit and spread salve on the man's face. He winced, but held still while she worked.

"What's your name, Sergeant?"

"Rawlings, sir."

"What happened to you?"

"I was at my waist gun when the fighters came in. I was firing at one firing at us when our airplane just came apart. I don't know what the hell happened."

"Your arms got burned?"

"Yeah, there was this big flash. We started spinning. I didn't feel anything at the time, but it hurts like a son of a bitch now."

"This is Katarina," Bogdonavich said. "She's a good gal. She wants to change your bandages. She knows it'll hurt, but she says she'll do the best she can."

"Thanks, sir. Please tell her I said thanks. Yeah, she's swell. How do you know how to talk Yugoslavian?"

"Serbian. Long story."

Greenbaum glanced over and waved. He stepped around the tents, ropes, and stakes to show Bogdonavich the roster on his clipboard.

"You got this gaggle organized?" Bogdonavich asked.

"Well, you know the old saying 'The key to airpower is flexibility.' And the key to flexibility is indecision."

Bogdonavich chuckled. But from the looks of the navigator's roster, he'd made plenty of decisions. The real key to flexibility was innovation and resourcefulness. Bogdonavich had seen plenty of that, from Vasa all the way up to Mihailovich, and from the downed airmen themselves.

The roster consisted of six sheets of paper, each marked Chalk One, Chalk Two, and so on. Twelve names appeared on each sheet. A *W* appeared beside most of the names on the first three chalks. *W* for wounded. As the fliers and the OSS men had discussed earlier, the C-47s needed to remain light to take off from the short field. Each would carry only a dozen men at a time.

"Good work, nav," Bogdonavich said.

"I wish we knew what happened to the rest of our crew," Greenbaum said.

"Me too. I haven't heard anything."

Bogdonavich wanted to hold on to hope for the other men of *Miss Caroline*, but he knew there was no point in speculating. Some of the crew may not have gotten out at all. And for those who did, bailing out of a stricken bomber was damned dicey business. You could smack into the tail on the way out. Flames could damage your parachute. Even without a fire, the chute could malfunction. The canopy could fail to inflate, and you'd streamer into the ground at about 120 miles an hour. Or a shroud line could tangle over the top of the canopy. The chute would partially inflate, and you'd spin around like a falling leaf.

You were lucky to reach the ground uninjured. Luckier, still, to fall into friendly hands. Maybe the other guys had been picked up by Partisans. Or maybe Krauts had caught them. In that case, the best that could happen was getting shipped to a stalag.

The possibilities were endless, and most of them not good.

A whistle blast interrupted Bogdonavich's thoughts. The signal for approaching aircraft caused no pandemonium this time; nearly everyone was hidden among the trees already. Bogdonavich peered upward through the branches. He strained to listen, and in a moment he detected the growling of pistons.

"Where do you think they're coming from?" Greenbaum asked.

"Marich just told me the Krauts have a unit at Kraljevo," Bogdonavich said, still scanning the sky. "That's only thirty miles away."

In aviation terms, thirty miles was nothing. An aircraft flying two hundred miles an hour covered that distance in nine minutes. And Messerschmitts flew even faster than that.

This thing didn't sound like a fighter, though.

"Do you see it?" Bogdonavich asked.

"Not yet," Greenbaum said.

The two men moved to the edge of the forest for a better look.

"There," Greenbaum said. He pointed to a spot low on the horizon, just above the tree line.

The approaching dot grew larger and louder. A single aircraft, not a formation. As it drew nearer, Bogdonavich discerned three engines: two on the wings and one on the nose.

"I think it's a Junkers," Bogdonavich said.

"Yep, it's a Ju 52."

Not a killer aircraft with rockets and guns, but a light transport. To Bogdonavich, the thing looked like a Ford Trimotor, only bigger. Useful for carrying passengers and small cargo.

Or for reconnaissance.

The Junkers growled straight over the airfield, no more than a thousand feet above the ground. Green-splotched camo paint covered the aircraft. White-and-black cross on the fuselage. Swastika on the tail.

Bogdonavich held his breath. *Nobody fire,* he thought. *Please, nobody fire. Not here.*

Discipline prevailed. No one took a shot.

The aircraft banked and came around for another pass.

"Oh, shit," Greenbaum said.

Three whistle blasts sounded. Bogdonavich had not been briefed on that particular signal. He looked around to see what was happening. Under the radio tent, General Mihailovich tapped Marich's shoulder and pointed to the makeshift cattle pen. Then he folded his arms. To Bogdonavich, it seemed a strange gesture for a commander whose airfield might have just been discovered by the enemy.

A guerrilla armed with nothing more deadly than a walking stick opened the cattle pen's gate. Two of the four cows were lying down. The man prodded them to their feet.

One of the animals wore a bridle. He led the cow out into the airfield, striding at a leisurely pace. The other three cattle followed. In the middle of the dirt and grass runway, the man stopped. Stroked the cow's neck.

On its second pass, the Junkers flew over the airfield again. The guerrilla looked up and waved.

A *Luftwaffe* observer aboard the Junkers would have seen exactly what he expected to see: a harmless Serbian farmer leading his livestock to pasture.

# CHAPTER 27
# What the Dead Don't Know

*D*ESPITE SLEEP DEPRIVATION, VASA FELT ALERT. EARLIER IN THE morning, he'd hardly been able to keep from dozing; he had been awake for nearly forty-eight hours. Fatigue had weighed him down. He'd felt as if a lead ingot had formed somewhere behind his eyes. But the scene now before him invigorated him.

On orders delivered by radio, Nikolas, Miroslav, and Vasa had fallen back from the ridge where they'd observed the German mortar company. The map showed there were only two routes the enemy unit could take to reach the airfield. One of the routes used the road the team had guarded earlier, where a rock ledge overlooked a bridge and an abandoned mill.

The team had returned to that spot, only closer to the bridge. Instead of watching from the stone ledge, Vasa and the others now crouched along the road itself. They carried their new M1s, the field radio, and the Browning machine gun. Just meters from the bridge, they stood guard while a special unit went to work.

Vasa did not know these three men. Nikolas said they had served with General Mihailovich in the old Royal Army. "Sappers," Nikolas called them.

They were older, like the general, in their forties and fifties. One wore wire-rimmed eyeglasses. Gray streaked their beards. They bantered and laughed like old friends. The one with the glasses, Sergeant Srecko, seemed to be in charge.

The sappers carried knapsacks and canvas tool pouches. They hiked down to the river's edge, and they climbed the bridge abutments as easily as a cat might climb a tree. In various corners, they placed bricks of explosives. From a knapsack, Srecko pulled out what looked like a coil of wire.

"What is the wire for?" Vasa asked.

"That is not wire," Nikolas said. "That is detonation cord."

Vasa watched in utter fascination. The plan, he knew, called for guarding this bridge until the last American aeroplane departed. If the Germans attempted to cross, the sappers would blow them to perdition. Another team was guarding the other road to Pranjani.

Srecko attached a length of detonation cord to one of the bricks. He held a pair of pliers in his teeth. While holding on to an abutment with one hand, he took the pliers from his mouth with the other. Twisted something with the pliers. Then he tossed the pliers to one of the other men.

"They have done this before," Vasa observed.

"Oh, yes," Nikolas said. "Many times."

"Brave men," Miroslav said.

"Yes," Vasa said. "It must take courage to handle explosives."

"It does," Miroslav said, "but that is not what I mean. Can you imagine what the Gestapo would do to them if they caught them?"

Vasa sat on the ground and leaned against the trunk of a spruce. He placed his rifle across his legs. A light breeze brought the scent of heather from within the forest. Vasa's fatigue returned, and his eyelids began to flutter. He bolted awake and apologized for drowsing on guard duty.

"It's all right," Nikolas said. "You have been up for a long time. Rest for an hour."

Vasa rolled onto his side and unclipped his ammunition belt. Folded the belt double to use it for a pillow. He placed it on the ground and lay with his head on pouches of .30-06 rounds. Vasa drifted off to sleep again.

When he woke up, the sapper team had finished its work. Sergeant Srecko and his two friends sat in a circle with Nikolas. They were sharing lunch while Miroslav manned the Browning. Vasa sat up and rubbed his eyes.

"Ah," Srecko said, "your young friend is awake now."

"I am sorry I slept so long," Vasa said.

"From what Nikolas tells me," Srecko said, "you have earned a rest. Care for a drink?" The sapper held up an old-fashioned wineskin. He spoke Serbian with a slightly different accent. Vasa took him for a native, but not from Ravna Gora.

"Thank you, sir," Vasa said. He took the wineskin and untied the leather thong that held it closed. Lifted the wineskin and took a drink.

The wine tasted almost like liquid soil. Not good, but strong. Vasa felt the heat all the way down. He passed the bag back to Srecko.

"That is brave work you do," Vasa said. "I have never seen this kind of thing before."

"Perhaps you will get to see the fireworks," Srecko said. "I actually hope the Germans come this way."

Srecko took two packages from a knapsack. Oiled paper covered both. He unwrapped one to reveal a loaf of rye bread. The other contained four apples. With dirty fingers, he tore off a chunk of bread and passed the bread and an apple to Vasa.

Vasa thanked him and said, "Where are you from, sir?"

Srecko crunched into an apple. Chewed, swallowed, and said, "Croatia, originally."

"Srecko shares your grief," Nikolas said. "He, too, has lost family and friends. He was just telling us that is why he fights so hard."

"We all fight hard," Srecko said. "We all have our reasons."

"I am sorry to hear of your loss," Vasa said. "Then you know how . . ." Vasa's voice broke. He stopped talking to keep from crying.

"I do, son."

The rumble of an approaching vehicle interrupted the conversation. Srecko leaped to his feet and ran to a box he had wired up on the ground. The wires extended to the bridge.

When the vehicle appeared from around a bend, it turned out to be a single truck. A rusted old thing, swaying on its suspension. The open bed carried crates of live chickens. Dust and feathers swirled behind the truck. The guerrillas let it pass. Srecko returned to his lunch.

"If you do not mind the question," Vasa asked, "what happened to your people?"

"Have you ever heard of a place called Jasenovac?" Srecko asked.

Vasa shook his head.

"It's a concentration camp in Croatia," Srecko said. "Actually, it is a complex of five camps, run by the *Ustaše*. Do you know of these people?"

"I have heard of them."

Vasa knew the *Ustaše* were Hitler's allies in Croatia, a fascist ultranationalist group. They were Catholics, and they despised Jews, the Roma, and Orthodox Serbs. Beyond that, Vasa had heard little.

"Whatever you have heard," Srecko said, "the reality is worse. Their crimes have sickened even the Germans."

Srecko described growing up in Dubrovnik, a beautiful town on the Adriatic Coast. Serbs were a minority there, and the *Ustaše* sought an ethnically pure homeland. More than a decade ago, he explained, *Ustaše* leader Ante Paveli had published an editorial. Srecko recalled a part of its chilling message. "'The dagger, revolver, machine gun, and time bomb; these are the idols, these are the bells that will announce the dawning and the resurrection of the Independent State of Croatia,'" he recited.

"He meant it, too," the sapper said. "Quite literally. The German death factories kill with gas, according to the rumors. But the *Ustaše* like to kill us one at a time, as horrifically as they can."

Srecko said he'd been home on leave when his family was rounded up. He'd known it was dangerous to travel there. But, like so many people, he didn't think the fascists would take matters to such an extreme.

"Jasenovac was—is—the deepest circle of hell," he said. "The commandant lets the guards kill for fun. They take bets on who can inflict the most pain."

Guards beat people to death with mallets, Srecko reported. They sliced open prisoners' stomachs. They threw prisoners alive into incinerators. They designed a special knife, the *Srbosjek*, or Serb-cutter, mounted with a wrist strap for leverage. With these knives, they slashed throats and sliced off breasts.

"They let me live because I was strong enough to work," he said. "They made me dig graves. I buried my parents. I buried my wife, or what was left of her."

Srecko stopped speaking. He gazed through the trees toward the river and the bridge. He did not cry; his eyes did not water. But his face blanched.

"How did you escape?" Vasa asked.

"The guards got sloppy. They thought they were supermen, and they learned otherwise." He related a story that horrified Vasa.

The *Ustaše* ordered Srecko's six-man grave-digging detail to travel from Jasenovic One to Jasenovac Three to clean up after a night of carnage. The men piled into the back of a truck. Two guards armed with Mausers rode with them. A driver and another guard rode in the front.

Along the way, the truck broke down.

"We saw our chance," Srecko said. "We had nothing—absolutely nothing—to lose."

With their shovels, the gravediggers attacked the guards in the truck bed. One guard fired his rifle, and the man beside Srecko tumbled over the tailgate. The other guard fired, and in his panic, he missed even at such close range. Before the guards could work the bolts on their Mausers again, shovel blades cracked into their skulls.

The two men up front jumped out of the cab and began firing their pistols. Two more of Srecko's comrades fell. But the guards couldn't shoot fast enough to save themselves.

Srecko struck the driver in the head with the flat of his shovel. The blow knocked the driver to the ground and caused him to drop his Luger. The driver crawled for his weapon. He swung his shovel again. This time he used the shovel's edge, and he struck the driver's neck. Blood spurted from the open gash.

Again and again, Srecko swung the shovel. Slammed the blade until he had decapitated the driver. He ignored the screams and pistol shots behind him. Gouts of blood soaked the gravel on the shoulder of the road. Blood spattered Srecko's shirt and face.

When he turned around, he saw that the guard who'd ridden on the passenger side of the cab was dead, too. The gravediggers had bashed in his skull. The head resembled a smashed melon. Brain matter littered the pavement like bloody scrambled eggs. The man's pistol and several expended cartridge casings littered the ground beside him.

It had been a fight to the death for both sides. Four of Srecko's fellow prisoners lay dead. The fifth sat up against a truck wheel, clutching his abdomen. He'd been hit at least twice, that Srecko could see.

"Shoot me," the man said.

"Come with me," Srecko said. "We need to get out of here."

The man shook his head. "I cannot," he said. "I'll just slow you down, and they will catch us both."

"Goran, you must . . ."

"Shoot me, Srecko. Please. When they find me, they won't just kill me. They'll cut me to pieces as slowly as they can. You know they will."

"We killed them, Goran."

Goran gave a weak smile. Then he coughed and spit blood.

Srecko picked up the driver's pistol. When he reached down, he realized some of the blood on his shirt was his own. He'd been shot in the shoulder. Until now, he had not felt a thing.

"Hurry," Goran said. "You must escape."

Srecko pressed the muzzle against his friend's forehead.

"Go be free," Srecko said. "May God bless you."

Srecko pulled the trigger. Then he fled into the woods.

"I eventually made my way back to Chetnik forces," Srecko said. "And here I am."

"You are a formidable soldier," Nikolas said.

"I am merely a husband and a son," Srecko said. "Or I was, anyway. Now I am just a man who lives for justice."

*Justice,* Vasa thought. *He didn't say vengeance.* In Srecko's case, a desire for vengeance certainly would have been justified. *Same with me,* Vasa considered.

Sitting in the forest amid the scent of heather and evergreen, bearing a rifle, a pistol, and many rounds of ammunition, Vasa pondered these things. What was the difference between justice and vengeance? Vengeance was sweet, and surely part of human nature. Part of Vasa wanted it so bad. But Father Milos had said vengeance was God's alone. The priest said he certainly didn't mean Vasa shouldn't fight. But he talked about the *spirit* with which Vasa should fight.

At the time, Vasa found those words confusing. All the roads in his mind led to a dead end of grief. He appreciated the priest's concern. But he thought the spirit with which one fights was a matter of hairsplitting for clerics in an abbey. Not for soldiers in the field.

But now, hearing another soldier speak of justice, Father Milos's point became clearer. Maybe the old man was wiser than Vasa realized. Vengeance had its place, but vengeance looked backward. It was about settling scores. Blood for blood. However, the dead don't know they've been avenged. Justice looked forward. Offered hope for a better future.

*You seek vengeance for yourself,* Vasa concluded. *You seek justice for everyone else.*

Vasa's tormented mind settled a little. He counted himself fortunate to be here in this place with these men. He had a job to do, and he knew how to do it.

Srecko offered another sip from the wineskin. Vasa drank and passed the wine around. He shifted his M1 and held on to it with the stock resting on the ground. He watched the river flow past the old mill. And he watched the road.

# CHAPTER 28
# Chariot Flight

*C*UMULUS, SHOT THROUGH WITH SCARLET BY THE LAST RAYS OF sunset, hovered over the ramp at San Pancrazio. In the gloaming, six C-47 Skytrains stood fueled and ready. Ground personnel took fireguard positions, extinguishers close by in case an engine start went bad. In the cockpit of the number three ship, Drew noted when the second hand of his watch swept through the 12.

"Start left engine," Drew said.

Torres reached overhead and moved the left starter switch and safety switch. The Pratt & Whitney barked, sputtered, and caught. Drew set the mixture lever to auto-rich and eased the throttle back to 800 RPM. Vibration spread from the wing into the entire airframe. Drew felt the trembling through the seat, in the back of his thighs.

Across the ramp, the left propellers on all six airplanes began turning at once. The precision and choreography implied a kind of inertia, a massive operation gaining unstoppable momentum. Drew couldn't get out of this now even if he wanted to. At the very least, he knew that once he released the brakes on his C-47, this object would remain in motion until it met with fate, one way or another.

The interphone came alive with terse commands and responses as the crew ran checklists. Torres started the right engine, and Drew scanned engine instruments. In the deepening darkness, he tweaked a rheostat to turn up the instrument lighting. Everything looked normal: good temperatures, pressures, and voltages.

A signal from the control tower's Aldis lamp started the procession moving. The lead ship lumbered off the ramp and entered the taxiway. The others followed in turn. Drew released the parking brake, eased off the toe brakes, and nudged the throttles. The C-47 began to roll.

Drew considered a Latin phrase he'd learned recently: *Memento mori.* "Remember that you must die."

*Tonight,* he thought. *Or seventy years from tonight. Whatever the time, use it well.* Once again, he carried an L-pill in his left shirt pocket. But this time, the cyanide capsule carried different meanings for him. The gift of life could not last forever. Drew was alive for now, though, perhaps more alive than he'd ever been. And, like Sienna had said, his story wasn't over yet. In his right shirt pocket, he carried her necklace.

Sweat from Drew's palms slicked the control yoke and the throttle knobs. He prayed his nerves wouldn't fail him. The men on the ground in Yugoslavia were counting on him. The Germans would surely capture or kill the downed airmen soon if this mission didn't succeed. It was a miracle they'd evaded capture this long.

The wind was blowing hard tonight. The wind sock stood straight out, at a right angle to the runway. Direct crosswind, naturally.

Up ahead, the lead ship took the runway and began its takeoff roll. The lead aircraft, and the formation itself, was commanded by Captain Geiser, the officer who'd told Drew at his review board that he was downgraded to line pilot. The lead ship's tail came up, and the aircraft lifted into the twilight. Number two began rolling, and Drew taxied into position behind it.

"Here we go," Drew called. He rotated the yoke a bit to counter the crosswind with his ailerons. Shoved the power forward. Guarded the throttles with the heel of his hand so they wouldn't creep back.

The airplane gathered speed, grew light on its tires, and flew. Drew eyed the number two ship ahead of him as he climbed through choppy turbulence. Number two appeared as a mere shadow; the C-47s were flying with all external lights off to avoid detection. Drew took his position in a loose formation forming up over the Adriatic. By now it was full dark. The water below appeared as a sea of ink.

Drew gave the controls to Torres. When they leveled at cruise altitude, they put the plane on autopilot. Drew switched on a utility light and aimed its beam at the aeronautical chart on his kneeboard. He reviewed the mission's planned headings and course changes. Static popped and fried in his headset. Behind him, Chisholm was warming up his Rebecca set. The lead aircraft was primarily responsible for navigation. But every ship needed to be able to find the objective on its own, in case the leader got shot down or suffered equipment failure.

Underneath the aeronautical chart, the clip on Drew's kneeboard also secured an aerial photo. A P-38 photoreconnaissance plane had taken a shot of the landing zone. The image showed an opening surrounded by forest and bordered by a road. The airfield offered roughly three thousand feet of usable runway. Haystacks stood at one end. The runway was oriented southwest to northeast. Pen marks, drawn by hand, indicated expected location of signal flares.

"Want to see the picture again?" Drew asked. Torres nodded, and Drew passed the photo to him.

"Burning hay bales for flares, huh?" Torres said.

"That's what they said in the briefing."

"Necessity's the mother of invention."

Drew tried to dwell on the tasks rather than the danger. He hoped that would keep his mind focused and clear. And missions always seemed to go more smoothly when pilots constantly looked toward the next step. "Staying ahead of the airplane," they called it.

A waning gibbous moon rose above the horizon. The light gave form to the waves heaving below. Drew hoped for good visibility at the landing zone. If necessary, he could turn on his landing lights on short final, but that was an absolute last resort. That could alert the enemy, and also spoil the night vision of everyone on the ground.

A radio call from one of the other aircraft interrupted Drew's planning.

"Chariot Lead, Chariot Four," a pilot called.

"Chariot Four, go ahead," Geiser answered from the lead ship.

"Our right engine just failed. We've got the prop feathered. Ah, we're gonna need to RTB."

Wordless hiss on the radio for a few seconds. Then: "Copy that. Return to base."

"That ain't good," Torres said on the interphone.

The formation crossed a dim coastline marked by waves crashing into a rocky beach. From altitude in the moonlight, the surf appeared as light smudges across a dark canvas. And the problems for Operation Halyard continued.

"Chariot Lead, Chariot Two," a pilot called on the radio.

"Go ahead, Two."

"Ah, sir, be advised we've lost some hydraulic fluid."

Long pause. Static.

"How much?"

"Engineer advises at least half."

Drew and Torres glanced at their own engineer, Montreux, who sat behind them in the jump seat.

"If he doesn't have hydraulic pressure, he doesn't have brakes," Drew said.

"He can't land on a short strip," Torres said.

"If he keeps losing fluid, he won't get the flaps down," Montreux said. "Not even with the hand pump."

In the lead ship, Geiser reached the same conclusion. "Chariot Two, RTB," the commander ordered over the radio.

"Chariot Two copies, RTB."

"And then there were four," Torres said.

*Two aborts already,* Drew considered. He thought back to his short time as a bomber pilot, and his own aborts. His had been gray areas, judgment calls. These two were not: Engine failure and hydraulic loss left no choice. *Don't think about the past,* Drew told himself. *Just fly.*

Drew scanned his engine and systems gauges once more. Everything still looked good. Below, the outline of hills and ridges took shape against the night horizon. Against one hillside, he saw flames. From altitude, the fire appeared as a flickering yellow dot.

"Something's burning down there," Drew said.

"Can you tell what it is?" Torres asked.

"Not really."

Drew checked his chart. The fire wasn't near the airstrip; that was still miles ahead. The fire could have been an accident, or it could have been Nazis razing a village. It reminded Drew that a war raged down there—and that he had no idea what awaited him on the ground. What if a security breach happened and the Germans got wise? They'd overrun the airfield. The C-47s could land into a storm of machine gun bullets.

*Don't think about it,* Drew told himself. *Just do your job.* He followed the formation's progress on his chart. After a while, he checked his calculations against Chisholm's.

"Navigator, pilot," Drew called on the interphone. "How far out are we?"

"Fifty-six miles," Chisholm said. Drew had estimated fifty. Close enough.

"All right, crew," Drew said. "We're about twenty-two minutes out. Suit up, if you haven't already."

Drew and Torres had donned their flak vests before engine start. The heavy armor made it impossible to get comfortable in the seat, but Drew knew they'd need it if the aircraft came under fire. He reached to the floor and picked up his M3 flak helmet.

Strapped it on over his headset. Torres and Montreux did the same.

Another call came over the radio: "Chariot Flight, Chariot Lead. Radio check."

This call, Drew had expected. Soon the formation would reach the objective. According to the mission plan, the lead ship would follow a Eureka beam to the airfield. Then it would look not just for the burning hay bales, but for an all-clear signal as well. An OSS man on the ground would flash a code word with an Aldis lamp. The lead pilot needed to know everyone could hear him report whether he saw the signal.

"Chariot Three, loud and clear," Drew called.

"Chariot Five."

"Chariot Six."

"Okay, it's almost showtime," Drew said on the interphone. "Let's make this happen." He tried to sound more confident than he felt. The terrain scrolled underneath his wings, forested ridgelines limned by moonlight. What dangers lurked in those hills?

"Chariot Flight, begin descent," the lead ship called.

Drew eased back his throttles and watched the manifold pressure drop. Established a gentle descent of a thousand feet per minute. His palms began to sweat again. His forehead too. A bead of sweat rolled down the bridge of his nose, though he didn't feel hot.

Another radio call interrupted his concentration:

"Chariot Flight, this is Lead. Ah, we're not getting a Eureka signal. Anybody picking it up?"

"Nav," Drew called on the interphone, "anything on your scope?"

"Not yet," Chisholm said. "He's a little ahead of us."

"Either the OSS guys aren't there, or lead's Rebecca isn't working," Torres said.

*And we gotta figure this out fast,* Drew thought. *If the Krauts have overrun the field, we sure as hell don't want to fly over it.*

Drew leveled off at the planned step-down altitude. Pushed his throttles forward. Held his breath.

"Still nothing?" he asked Chisholm.

"Negative."

"Chariot Flight," Geiser called, "anybody got a signal?"

"Nav?" Drew asked.

"Negative. Wait—I got it. They're on. Right turn zero-two-zero."

"Zero-two-zero," Drew said. Then he pressed his transmit switch. "Chariot Three has the Eureka. Heading zero-two-zero."

"All right, Three," Geiser called. "Our Rebecca must be busted. I'm gonna turn out of formation and rejoin at the back. You got lead."

"Roger that," Drew transmitted. Then on the interphone: "Guys, we're the lead ship now. You know the ground signals." *The guy who told me I was downgraded just had to put me in charge,* Drew thought. *Don't screw this up.* Once again, he called out the new heading, and the formation began its turn.

Drew craned his neck to look as far ahead as he could. For several seconds he saw only undulating dark hills. Then a dim point of light. Then two, three.

Two parallel lines of tiny fires took shape in the distance.

"Nav," Drew called, "I think I got it about ten miles ahead. Does that check with your Rebecca?"

"Affirm."

"All right, let's see if we get the all clear."

Drew held his heading, and he throttled back to one hundred miles per hour. The fires grew larger. He glanced down once more at the photo on his kneeboard. The edges of the airstrip, outlined by the fires, oriented roughly with the image taken by the P-38. Torres peered out the right window.

"I got a light signal," Torres called.

Drew saw the flashes from an Aldis lamp. He concentrated on heading and altitude and let Torres decode the Morse.

"X-ray," Torres said. "Able. Easy. Ah, yeah. *X-A-E.*"

"That's it," Drew said. "*X-A-E.* Sounds like a fraternity." Then he transmitted: "Chariot Flight, we have an all clear."

The other three aircraft acknowledged. Geiser added, "Good job, Chariot Three. Take us in."

Drew inhaled a deep breath. His ribs strained against his flak vest. He banked left to set up for the downwind leg for landing. Watched his flight instruments and scanned the ground. And prayed to see no tracers.

# CHAPTER 29
# The Black Hole Effect

*C*HEERS ROSE FROM THE FIELD AS THE FIRST C-47 OVERFLEW THE airstrip. Bogdonavich pumped his fists into the air.

"We're going home, boys!" Bogdonavich shouted.

Greenbaum slapped him on the back. Oliver, Higgins, and dozens of other crewmen in the woods alongside the landing strip laughed and embraced. Marich put down his Aldis lamp. Reached into his gear bag and pulled out a Very pistol. Raised the pistol above his head and fired the final "cleared to land" signal.

A green flare soared into the sky. Another swell of cheers and laughter rose with it. The flare arced over the field like an emerald comet, burned out, and vanished.

"I can't believe this is actually working," Greenbaum said.

"It hasn't yet," Oliver said. "Let's see if they get in."

Three other aircraft roared overhead and turned to set up for landing.

"I count just four," Marich said. "There were supposed to be six."

"I hope they're all okay," Bogdonavich said.

Bogdonavich squinted to catch sight of the first plane as it rolled onto final approach. For a few minutes, all of the aircraft disappeared in the darkness. But then he made out a shape ghosting along in the moonlight. Yes, there it was. Lower now. On a glide path for landing.

"Come on, baby," Oliver said. "Come on."

"They gonna make it?" Higgins asked.

"It'll be tight," Oliver said.

The first plane floated over the trees at the approach end of the field. Engines at idle, the machine seemed to whisper as the wheels neared the ground. In the moonlight, Bogdonavich discerned the C-47's tail, with a rudder big as a barn door.

And then the engines screamed.

The aircraft leveled off, then climbed. The pilot was aborting the landing.

Drew pulled back on the yoke and held the throttles against their forward stops. Watched the vertical speed indicator register a climb. Held his breath until his wheels cleared the trees at the far end of the field.

"Tell the others to extend downwind and let me try again," Drew told Torres.

Torres pressed his transmit switch and said, "Chariot Flight, Chariot Three going around. Extend your downwind."

The other aircraft acknowledged.

"Field too short?" Montreux asked.

"It's short, and I was ten miles an hour hot," Drew said. "It would help if I could see a little better."

*The black hole illusion,* he thought. Drew had warned student pilots about it, and he was still subject to it himself. When approaching a lit airstrip from over dark terrain, you can think you're too high when you're not. You tend to push down the nose when you don't need to. That's why he'd gotten too fast. Too low, too. He'd damn near clipped the trees at the approach end.

Drew leveled off at a thousand feet above the ground. He turned onto his downwind leg, parallel to the runway. Kept the flaps and landing gear extended. Throttled back to approach speed. Glanced down through his side window. The burning hay bales still beckoned him. Two of them burst into brighter flame.

Sparks rose skyward. Someone adding kerosene, perhaps, to keep them alight.

"Damn," Torres said. "We got planes going around, burning hay, flares, and Aldis lamps. Can we do *anything* else to alert the Germans?"

Drew eyed the two burning bales that marked the approach end of the runway. He mentally marked the space between them as his aim point. When he had to look over his left shoulder to see them, he throttled back and turned onto his base leg. The aircraft began descending.

"Call my altitudes," Drew said.

"Got you nine hundred above ground level," Torres answered. "Looking good."

*So far,* Drew thought. *Please don't let me screw this up.*

"Seven hundred," Torres called.

Drew glanced at his vertical speed indicator. He was descending at about seven hundred feet per minute. About right. He turned again, to roll out onto final approach. The burning bales swung into view. Two lines of fires stretched before him. *Like a visual approach into hell,* he thought.

"Five hundred feet," Torres called.

"Rog," Drew said.

"Three hundred," Torres said. "On glide path."

The fires loomed larger in the windscreen now. The brightness washed out much of Drew's night vision. The airstrip between them now appeared as a black void.

"One hundred," Torres said.

Drew retarded the throttles to idle. Pulled back on the yoke to flare for landing. Now he couldn't see the ground at all. He simply held the aircraft in the landing attitude.

The main wheels thumped to the ground. Rolled smoothly with no bounce.

As soon as the tail came down, Drew pressed on the toe brakes. The C-47 rolled to a stop.

Drew let out a long breath. Wiped the sweat from his palms onto the thighs of his flight suit. He was on the ground in Yugoslavia. With an aircraft that could still fly.

* * *

Vasa heard engines, faint in the distance. All day and into the night, he had strained to listen. First a bomber formation passed during the afternoon. They appeared as gnats, their motors a distant hum. At twilight, two German fighters flashed low overhead. A grating whine accompanied them. Then an old farm truck sputtered across the bridge. Vasa smelled exhaust smoke as the vehicle coughed past.

This new sound was different. Powerful engines, low to the ground. More than one. Perhaps many more than one.

"Is that the American aeroplanes?" Vasa asked.

"I hope so," Nikolas said.

Vasa kneeled in the brush with his M1 across his forearm. Srecko crouched at his detonator, with the other two sappers close by his side. Miroslav took position behind the Browning. If the Germans came and the explosives failed to drop the bridge, Miroslav would sweep the entire span with bullets. Nikolas lay prone with his rifle across a log. He kept the field radio close beside him, switched on with the volume low, in case any other units reported enemy movement.

If the German mortar company came, Vasa knew, his team would face a hellish battle even if Srecko blew the bridge. The enemy would pour gunfire from across the river. Eventually they would probably ford the river.

*If we cannot stop them,* Vasa told himself, *we must at least slow them down.*

But thus far, there was no sign of movement from beyond the bridge. There were no warnings over the field radio. Perhaps the Nazis were spending another night in their valley encampment. Or perhaps they'd moved on in other directions.

Regardless of the quiet, Vasa remained wide awake. His senses felt turned up to maximum, as if by a knob on that radio. He kept a fresh clip for his M1 on the ground in front of him, ready to reload fast. Other clips waited in his ammunition belt, pouches already unsnapped for quick access.

Nikolas had forbidden smoking, so that the fire at the end of a cigarette wouldn't give away their position. But the order had an additional benefit: Since sundown, Vasa hadn't seen any artificial light, not even the brief flare of a match. His irises had fully adjusted to the darkness. Moonlight illuminated a curve on the other side of the bridge, and if so much as a squirrel passed along that road, Vasa would see it. As an experiment, he raised his rifle to his shoulder as if to aim. Yes, he could even make out the front and rear sights, though just barely.

With his body alert and focused, Vasa's mind grew clear and untroubled, at least for the moment. He liked this place where his thoughts had settled. The soldier place, he named it.

*I have feared the Germans so much,* he thought. *I have grieved the things they have done. They have determined my feelings and actions. But not tonight. This is no longer about what they have done to me. This is about justice, and what I will do to them.*

Bogdonavich watched the first C-47 lumber across the grass. Using a pair of flashlights as marshaling wands, Marich guided the pilot to a parking area. As the propellers spun down to a stop, cheers rose from the adjacent woods. A few minutes later, the cargo door swung open. A crewman unfolded a metal ladder and placed it beneath the door. Bogdonavich trotted over to the aircraft to see if he could help.

"What's your name, soldier?" Bogdonavich asked.

"Montreux, sir. I'm the engineer."

"We're mighty glad to see you. What can I do to help you?"

"We got a few things to unload. I can bring them to the door if you want to take them down the ladder."

"You got it."

To Bogdonavich's pleasant surprise, the C-47 had brought more supplies for the guerrillas and villagers. Not nearly as much as the airdrop, but any amount would help. The engineer passed him a wooden box labeled: U.S. ARMY MEDICAL DEPARTMENT, HUMAN PLASMA. Bogdonavich placed it on the ground beside the ladder. He motioned for some of the other downed fliers to come and help him. They unloaded boxes of blankets, rations, bandages, and even cigarettes. But no boots. The army or the OSS or whoever loaded these planes had been wonderfully generous, but no-body had thought about footwear.

By now, the second aircraft had landed. Windblast from its pro-pellers stung Bogdonavich's eyes and flung grit into his face. He didn't mind, though. It felt like success. He picked up the box of plasma and took it straight to Katarina. Placed it on the ground with her other medical supplies. The nurse already had her first four patients lined up on makeshift stretchers.

"Can you help me move them over to the aeroplanes?" Kata-rina asked in Serbian.

"Da," Bogdonavich said. He kneeled to lift one end of a stretcher. On it lay Sergeant Rawlings, the waist gunner suffering from burns. "How are you feeling, Rawlings?" Bogdonavich asked.

"Better now," the gunner said. "That's for damn sure. Ready to go home."

"Let's get it done, then."

Katarina took the other end of the stretcher. They lifted Rawl-ings and began carrying him across the field to the first C-47.

"Sir," Rawlings said, "tell Katarina we all love her. That woman's an angel."

Bogdonavich translated, but Katarina ignored the compliment. Too busy and focused right now, Bogdonavich figured, to bother with pleasantries.

At the aircraft, Montreux helped lift the wounded gunner into the cargo compartment. As they finished, another plane was land-ing. At first, the approach looked normal. But when the main wheels touched down, the plane bounced back into the air.

"Go around," Bogdonavich whispered to himself.

The pilots did not go around. The plane hit the ground again, hard enough to flex the wings. Swerved toward the side of the airstrip. For a second, Bogdonavich feared the aircraft would crash into the trees. Then it veered away from the tree line. And spun its right wing into a haystack.

The impact filled the air with straw. Prop blast sent the straw flying farther. The crew shut down the engines, and the propellers spun down to a stop. The odors of exhaust, hot brakes, and burning hay filled the air. Men ran toward the aircraft.

Drew, Torres, and Chisholm jumped down from their own plane and joined the rush to the aircraft that had ground-looped into the haystack. To Drew's relief, it didn't look too badly damaged. Then the last aircraft, piloted by Geiser, the flight commander, landed safely. Now four C-47s sat in the brandy-colored light of the moon. The hay bales that had guided them in burned down to embers. Piles of flickering, smoldering ash lined the airstrip on both sides.

One of the engineers set up a ladder and climbed for a better look at the wing that had smashed through the haystack. He played a flashlight along the leading edge. The man shrugged, switched off his flashlight, and climbed back down. Drew recognized Captain Marich, the OSS officer, among those waiting for the engineer's assessment.

"Just a minor ding," the engineer said. "She'll fly out."

"Thank God for that," Marich said. "Good work getting in here, boys. You made it happen. We want to get you out of here quick, too. But first, we gotta have a talk. Officers, bring it in."

Marich waved his arms, motioned for the pilots and navigators to gather around him. The enlisted men checked over the planes and helped load wounded men aboard.

"I always assumed this had to be a night operation," Marich said. "We're working right under the Krauts' noses. But, damn, we just had a real close call. We can't afford a crash."

"It's like threading a needle, sir," Drew said. "I had to go around on my first try."

"And I should have," the pilot from the damaged aircraft confessed. "I almost blew it for everybody."

"Yeah, but you didn't," Marich said. "It's all right. But listen, can we keep doing this in the dark? I'm not a pilot; you guys gotta tell me."

"I almost went around, too," a pilot added.

"Except for the signal fires, it's really black around here,"

Geiser offered. "There aren't any other lights for reference points. You get on final, and you lose your depth perception."

Geiser and the OSS officer reached a consensus: Operation Halyard could not afford a botched night landing.

"You can't rescue anybody if you turn your airplane into a fireball," Marich concluded. "Tomorrow we'll do this in broad daylight."

The crews would need to trade one set of risks for another and pray they made the right decision. Better visibility versus greater risk of detection? Everything about the mission presented dangers. Perhaps landing in daylight presented slightly fewer.

*But first,* Drew thought, *we gotta get off the ground tonight.*

# CHAPTER 30
# A Time for Every Purpose

WITH A DOZEN PASSENGERS LOADED, CARGO DOOR LATCHED, AND engines running, Drew held his brakes with the tips of his boots. He eyed the trees at the end of the airstrip. To live through the next two minutes, he needed to make best use of every inch of runway. Every foot-pound of propeller torque. Every molecule of lift-producing air.

"Gimme a notch of flaps," Drew said.

Torres pulled the flap handle. That setting would help the wings generate more lift and shorten the takeoff roll.

"Flaps set," Torres said.

"Thanks. Don't let me do anything stupid."

The other three C-47s waited behind Drew's aircraft. Because he'd led the formation into Pranjani, Captain Geiser let him lead it out. It was a mixed honor: He'd get to demonstrate whether getting out of this field was even possible.

"Engineer," Drew said, "scan the gauges with me when I push up the power."

"Rog," Montreux said.

With the heel of his hand, Drew bumped the prop control levers to double-check they were in the full high RPM setting.

Took a deep breath. Pressed the throttles forward. The needles for manifold pressure and cylinder head temperature began to rise. The engines howled. The airframe rattled and trembled. This inanimate, unfeeling object seemed to yearn for the sky.

"Power's good," Montreux said.

"Call my speeds," Drew said to Torres.

Drew released the brakes. The C-47 lurched forward. For an instant, it wanted to veer left, but Drew corrected with the rudder pedals. The aircraft swayed across a low spot in the field.

"Forty," Torres called.

Drew pressed forward on the yoke just enough to start bringing up the tail.

"Fifty," Torres called.

The moonlit trees along the side of the airstrip began to blur. The trees at the end of the field loomed larger.

"Sixty."

The tail lifted clear off the ground. By subtle pilot instinct, Drew felt the wings begin to take weight off the wheels.

"Seventy."

No stopping now. Not even if an engine failed. There wasn't enough runway left to stop.

"Eighty."

Drew eased back on the yoke. The rumbling of the tires hushed. The airplane lifted off the dirt and grass, and began to climb. The trees in their moon shadows passed just feet beneath the wheels.

Cheers sounded from the cargo compartment. Drew smiled for a second. But apart from that, he ignored the celebration. He needed to concentrate. He still had terrain to clear.

"How's it looking, navigator?" Drew asked.

"Keep this climb rate going, and we're good," Chisholm said.

"Crew, keep your eyes out there," Drew ordered. "Last thing we need is to get jumped by a night fighter."

Drew banked to the left. Stars tilted in his windscreen. He leveled the wings on an initial southwesterly heading. Chisholm would fine-tune the course from there.

As Drew climbed, the other three C-47s checked in by radio. Everyone had made it off the airfield safely. At cruise altitude, the aircraft formed up, and Chisholm plotted a course across the Adriatic.

The Americans still waiting their turns to fly out remained at the airstrip. No one knew exactly when the C-47s would return, and no one wanted to risk missing a flight. The field became a scene of celebration—and anticipation. Now that the plans for night ops had been scrapped, Bogdonavich, along with everyone else, wondered how things would go from here.

Through the rest of the night, Bogdonavich watched the activity at the radio tent. Marich and his radio operator made calls both by voice and code. Just before dawn, Jezdich, the OSS radio operator, removed his headset, placed it on the table, and rubbed his eyes. Bogdonavich decided to ask for an update.

"We've been on the horn with Fifteenth Air Force," Marich said. "We want to get fighter escort for the next flight in."

"Any luck?" Bogdonavich asked.

"Don't know yet. I'm sure every infantry unit between here and Normandy wants air support. It's not like we got squadrons of P-51s sitting around with nothing to do."

Bogdonavich knew firsthand how vulnerable a heavy aircraft could be against a nimble Messerschmitt or Focke-Wulf. And his B-24 had bristled with guns; it at least carried some means of fighting back. The C-47s were defenseless.

The pilots of fighters and bombers got all the glory, Bogdonavich realized. But you needed a set of brass balls to fly a cargo airplane into a combat zone. Fortune had smiled on this humble little airfield, but could that kind of luck continue long enough to evacuate more than five hundred men?

Word of the successful flights filtered through Pranjani. By midmorning, villagers came bearing farewell gifts for the men still on the ground. Several women brought *Pirot kilims*, a type of traditional rug named for the town of Pirot and considered a national symbol. The women crafted the brightly colored tapestries on vertical looms. Each one represented hours of work. The villagers draped the rugs around the men's shoulders and kissed their cheeks.

The sight nearly brought Bogdonavich to tears. These people who had risked so much for the airmen now brought gifts? As if they hadn't already done more than anyone could ask?

He tried to think of how to express appreciation. What could he do for the locals that would help them in some practical way? Bogdonavich considered the airdrop that had brought the guerrillas much-needed supplies. He recalled that the OSS had thought of practically everything except footwear. Vasa and some of the other fighters still made do with worn-out boots. What could be done about that?

Bogdonavich found Greenbaum and Oliver.

"Have you noticed how so many of these Serbs have holes in their shoes?" he asked.

"Ah, yeah, now that you mention it," Greenbaum said.

"When the airplanes come back," Bogdonavich said, "right before you leave, throw your boots out. Once we get back, we can get new ones from supply anytime."

"That's a great idea," Oliver said.

"Thanks," Bogdonavich said. "Spread the word."

At the overwatch site, Vasa woke to Nikolas shaking him by the arm.

"Good morning," Nikolas whispered. "Did you catch up on your sleep?"

Vasa sat up, rubbed his eyes. Glanced around to make sure his rifle and pistol remained close at hand. He and Miroslav had kept watch until two a.m., and then Nikolas and Srecko had taken over.

"I did," Vasa said. "Anything new?"

"No, still quiet. Do you want some tea?"

The question surprised Vasa. He'd assumed there would be no cooking fire, no smoke to give away the ambush site. He expected the team would drink nothing but water and the occasional sip from the wineskin.

"Yes, thank you. But how?"

"You have to see this."

Vasa sat up, adjusted his clothing. Took a sip of water from his canteen. Sloshed the water around in his mouth and swallowed it. Stumbled over to join the rest of the team. Most of them sat on the ground in a circle. Miroslav and one of the sappers watched the bridge with weapons ready.

At the center of the circle, Srecko kneeled over a small hole he'd dug in the ground. He glanced over at Vasa.

"You are just in time," he said.

Above the fire hole, Srecko held a brick of explosive like the ones he'd set under the bridge. He'd opened the paper at one end. Whatever the explosive was made of, it wasn't terribly hard, because Srecko was shaving chips off it with a knife. The slivers fell from the blade and collected in the fire hole.

"What is that?" Vasa asked.

"The Yanks and the British call it Composition C," Srecko said. "It is useful for many things, including making coffee and tea."

Puzzled, Vasa watched Srecko work. From a mess kit, Srecko produced a wire grate, which he placed over the hole. He poured water from his canteen into a tin pot, which he placed on the grate. Dug into his field jacket and found a box of matches. Struck a match and touched it to the pile of whitish shavings.

Instantly flames filled the fire hole. Vasa had never seen fire start so quickly, not even with kerosene. The fire gave off a chemical smell, and it burned almost without smoke.

"That is quite a trick," Vasa said.

"This is amazing stuff," Srecko said. "A little bit warms your tea. More kills a man. Still more blows a bridge."

There was a lesson in there, Vasa considered. Something about proportions and purposes. Father Milos had spoken about a time for every purpose.

Srecko and the sappers shared their breakfast with Vasa, Nikolas, and Miroslav. In addition to the usual stale bread, Srecko offered *burek*, a traditional Serbian pastry. Vasa wondered how Srecko could have found such a treat in the midst of guerrilla warfare. Perhaps he had baked it himself somehow with that magic explosive.

The men ate while keeping a close watch on the bridge. Nikolas also kept a listening watch on the field radio. The radio, resting on the ground in its backpack, gave off a faint hum. Mist hung in the treetops. The landscape lay quiet; no traffic passed along the road. The forest filled with the chirp and twitter of birds.

Vasa sipped his tea from a metal cup. He savored the unexpected luxury, watched steam rise from hot liquid. He took a bite of the *burek*; it even had cheese inside.

A radio call interrupted the meal.

"All stations," the set hissed, "this is Archangel. Radio check."

Nikolas put down his cup and reached for the handset.

"Archangel, Jeferdar Three," he called. "Loud and clear."

"Jeferdar One, loud and clear," another team called.

"Jeferdar Two," another answered.

Nikolas had explained that Jeferdar Two was on the ridge overlooking the German mortar company. Jeferdar One was manning another ambush point. If the enemy took either of two roads that could lead them to Pranjani, they would meet with fire and lead. If they took routes away from Pranjani, they would never know how close they had come to disaster. They would be allowed to leave, and perhaps the Chetniks would kill them another day.

The morning passed into noontime with no action, not even any traffic. Srecko shared tales of life in Dubrovnik. This time, he spoke of happy memories from before the war: fishing with his father, watching boats in the harbor. Wandering the streets, admiring the women. Dining in restaurants that spread aromas through the neighborhoods.

The sapper chief seemed to enjoy telling these stories. He spoke without tears. Vasa thought perhaps the man wanted people to know how his family had lived in peacetime. That way, he kept them alive in memory.

But the radio broke into the fond recollections.

"All stations," the radio crackled. "This is Jeferdar Two. Be advised the Germans are moving."

# CHAPTER 31
## River Afire

*I*N A CHOW TENT FOR TRANSIENT FLIERS AT BARI, ITALY, DREW AND his crew ate a late breakfast. They'd landed before dawn, gotten a few hours of sleep, and planned to launch again in the afternoon. Despite the limited rest, Drew felt refreshed. The chow hall's trash can coffee tasted like the finest espresso. The powdered eggs might have been a crabmeat omelet at the Ritz. The flaccid bacon, filet mignon.

The wounded airmen they'd brought back were already being treated. Some were scheduled to fly out today to a military hospital in Naples. With great satisfaction, Drew watched the trucks with red crosses on their sides trundle around the base. The men would heal, and then they would go home.

Drew took another sip of black coffee. Through steam rising from the cup, he noticed his navigator, Chisholm, looking at him.

"It's a good feeling, isn't it?" Chisholm said. The navigator slathered butter across a piece of toast and took a bite.

"You mean bringing those guys out?" Drew said. "Yeah, it is."

"You ever heard of Antoine de Saint-Exupéry?"

"Can't say that I have. Who's that?"

"French writer and aviator. In one of his books, he said every pilot who has flown to the rescue of a comrade knows all other joys are vain in comparison."

"He sure got that right," Drew said. "Who is this guy again?"

Chisholm repeated the name. Then he said, "He went missing just the other day. Not too far from here, either."

Chisholm explained that Saint-Ex, as he called the writer, had been flying recon missions from a base in Corsica. In his forties, he could have gotten out of combat flying, but he insisted on serving. On July 31, he took off in a P-38 Lightning and never came back.

"Heard about it on the radio a little while ago," Chisholm said.

"Damn, that's awful," Drew said.

The news dampened Drew's good mood. Reminded him that death hovered over every combat aviator. What happened to this Frenchman could happen to him. With every mission, he would need to battle his fears. Drew tried to focus on the positives: The reward for controlling his fear was all around him now, represented by the rescued fliers who would see their families again. And—just maybe—Drew would get to see Sienna again. After all, he'd made it this far.

After breakfast, in a flight planning room, the crews debated tactics. All along, they'd planned on night ops. Now, with the sudden change in plans, they had to adjust to working in broad daylight. In enemy territory.

"Should we go in high?" a pilot asked.

That idea offered one advantage: If they flew in at ten thousand feet—or if they carried oxygen and flew still higher—small arms posed less threat. A bullet would not likely reach that high and punch through aluminum with enough force to continue into flesh and bone.

"But the Krauts can't miss a formation of six C-47s waltzing in at altitude," Geiser, the flight commander, said.

"He's right," Drew said, "and they've got a *Luftwaffe* squadron at Kraljevo."

Drew let his fellow aviators put together the rest: Kraljevo was only thirty miles from the airstrip at Pranjani. At first sighting of the C-47s, the Germans could launch their fighters. Even if the C-47s had fighter escort, the enemy would still have an advantage. Just off their base at Kraljevo, the Messerschmitts would have nearly full tanks of gas when they engaged the P-38s. The American escorts would have burned through much of their fuel. The Germans could toy with the American fighters—approach and break off, approach and break off—while the American tanks ran low. At bingo fuel, the P-38s would have to turn for home. And then the Messerschmitts could slice in for the kill.

On this mission, climbing to high altitude would amount to climbing a gallows.

"Then we'll go in low," Geiser said. "I mean, *real* low."

Low flying offered several advantages: Down at treetop level, the formation would be hard to spot. It would have to fly right over a German unit to be discovered. And if the Germans had installed their Freya radar system at Kraljevo, the C-47s would sneak in below radar. Low altitude would put the aircraft within range of Mauser bullets, yes. But to a ground observer, the planes would appear and disappear quickly. Very little time to get off a shot. In USAAF lingo, the aircraft would present a "high angular velocity."

"We'll be gone before they can say '*Heil* Hitler,' " Torres said.

"All right," Geiser said, "but I still hope we get those P-38s to ride shotgun."

That was still being worked out, the flight commander added. They might not know about fighter escort until takeoff time.

After the flight-planning meeting, Drew pulled together his gear. In the shade of an open-sided tent, he piled his flak vest and helmet next to his flight case. Strapped on his .45. Stuffed his survival kit in the lower leg pocket of his flight suit. And waited.

During the wait, he thought about Sienna. He would have loved to tell her about what he'd accomplished so far. That was impossible, of course. When not flying, he was restricted to base until completion of Operation Halyard.

In his mind's eye, he saw himself holding her close. Stroking her hair. Making her feel she was not damaged goods, but something to cherish. And he began to see himself as perhaps, almost, maybe . . . worthy of her. That is, if he could hold it together just a little while longer. Keep his focus. Keep his fears in check.

He pulled an aeronautical chart from his pocket and spread it across his lap. Reviewed the route of flight and the terrain around the airstrip in Yugoslavia. Mentally rehearsed short-field landings. Forced his mind to the task at hand.

Vasa began to think the Germans weren't coming his way, after all. So much time had passed since the radio had warned about enemy movement. No traffic passed along the road. No sound rose through the forest except the surge of water beneath the bridge. In the quiet, Vasa heard wings flapping overhead. Three ravens circled the bridge and settled on the railing. Sunlight illumined the black sheen of their feathers. One of the birds cocked its head toward the ambush team and cawed.

The ravens were the last living things to cross that bridge.

From around the bend beyond the bridge came the sputter of diesel. The grinding downshift of gears. The rumble of tires.

The noise lifted the ravens from the railing. Their wings beat the air until they soared above the treetops. The birds disappeared in the direction of Pranjani.

An open-bed truck filled with soldiers appeared from around the curve. Behind it came a four-door *Kübelwagen.*

The railings vibrated when the bridge took the weight of the traffic. Srecko hunched over his detonator like a cat ready to pounce. The truck reached the middle of the bridge.

A crack split the afternoon.

The noise assaulted Vasa's eardrums. The shock wave flapped his sleeves. The heat wave stung his face. Fire and debris boiled from the abutments. For a moment, the bridge lifted as if on a hinge, then collapsed to the river.

The truck sank with the remains of the bridge. Rolled onto its side, burning. The *Kübelwagen* fell with it. The water flowed too shallow to extinguish the fire, which billowed into an orange-and-black miasma. The fuel tanks in the truck and the *Kübelwagen* ignited, and the explosions spread the fire farther through the bridge's wreckage.

Men poured out of the vehicles like flaming ants. Miroslav opened up with the Browning. When he cut them down, they fell smoking into knee-deep water.

At the field radio, Nikolas lifted the handset. "All stations," he shouted, "Jeferdar Three is engaged."

Behind the *Kübelwagen*, a second truck screeched to a halt. The vehicle managed to stop just as its front wheels dropped over the edge of the void. Soldiers leaped from its bed. They dropped into kneeling or prone positions and fired into the trees without aiming.

Vasa's thoughts came quick and clear: *I see them, but they do not yet see me.*

His sights settled on a German blasting away with a machine pistol. Vasa fired once. Red mist spewed from an exit wound. The man dropped his weapon and fell.

Gunfire zipped into the woods. Vasa lay flat to the ground. The rounds scorched over his head. Some smacked into trees and sent bark and wood chips showering over him.

Beside Vasa, the rest of the ambush team kept firing. Nicholas squeezed off shots in rapid succession from his Garand. Srecko worked the bolt on an old Springfield. The sapper's rate of fire was slow, but he made every shot count. Enemy soldiers fell to his rifle. Two tumbled off the shattered bridge timbers and dropped into the river.

More vehicles backed up behind the truck on the lip of the bridge. More soldiers piled out of them, and Vasa kept firing. The Chetnik team was badly outnumbered now, but the terrain gave them an advantage: Only so many German soldiers could fire from the embankment across the river with any accuracy. The rest, crowded behind them, couldn't aim low enough without hitting their comrades.

Vasa emptied his weapon. The expended clip pinged from the breech. He smacked another clip into the M1. Let the bolt slam closed. Fired again.

At the Browning, Miroslav burned through a belt of ammunition. When he kneeled to open an ammo can, a bullet struck his throat. He collapsed onto the leaf carpet. Blood pulsed from his wound, spattered his face. Miroslav looked at Vasa as if to plead for something. Then his eyes went still.

Vasa took Miroslav's place at the machine gun. Enemy bullets cracked and zinged around him. He fed a belt of cartridges into the breech. Racked the charging handle once, twice, three times, until the first link came out. Placed both hands on the weapon's grips. Swung the barrel and aimed through a ring sight meant for downing aeroplanes.

He pressed his thumb against the trigger lever. His rounds stitched through the first rank of soldiers on the embankment. Three of them slid into the water below—into a liquid pyre. By now, the river itself was flaming. Fuel had spread across the ripples. Lighter than the water, the diesel floated on top and burned.

More Germans came under Vasa's sights. Some died where they stood. One tossed an object. For a second, Vasa thought the man had, absurdly, hurled a stick. Then he realized the thing flipping end over end was a potato masher grenade. Its long wooden handle made for better throwing.

With calm detachment, Vasa watched the grenade arc toward him. The thing seemed to move in slow motion, as if the flow of time had thickened and clogged. With perfect clarity, Vasa saw that the grenade's trajectory would place it practically at his feet. Then the grenade's handle struck a branch. The grenade deflected downward, its trajectory interrupted. It fell next to Srecko, who lay prone with his outdated rifle.

Without hesitation, Srecko let go of the Springfield. He rolled to his left. Now he lay on top of the grenade. Bullets whined over his head and showered him with bark and leaves. The debris fell through a ray of sunlight that lit the particles like stardust. For a moment, the sapper appeared transfigured, as if heaven opened to take him.

With a muffled thump, the grenade detonated. The blast lifted Srecko's chest off the ground. Wisps of smoke curled from underneath him when he dropped back to the forest floor. The smoke rose into the ray of sunlight. His left leg twitched. Then he lay still.

And then Vasa's gun went silent. The Browning had reached the end of the ammunition belt.

The Germans parted. They looked behind them and opened a space as if to make way for something.

Nikolas dropped his M1. He grabbed a fresh can of ammo for the Browning, flipped open the cover, and lifted a belt of cartridges.

On the embankment, the Germans brought up a heavy weapon. Some sort of crew-served machine gun.

Nikolas fed the first round into the breech. Vasa yanked the charging handle.

The German machine gun cackled. Rounds flayed the forest. The first stitches flew high. But the enemy adjusted fire. Nikolas grunted as if air had been slammed from his lungs. He crumpled to the ground. Blood poured from fist-sized holes in his chest and stomach.

Vasa thumbed the trigger lever.

This time, the ammo belt included tracers. A tongue of fire lashed from the Browning. Vasa swept the fire like an artist might sweep a brush over a canvas. He painted the German machine gun, and men fell away from it.

But other Germans continued shooting. One threw another grenade.

Vasa did not hear the grenade detonate. The blast overwhelmed his eardrums so fully that the world went silent. But the force of the explosion seemed to rupture every cell in his body. Hot metal lacerated him all over. He felt himself burned and crushed all at once.

Stunned and deafened, Vasa stumbled back from the Browning. Then another assault mauled him. This time, something struck his shoulder so hard it spun him around. Vasa's legs went to rubber. He found himself on his back, looking up through the forest canopy at a blue sky.

The blue faded to gray. The gray tunneled to black. Robbed of sight and hearing, Vasa now sensed only heat and pain. His mind's rational lobe, which normally served him so well in combat, now told him only one thing . . .

He'd been shot.

# CHAPTER 32
## Horror and Wisdom

$A$T THE PRANJANI AIRSTRIP, THE EXPLOSION IN THE DISTANCE REG-istered as a muffled slam. A beat of silence followed. Then came an eruption of gunfire that never seemed to stop. The airmen exchanged glances with widened eyes.

Bogdonavich muttered curses under his breath. He'd known things had gone too smoothly.

"All right," Marich shouted. "Heads on a swivel." The OSS man carried a carbine. Throughout the woods alongside the field, men rechecked their weapons. Most possessed only their USAAF-issued handguns. A few had scrounged old rifles from guerrillas and villagers; all the M1s had gone to Mihailovich's most active fighters. One pilot brandished a British-made STEN gun. Its long magazine jutted from the left side of the weapon. Some of the fliers took positions around a perimeter they'd marked earlier. They crouched in underbrush and behind tree trunks. They stacked extra magazines and peered into the forest.

In Bogdonavich's estimation, they were preparing for nothing better than a last stand. If a German outfit broke through and reached the airfield, that perimeter would amount to little more than a speed bump. Downed flyboys armed mainly with .45s would stand little chance against a battle-hardened enemy ground unit.

At the radio tent, Mihailovich wore a grave expression. He sat in a folding chair beside the OSS radio operator, and he began speaking into a microphone. Bogdonavich couldn't hear the words. He hoped the Chetniks had reinforcements they could bring up from somewhere, but he wasn't privy to all their plans.

He tried to imagine the scene as Germans arrived. Bogdonavich had never experienced ground combat, but he'd seen enough of the newsreels. A few mortar rounds could send hot steel slashing through the trees, through flesh and bone. And what if the Krauts came with even more? Heavy artillery? Flame-throwers?

*Don't dwell on it*, Bogdonavich told himself. *The operation's in motion; the wheels are turning. Whatever happens will happen.*

He let the thought settle in his mind. He felt the fear's sharp points and edges like a nail gripped in his palm. He could not control events, but he could control his fear.

At the radio tent, Mihailovich finished his call, and the radio operator donned a headset. The man scribbled at a notepad; he appeared to be taking down a message signaled in Morse. He tore off a sheet and handed it to Marich.

"The second flight's en route!" Marich shouted.

The azure iridescence of the Adriatic glowed as if lit from within. Drew banked over the Italian coastline as the C-47s formed up. Below, submerged reefs and rock formations appeared as darker blue shadows in the water. A squadron of gulls passed underneath, white wings outstretched and motionless, gliding on a maestro headwind. Drew leveled at five thousand feet. Today he piloted the number two ship, right behind Captain Geiser in the lead.

For now, number two was good enough. Drew felt he'd earned Geiser's confidence on that first night. Now, if Geiser's aircraft experienced problems again, Drew could take lead once more.

Behind him, four other C-47s assembled. A few minutes later, a glint of silver caught Drew's eye. He looked to his left and saw a flight of P-51 Mustangs vectoring toward him.

"Here come our little friends," Drew said. "I count four, five, six of them."

In bright sunlight, the fighters gleamed like minnows flashing in clear water. Their polished aluminum fuselages sparkled. Perhaps the deadliest of American fighter aircraft, their grace belied their purpose. P-51s carried six .50-caliber machine guns and mounting points for up to ten rockets. As the aircraft flew nearer, Drew saw that each carried a full set of rockets beneath the wings.

"I got some joining up on my side, too," Torres said.

"Mustangs?" Drew asked.

"Ah, no, they look like P-38s."

Drew felt glad to get those, too. They didn't have the range of the P-51s, so they might not be able to loiter while the C-47s loaded passengers on the ground. But Drew would take whatever coverage they could provide.

The C-47s assumed a V formation as they set a course for enemy airspace. Drew and Torres put the aircraft on autopilot. Drew cracked the throttles back a couple of inches of manifold pressure to set cruise power, and he rested the heel of his right hand on the throttle knobs. To the left and right, the fighter escort flanked the Skytrains like a swarm of hornets ready to destroy any threat. Drew felt a tingling in his fingers and toes. Nervous, but not panicky. Alert, but not frightened. After the formation droned along for a while, he called Chisholm on the interphone.

"Nav, pilot," Drew said. "How long to combat entry?"

"Fifteen minutes."

The answer came quick and sure. The navigator was probably updating his position every couple of minutes.

Drew recalled his most recent conversations with Chisholm. Chisholm had talked about the Stoics' thoughts on handling adversity—how facing danger became easier with experience. By *living* the struggle each day. The way a sailor grows accustomed to the pitch and roll of waves, the way a farmer's hand forms calluses against the plow, the way a spearman's shoulder strengthens with each throw, a man stands against dangers and learns to defy them.

An aerial armada over the waters of ancient Roman trade routes seemed as good a place as any to learn these lessons. Wisdom of the first and second centuries might steel Drew against the horrors of the twentieth. He scanned his engine instruments, flipped gauge selectors from engine one to engine two. Drew found good temperatures and pressures, all systems normal. Everything shipshape.

When he looked up from his panel, the Dalmatian Coast hove into view. Land appeared first as a chalked streak on the horizon. Then it took firmer form as combers crashed white against stone. Behind the beach, terrain materialized into a patchwork of hills, forests, and fields.

"Chariot Flight," Geiser called from the lead ship, "descend now."

Shock and blood loss dulled Vasa's senses. The battle noises faded. He looked up through the forest canopy. High clouds like white blankets sailed above him. Vasa wondered if he was dying, if God was somehow pulling a blanket over him and bidding him to eternal sleep.

But then the noises returned. Gunfire thumped all around him. The reports sharpened into cracks and booms. Vasa took in a deep breath, and it did not bring coughing or pain. The calm part of his mind that emerged in crises told him: *You are not shot through the lungs. You are not dying. At least not yet.*

He tried to raise himself on his left elbow. The arm collapsed, and Vasa fell back onto his side. He found he had little control of his left arm. Blood throbbed through a hole in his shoulder. Red droplets spattered onto the leaves that carpeted the ground.

Vasa turned onto his right elbow. That arm, still strong, supported him. He squinted through the smoke drifting through the trees. The odor of burning fuel and gunpowder salted the air.

Amid the haze, Vasa saw the two surviving sappers. Both were firing their rifles across a fallen log. Expended brass flipped and somersaulted from their weapons.

With his good arm, Vasa pushed himself upright. He kneeled, then staggered to his feet. Blood that had pooled in his left sleeve oozed down his arm and dripped off his fingers.

He did not know how long he'd been down. It could have been seconds or hours. The Browning stood idle, its barrel angled to the sky. A partially expended belt of cartridges hung from its breech, just as Vasa had left it.

Vasa felt his body growing weaker. By sheer will, he forced himself to function. One-handed, he took hold of the weapon. Leveled the barrel, swung it toward the field-gray uniforms across the river. Thumbed the trigger.

The bolt jackhammered as Vasa hurled fire toward the Germans. The weapon rattled and shook. Expended casings trailed smoke as they flipped through the air. The empty brass clattered at Vasa's feet. Using only one hand, he found it harder to aim. Still, his rounds ripped through three of the enemy. One burst tore a soldier's arm away, but other Germans took the places of those who fell.

Vasa's thoughts remained clear, and he realized: *There are more of them than us. We cannot win this. We can only delay them.*

Despite Vasa's suppressing fire, the Germans again manned their heavy machine gun. Vasa tried to train the Browning on them, again, but sweat and nausea clouded his vision. He aimed through the ring sight and pressed the trigger once more. Loosed another stream of fire. This time, his rounds struck low and chewed into the riverbank. The bullets struck only knotted roots and exposed clay. Then his weapon fell silent.

He had run through another ammunition belt.

Reloading took time even with two good arms. With one, it became nearly impossible. Vasa lifted the end of a fresh cartridge belt and tried to feed it into the weapon. He dropped it. Picked it up. Dropped it again.

One of the sappers looked over his shoulder and saw Vasa struggling. He ran to the Browning, put down his own rifle, and inserted the cartridge belt. With his good arm, Vasa yanked the charging handle.

From across the shattered bridge, the German machine gun chattered. The sapper staggered backward like a marionette jerked by strings. Red mist fouled the air. The man slumped to the ground. Intestines slid from underneath his tunic.

The Germans lashed the forest with bullets. Now there was no one left to return fire except Vasa and the single remaining sapper. Vasa could not remember the man's name. The stranger fired from over the log. Emptied his rifle, rolled onto his side to reload. The enemy must have spotted the movement; they adjusted aim and swept the sapper with fire. Several rounds spiked through him. The man lay still.

Vasa opened up with the Browning again. The Germans returned fire with tracer rounds. Spears of light stitched the ground in front of him. Something struck his right shin. The bone snapped as if crushed by a maul. Instantly Vasa dropped. He collapsed beneath the big machine gun. Tried to crawl for cover behind a tree, but found he could not move. He closed his eyes. Waited for the German fire to finish him.

Instead, he heard the rattle of gears.

The sound came from his own side of the bridge. He turned his head to see a guerrilla team, men he did not know, leaping from a truck that had veered off the road. One man kneeled with a tube across his shoulder. Another loaded a rocket into the back of the tube. Vasa had heard of such antitank weapons, called bazookas, but had never seen one.

When the weapon fired, flame spewed from both ends of it. Backblast kicked up dust along the roadway. The rocket speared into the Germans massed across the river. The round detonated with a distinct clap and sent streamers of smoke and sparks in all directions.

The explosion parted the enemy like a scythe. Still, some of the Germans kept shooting. Vasa saw two guerrillas crumple to the ground. The bazooka team reloaded. The man holding the weapon across his shoulder shuffled around on his knees, adjusted his aim. Steadied the tube. Fired again.

The second rocket smoked a trail into the enemy position. The round spattered fire and metal across the far side of the ruined bridge. Smoke from the burning vehicles made it difficult for Vasa to see, but it appeared the Germans were faltering. Their muzzle flashes slowed; their guns relented.

From the guerrillas' truck, automatic fire chattered. A Chetnik leaned a machine gun barrel across the hood and raked the enemy side of the river.

Behind the gunfire and shouts, Vasa perceived a whistling growl. At first, he thought his ears were ringing from noise of the firefight. But the strange sound intensified.

The reverberation came from above and behind him. Vasa realized it was aeroplanes, but not like any he had heard before. He raised himself on his good arm, peered upward through the forest canopy.

Silver flashed in the sunlight. Two machines bored toward him. Not high like bomber formations, but barely above the treetops. Small aeroplanes, but fast. Faster than anything he'd seen.

When they scorched over the river, Vasa recognized the white stars on their fuselages. So these strange machines were American. Their polished aluminum wings shone like jewels.

The pilots must have spotted the smoke from the battle. The aeroplanes pulled up into a climbing turn. They came back for another pass.

On the Germans' side of the riverbank, the gunfire died away until no sound remained except that of snarling engines. The aeroplanes seared across the shattered bridge so low that trees swayed in their wakes.

The pilots did not fire their weapons. They didn't need to.

The Germans had fallen back.

# CHAPTER 33
# Halfway to Heaven

*H*ILLOCKS AND PASTURES FLOWED BENEATH DREW'S WINGS AS IF the terrain were as fluid as the Adriatic. At low level, speed set the land in motion. Forests and crops undulated like a verdant sea. Ahead, the fighter planes scissored across the landscape. They dipped over intersections and bridges, searching for the enemy, daring the Germans to open up and reveal their positions. As far as Drew could tell, the Mustangs and Lightnings drew no fire. Smoke rose from a spot along a river. A pair of P-51s investigated. After a couple of passes, they pulled up without shooting.

Drew directed his attention back to his instruments. With constant glances at his altimeter and airspeed indicator, he held his place in formation as Chisholm called out distances.

"The field should be right off your twelve o'clock," Chisholm said, "five miles out."

In daylight, the airstrip looked even smaller than Drew remembered. Just a scratch on the earth, a nondescript rectangle of dirt and grass. Drew counted that as a good thing. A German recon pilot might dismiss it as another paddock for livestock, or perhaps a meadow seeded with late-planted grain.

Moments later, the C-47s overflew the field. An Aldis lamp

flashed green, and Drew followed the lead ship in a left turn onto a downwind leg. He eased the throttles back and called for Torres to lower the landing gear. Then he glanced at the runway. In broad daylight, it looked so very short. *If I did this in the dark,* he thought, *I can certainly do it now.*

The lead C-47 rolled onto final approach. Drew turned to follow. Pulled his throttles to idle and continued descending. He found himself a mile from the touchdown point, lined up with the airstrip, but a little high.

Torres confirmed the suspicion. "Let's get her on down," the copilot said.

Drew responded as if the aircraft were an extension of his own limbs. He kicked a rudder pedal and turned the control wheel to place the C-47 into a slip. That attitude presented more drag, and the aircraft's descent rate increased. At one hundred feet, he straightened her out. At fifty, he pulled back on the wheel to flare for landing. The ship touched down and stayed down, with no hint of a bounce.

"Very nice," Montreux said from the engineer's jump seat.

Drew tapped the toe brakes and slowed to taxi speed behind the leader. Both aircraft lumbered off the dirt strip and onto the grass to make way for the rest of the formation. Two P-38s orbited above the field, riding shotgun. Drew couldn't see the other fighters at the moment, but he knew they were buzzing around. By now, the Lightnings had to be low on fuel.

"I'll keep the engines running," Drew said. "Let's load up quick as we can and get moving again. Our little friends up there can't loiter forever."

Montreux popped the release on his harness. The buckles clattered to the floor. "I'll get things moving," he said. The engineer disappeared through the companionway.

On the airstrip, the number three ship landed. Dust swirled in vortices kicked up by the wingtips. Number four came in close behind. Drew watched five and six turn base-to-final.

Men began emerging from the tree line. An odd assortment of fliers in USAAF uniforms and bearded guerrillas laden with bandoleers assembled around the C-47s. Officers pointed, directing groups of men to the airplanes.

"What's happening back there?" Drew asked on the inter-phone.

"Montreux just opened the door," Chisholm reported from the navigator's station. "He jumped out, and he's talking to a captain with a beard. I think it's that OSS guy, Marich."

A few minutes later, bangs and rattles sounded from the cargo compartment. The noises rose above the general vibration of the airframe as the engines idled. In the cockpit, the temperature climbed, even though Drew and Torres had slipped open their side windows. A bead of sweat dripped from the end of Drew's nose. He realized the sweat resulted not just from the heat, but also from his nerves. Drew tried to enjoy the moment, to calm those nerves and take satisfaction in what he'd just accomplished. He drummed his fingers on the control wheel, eager to fly again. Took off his aviator's shades. Wiped the lenses with his handker-chief. Put the shades back on. He considered the fact that he'd performed this casual gesture in the middle of a combat zone.

"All right, we got a dozen guys on board," Chisholm said on the interphone. "Wait a minute—this is weird."

"What's weird?" Drew asked.

"They're taking off their boots and flight jackets," the navigator answered. "They're throwing them out the door. These guys are gonna fly home in their socks."

"That'll look pretty funny when we get them back to Italy," Tor-res said.

"Okay, they're strapping in," Chisholm said. "Man, you could light up New York with the smiles on their faces."

Montreux returned to the cockpit. Lowered himself into his seat and buckled his harness. Sweat darkened the armpits of his flight suit. He plugged in his throat mic. Scanned the engine in-struments and said, "We're all buttoned up in the back. Let's get outta here."

Drew placed his feet on the toe brakes and released the park-ing brake. Leaned forward for a better view out his side window.

The lead ship had already begun to taxi. Drew knuckled the throttles forward. The propellers chopped at the air, and the aircraft began to roll.

Bogdonavich started collecting boots and jackets from the ground. Prop blast had coated them with dust, but it didn't matter. The first two C-47s lumbered to the departure end of the airstrip. Dust, exhaust, and bits of grass billowed behind them. The lead ship ran up its engines. The pistons emitted a chain saw roar, and its propellers bit into the air. The aircraft trembled, then powered along the runway. At midfield, the tail lifted. At the end of the strip, the plane rose from the ground. The wheels barely cleared the trees at the departure end of the runway.

As the second aircraft departed, a commotion along the road drew Bogdonavich's attention away from the airstrip. A truck had pulled up. Chetniks leaped from its cab and bed. They unloaded a wounded man on a stretcher. *Why would they bring their wounded here?* Bogdonavich wondered.

Katarina emerged from the trees and ran toward the vehicle. That answered Bogdonavich's question: She was the nearest thing to a doctor for miles around. The guerrillas must have known their nurse was here to help with injured airmen.

Bogdonavich joined her at the truck. He saw that the wounded man was Vasa.

Katarina pointed into the forest. "I have a tent with medical supplies over there," she said.

Vasa lay bare-chested on the stretcher. A bloody bandage covered his left shoulder. Another bandage had been wrapped around his right shin. His right foot twisted at a strange angle; a bullet had apparently shattered the bone. Bloody streaks matted the hair on his chest. In addition to the bullet wounds, small puncture wounds flecked his neck and arms. Shrapnel, evidently. His skin had gone pale, and his eyelids fluttered.

"What happened?" Bogdonavich asked.

"His detachment blew a bridge when the Germans tried to cross it," a guerrilla said. "But then they almost got overrun."

Bogdonavich helped Katarina and two Chetnik fighters lift the stretcher. They carried Vasa toward the trees as another C-47 lifted off. Dust swirled over them, and grit irritated Bogdonavich's eyes. He blinked to help tears clear the dust. At the edge of the woods, he pushed aside a branch and led the stretcher team into the shade.

They put Vasa down beside a lean-to, where Katarina had stacked bandages and medicines. She had applied new dressings to some of the wounded airmen before they left on the first flights. Evidently, she'd thought her work here was finished; she'd begun packing up her supplies. She unbuckled a musette bag, opened the flap, and dug out a pair of scissors. She cut open the dirty rags that covered Vasa's most serious wounds.

The sight of Vasa's leg turned Bogdonavich's stomach. Blood oozed through what resembled hamburger flecked with bone chips. The fighters had applied a makeshift tourniquet above the wound; it was merely a length of rope tied with a square knot.

Katarina felt Vasa's neck. "He's lost a lot of blood," she said. "His pulse is racing like a bird's."

From a crate underneath her lean-to, Katarina took a bottle of blood plasma. She unsheathed a bayonet, stabbed it into the ground next to Vasa's arm. Kneeled beside him. She unspooled a length of rubber tubing and connected one end of the tubing to the plasma bottle. Inserted a needle into the other end. Then she placed the bottle into a metal bracket with a hook at the top. Hung the bottle from the bayonet's barrel ring.

She yanked Vasa's sleeve upward to reveal his wrist and lower arm. Unscrewed a bottle of alcohol, dabbed alcohol onto a gauze pad, and scrubbed the arm. Slapped his arm to reveal a vein. Jabbed in the needle.

If Vasa felt the needle, he did not show it. But he opened his eyes and stared up into the trees. Let out a low moan.

"I'm surprised that plasma is still good," Bogdonavich said.

"It was dried plasma," Katarina said. "It keeps until you need it. I added water to it just this morning. I did it in case a plane crashed."

"Will he make it?"

Katarina brushed hair from her eyes. With her sleeve, she wiped sweat from her face. Looked up at Bogdonavich as if he'd asked a stupid question. Shrugged.

"Maybe," she said finally. "But that leg needs surgery. It might have to come off. He needs more than what I can do for him."

"Where's the nearest doctor?"

Katarina just shook her head. Then her expression changed. She shifted from one knee to another. Looked up at Bogdonavich again.

"For him," she said, "the nearest doctor is in Italy."

It took a moment for her meaning to sink in. Then Bogdonavich understood.

"You mean take him with us?"

"That is exactly what I mean. Your bases in Italy have hospitals, do they not?"

"Yes, but . . ."

"Then that is his best chance. If he stays here, he will be a cripple, if he lives at all."

As they spoke, the sixth C-47 roared off the runway. Climbed over the tree line and banked toward the southwest. If all went according to plan, the planes would return in the late afternoon. Vasa could take one of the last flights out that day. But there were no orders, no manifest, no anything that authorized a Yugoslav national on an Operation Halyard flight.

"I'll see what we can do."

Bogdonavich found Captain Marich and General Mihailovich at the radio tent. Explained what Vasa needed.

"You're really trying to get me in trouble, aren't you?" Marich said.

"I know it's out of the ordinary," Bogdonavich said, "but if not for his unit, the Krauts might have rolled up this whole operation by now."

"Yeah," Marich said, "when I heard that shooting, I thought we were done."

Mihailovich stroked his beard. "We should do what we can for the boy," he said. "But this mission is more sensitive than you know."

The general reminded them of the tensions among the Allies about whether to support Chetniks or Partisans. Operation Halyard was already controversial. A Chetnik guerrilla showing up at a U.S. Army hospital wouldn't help matters.

"Due respect, sir," Bogdonavich said, "I don't care."

Mihailovich smiled. "Neither do I," he said.

"I think this is a time," Marich said, "when it's better to ask forgiveness than permission."

The pain set in.

In the heat of battle, Vasa had ignored his wounds. He'd known he was injured, but the swirling action and the shock had dulled the agony. Like the Serbian heroes of old, Vasa had fought on despite his wounds.

But now, by God, it hurt. Everything hurt, not just the two bullet wounds. He felt as if his whole body had become a mass of nerves, all overloaded by pain. His mind could process little else. He could not even remember how he came to be lying here in the woods next to the airfield. His fingers trembled; his teeth chattered from the torment.

*So this is what it is like to die,* Vasa thought. Not an easy thing. Dying would come hard. His body was strong; it would hold out for a long time. Until then, every cell would sear with pain.

A woman kneeled beside him. She stroked his cheek. Sunlight filtered through the branches and illuminated her hair, and glare blurred her face. Her features remained indistinct. Vasa sensed only kindness from her. Surely, this was a *veela* who would escort him into heaven.

Then she spoke. The voice was familiar. She was no *veela*, but rather Katarina.

"This will ease you, Vasa," she said.

Something pricked his arm. The tiny pain came amid a crescendo of pain, like a bird's chirp amid a booming thunderstorm. But a warmth spread from the prick. In moments, every muscle and sinew relaxed. The pain remained, but now it hushed, as if the thunderstorm receded a few miles into the distance.

"Is that better?" Katarina asked.

Vasa closed his eyes. Sighed a long breath. Now his brain could function again. The morphine and blood loss made his thoughts fuzzy and indistinct, but he could at least form words.

"Yes," he whispered.

"Very good, Vasa. Lie still and rest. We are putting the blood back into you."

"Am I dying?"

"No, Vasa. You are not dying. But you need a doctor. The Americans are going to take you in their aeroplane."

"But my detachment . . ."

"Shhh. Don't worry about that. General Mihailovich says you can go. You can come back when you get better."

"Where is Nikolas? Where is . . ."

"Nikolas is gone, Vasa. He has earned his place in heaven. So have you, but you will not go there today. You shall fly, but not quite that far."

"I'm going to fly," Vasa said.

Vasa tried to imagine lifting into the sky and riding among the clouds. What would it feel like to move so quickly? Would he see birds flying close? Would he look down on mountains and seas?

Before he could ponder those questions for long, the morphine put him to sleep. When he awoke, the sun hung low. Its orange rays slanted sideways through the forest. Katarina sat beside him and held his hand.

He heard motors overhead. The shadows of great wings danced across his body and flickered through the trees. Vasa remembered what Katarina had said right before he'd gone to sleep. The aeroplanes would take him toward heaven. Just not all the way.

# CHAPTER 34
## The Smell of the Ocean

$S$ IX C-47S IDLED ALONGSIDE THE WOODS. AT LOW RPM, THEIR EN-
gines trembled and spat clouds of smoke. The tips of their propellers, painted yellow, spun blurred circles that spread exhaust
through the forest where airmen waited their turn to board. The
fumes lent a tang to the air that smelled good to Bogdonavich.
He'd planned to take the last flight out—which might not come
for a few days. But now, he was leaving earlier so he could accom-
pany Vasa and translate for him.

General Mihailovich himself helped lift Vasa's stretcher. Bogdonavich raised the other end. Captain Marich held the plasma
bottle and kept its tubing clear while they carried the boy to the
airplane. Katarina followed them. She brought with her a canvas
bag of medicines and bandages.

"You can give him morphine in an hour," she said. "Do you remember how I showed you?"

"*Da,*" Bogdonavich said. "I do."

"And tell the American doctors I changed his dressings and put
in sulfa powder."

"I will, Katarina. You did a fine job."

At the C-47, the men raised the stretcher up to the open door.

Two enlisted men, an engineer and a radio operator, took hold of the handles. Marich passed the plasma bottle to an officer wearing navigator's wings.

"What's your name, soldier?" Marich asked.

"Chisholm, sir."

"This patient is a Yugoslav national. He needs surgery for gunshot wounds. Get him to the base hospital at Bari as soon as you land. If anybody gives you grief about it, tell them they can take it up with me when I get back."

"Yes, sir. But isn't this kind of irregular?"

"Yeah, it is. This whole damned operation is irregular."

"Yes, sir."

"He has earned it," Mihailovich said. "If not for this boy and his detachment, you might have landed in the middle of a German welcoming committee."

"Understood."

Bogdonavich climbed aboard. Katarina passed the medical bag to him. He opened the flap, checked the syringes and vials. Then he sat on one of the C-47's folding canvas seats, unlaced his boots, slid them off, and passed them down to her.

"Give these to someone who needs them more than me," Bogdonavich said.

"I will," Katarina said. *"Hvala vam."*

The enlisted crewmen strapped Vasa's stretcher to the floor, then passed another strap over Vasa's waist to hold him in place. One of the men ratcheted the strap down and asked, "Too tight?"

"He doesn't speak any English," Bogdonavich said. He translated for Vasa, and reached down to test the strap's tightness.

"It is fine," Vasa said. He was wide awake now, eyes moving constantly, taking in this new experience. The boy watched the Americans board the aircraft. Each man removed his boots and tossed them out the door.

"How are you feeling, Vasa?" Bogdonavich asked. "Are you in a lot of pain?"

"Not now. It was bad before."

"Tell me if it gets bad."

Vasa closed his eyes for a moment and smiled. "I am going to fly," he said.

"Yes, you are, Vasa the Wolf. We will take you to doctors who can fix you."

Vasa smiled again at the mention of his nickname. Bogdonavich wished the boy could sit up and look out a window. He wished Vasa could watch the ground fall away and see clouds at eye level. View the earth itself receding to the horizon. However, the young fighter would have to make do with whatever sensations he could experience from the floor. Sitting up might worsen his injuries.

*Can't wait to tell Dad about this,* Bogdonavich thought. He couldn't begin to repay the local Serbs for all they'd done for him. But bringing Vasa to medical help made a good down payment.

Bogdonavich wondered what the brass would do when he showed up with Vasa in Italy. Maybe nothing. Or maybe they'd court-martial everyone involved. Didn't matter. He recalled the stories he'd heard from Gregor and Stefan about how the Great Powers used the Serbs as pawns. *Well,* Bogdonavich considered, *the Great Powers can spare one damned hospital bed.*

When everyone got strapped in, the C-47's engineer slammed the cargo compartment door and checked the latches. The crewman made his way forward to the flight deck, nodding to his new passengers. Several grinned and offered thumbs-up gestures. A few minutes later, the aircraft began to roll, and it swung around into the takeoff position at the end of the runway. The engine noise rose from an idling growl to a banshee wail. Vibration coursed through the fuselage and transmitted into Bogdonavich's bones right up to his molars. When the pilot released the brakes, the ship lurched forward and began to accelerate. Bogdonavich glanced down at Vasa. The kid wore an expression of pure serenity, but his eyes widened when the tail came up.

The aircraft shuddered down the airstrip. The rumbling of wheels stopped when the ship lifted into the air, and the men erupted into cheers. Several laughed and clapped. Bogdonavich looked out his window and saw the landing gear clear the firs by mere feet. With the squeals and groans of hydraulic actuators, the wheels came up, and the ship banked into a climbing turn.

*We're actually getting out of here,* Bogdonavich thought.

When the aircraft leveled off at cruise altitude, Bogdonavich checked his watch. He opened the medical bag and uncapped a needle and syringe. Unbuckled his seat belt and kneeled beside Vasa. Bogdonavich pushed up Vasa's sleeve and gave him the injection, just like Katarina had shown him. Vasa showed little reaction, except that the lines around his eyes faded as his muscles relaxed.

Bogdonavich put away the medical kit. Then he excused himself past some of his fellow passengers to get to the navigator's station. By now, the cold of higher altitude had begun seeping through the airframe. As Bogdonavich padded around in his socks, the steel floor felt like ice. He noticed some of the other men picking up their stockinged feet and rubbing their toes.

At the front of the cargo compartment, Bogdonavich tapped the navigator's shoulder. The man looked up from his chart table and moved one of his headset's earpieces away from his ear.

"Can I talk to the pilot?" Bogdonavich shouted over the engine noise.

"I'll ask," the navigator said.

The man pressed his talk switch and spoke words over the interphone, which Bogdonavich could not hear. Then, with the wave of a pencil, the navigator motioned for Bogdonavich to step through the companionway.

In the cockpit, Bogdonavich found the pilots conferring over an aeronautical chart. The copilot, in the right seat, was a dark-haired man wearing aviator's sunglasses. The aircraft commander, in the left seat, had a lighter complexion. Patches of sweat darkened his flight suit, despite the coolness of altitude. His face conveyed deep concentration and maybe some nervousness. Bogdonavich regretted interrupting him, but decided to go ahead and say his piece, anyway.

"That was some fine flying back there," Bogdonavich said.

The pilot looked up from the chart and said, "I appreciate that.

Welcome aboard." Then he extended his hand and said, "I'm Drew Carlton. Nice to meet you."

Bogdonavich introduced himself as he shook Drew's hand. "Were you guys one of the crews that flew in that first night?" Bogdonavich asked.

"Yeah, we were the first plane in," Drew said. "We went around, and then we got in on the second try."

"I saw it. You guys need to get the Distinguished Flying Cross, at the very least. Maybe the Silver Star."

The pilot beamed at the comment, but then he swatted his copilot on the arm and said, "Couldn't have done it without old Torres here, and the rest of the guys."

The reaction impressed Bogdonavich. This man immediately wanted to share credit with his crew. Mark of a good leader.

"How long have you been on the ground down there?" Drew asked.

"About eight weeks. My dad came from Yugoslavia. He always wanted me to see it, but not like that."

"What's the deal with that wounded guy back there? Have you talked to him?"

"Yes, I know him. His name is Vasa. Just a teenager, but he and his detachment saved our asses. Yours too, probably."

"I heard there was a firefight."

"It was pretty bad," Bogdonavich said. "Vasa's the only guy left from his squad."

Bogdonavich leaned over to peer out the windscreen. The coastline took shape, and beyond it, the sea stretched into a cobalt haze. He considered the last time he'd viewed the Adriatic from this vantage point. He'd been going the other direction, on what turned into a one-way trip. Seemed a lifetime ago.

Vasa had expected the experience of flight would mark this day in his memory. Indeed, the excitement of takeoff thrilled him enough to forget his pain for a few minutes. But that paled in comparison to the elation he felt when the men broke into cheers. The fliers celebrated their freedom with loud hoots and applause. The ones within reach of Vasa's stretcher leaned down and patted him on the shoulder. They recognized he'd helped give them their freedom. Perhaps without realizing it, they had given him a gift, too. Their cheers created a moment he could savor for the rest of his life. He hoped that Nikolas, Miroslav, and Piotra, in heaven's halls of honor, had somehow heard the cheers as well.

Lying on his stretcher, Vasa enjoyed a clear view out one of the windows. From his position on the floor, he could not see the ground or even the horizon. But he watched the sky's color shift as the sun set. Blue yielded to white. White deepened to yellow. Yellow washed into scarlet. Scarlet darkened to purple. Then came full night: black velvet studded with silver. Vasa marveled that such a wondrous transfiguration came each evening, and most men ignored it. He vowed he would never ignore it again.

The motors hushed from a roar to a whisper. Vasa sensed a descent. The aeroplane turned once, then again, dropping all the while. When the wheels thudded to the ground, the Americans cheered once more. They loved to shout and applaud.

"Welcome to Italy, Vasa," Bogdonavich said.

The plane rolled for a few minutes. Then it stopped, and the motors shut down. One of the fliers opened the door. Harsh rays from floodlights lit the cabin. But no one moved to get out.

"You will leave first, Vasa," Bogdonavich said. "The medics are coming for you. The doctors will try to save your leg tonight."

Bogdonavich unbuckled the straps that held Vasa and his stretcher to the floor. Another flier held the bottle connected by tubing to the needle in Vasa's arm. Men climbed into the plane and lifted the stretcher. When they raised Vasa and moved him toward the exit, Bogdonavich saluted him. So did all the other fliers.

The gesture filled Vasa with pride and gratitude. To be treated with such respect by these aviators brought tears to his eyes. Then his tears of gratitude turned to tears of grief. He wished so much his father could see this. He wanted so badly to tell Aleksandra of this. Those things would never happen. But he recalled some of

Father Milos's words of consolation: *"In this mortal life, Vasa, every-thing you love will pass away. But love finds a way to return to you."*

The men passed him down to other men outside the aero-plane. Some wore white coats. They laid him down on a gurney, and a nurse in a white dress took the plasma bottle. The nurse began talking to him. She spoke in soothing tones, just like Kata-rina, though Vasa understood none of the English. Unlike the black-haired Katarina, this woman was a blonde. But she had the same kind eyes as Katarina, and she stroked his hair in the same way.

Bogdonavich jumped down from the aeroplane.

"They are going to roll you to the hospital, Vasa," Bogdonavich said. "I will see you when you wake up from surgery."

The American medics, babbling away in English, began push-ing the gurney across the tarmac. Vasa tried to take it all in: the nurse's touch, the glare of lampposts, the odor of hot engines. Farther from the aeroplane, a breeze freshened the air. Though Vasa had never seen the ocean, somehow he knew this was the smell of the sea. Bogdonavich had told him they were flying across the Adriatic to a base on the Italian coast. *Perhaps they will let me see the water before I leave,* Vasa thought.

His pain came and went in waves. He felt it rising again, but it was not yet so bad that he couldn't think of other things. He so hoped they could save his leg. If they did, he could return to the fight.

The medics pushed the gurney inside a building. Vasa's wounds throbbed when the wheels rattled over the threshold, but he did not cry out. The Yanks wheeled him into a room lit by the bright-est lights he had ever seen, so bright he had to squint.

Figures, backlit and blurry, moved over him. The medics began to cut away his bandages. Through his narrowed eyes under the bright lights, all the faces became indistinct. He could imagine them as anyone. When a black-haired nurse appeared, Vasa let himself believe she was Aleksandra, come from beyond to com-fort him in his hour of need.

Two doctors examined him. Voices tumbled with that incomprehensible language. Tools clanked on metal trays.

The black-haired woman placed a mask over Vasa's nose and mouth. He breathed in a cold vapor that dulled his pain and calmed his mind. The woman caressed his cheek with the side of her hand.

Vasa grew drowsy and comfortable. He pictured Aleksandra's face above him, imagined she was giving him the vapor. He thought of the sea breeze, and he drifted into sleep with the smell of the ocean.

# CHAPTER 35
# Everything That Is Beautiful

*A* RARE MORNING RAINSTORM SHOWERED THE AIR BASE AT BRINDISI. The first drops thudded heavy into hard-baked soil and threw miniature dust clouds to ankle height. Rain drummed the tin roofs of San Pancrazio's hangars and ran steaming into gutters. Clouds thickened and showers spread mist across the ramp and the rows of idled C-47s.

Fliers quickened their steps and ran inside the open front doors of the main hangar, their gabardine uniforms splotched with rain and sweat. They took their places among rows of folding chairs arranged before a rostrum. Drew sat with his crew in the fifth row. With their mission complete, the men of the Air Crew Rescue Unit gathered for a debrief.

At precisely 1000, a door opened at the rear of the hangar. A sergeant posted by the doorway came to attention and shouted, "Room, ten-hut!"

The men rose to their feet. Five officers entered, led by Captain Marich. The group included General Twining, the Fifteenth Air Force commander. Despite the heat, he wore his service coat, his stars and wings gleaming.

"As you were," Marich said.

The men took their seats. Drew wondered what had brought
General Twining back to San Pancrazio. Operation Halyard had
succeeded beyond expectations. The most recent flights from
Pranjani to Bari yesterday had brought the total number of rescued airmen to more than five hundred. The men of ACRU had
wrapped up their mission this morning with a quick hop from
Bari to their main base in Brindisi.

*Maybe this is the awards ceremony,* Drew thought. He recalled how
that bombardier, Bogdonavich, had said he deserved the Distinguished Flying Cross. Drew imagined standing with his crewmates
at the front of the hangar while Twining pinned DFCs on their
chests. At the very least, he supposed, they'd all get the Air Medal.
He could already imagine Twining reading from the citations:
*"For meritorious achievement while participating in sustained aerial
flight . . . under risk of enemy fire . . . Lieutenant Drew Carlton's courage
and airmanship reflect great credit upon himself and the United States
Army Air Forces."*

A final and official absolution. A decoration to sweep away all
murmurings of cowardice like a forgiven sin. A ribbon to wear
every day, a medal to wear on his dress uniform during formal oc-
casions, a citation his parents could frame and display over the
fireplace. The nearest thing to knighthood America could be-
stow.

Captain Marich offered words of welcome. Then he introduced Twining. The scene struck Drew as a little odd. The general approached the rostrum empty-handed. He carried no
notes, no documents. And no stacks of little boxes for medals.

"You gentlemen have made me proud," Twining began. "You
have pulled off something damned near impossible. In fact, there
were those who wanted us to scrub this mission because they
thought it couldn't be done. But you proved them wrong. And
you did not leave a single man behind. It is an honor to stand in
your presence."

The general paused. His expression darkened when he continued.

"You gentlemen deserve all kinds of recognition," Twining said. "Unfortunately, there will be none, at least in the public sense. I'm sorry to tell you this, but do not expect a lot of decorations. Do not expect a feature in *Life* magazine. Expect only the assurance that you have the eternal gratitude of your nation, your commander, and the men you brought out of harm's way."

Outside, the rain intensified. The tattoo on the tin roof grew louder, and the general raised his voice so the men could hear him.

"As you know," Twining continued, "this mission was classified, and it must remain so until further notice. That means not a word about it to wives, sweethearts, buddies, or relatives. Some of the Allies don't like the friends in Yugoslavia who helped us do this. It's a very sensitive matter, and that's all I'm going to say about that."

A collective sigh whispered across the hangar. For several seconds, no one spoke.

"That's all right," Torres said under his breath. "We know what we did."

Drew let that thought sink in as he tried to control his disappointment. Was he a coward or a hero? Did it depend on a scrap of parchment and an inch of ribbon?

He replayed the mission in his mind—the tight takeoffs and landings, the deft aircraft control, the cheers on liftoff. There was nothing in his memory marked SECRET. He could relive these moments whenever he liked, for the rest of his life.

Chisholm leaned back in his seat. Looked up into the rafters. "Everything that is beautiful is beautiful in itself," the navigator said. "Nothing is made better or worse by being praised."

"Sounds familiar," Drew said. "A paraphrase of Marcus Aurelius?"

"Yep," Chisholm said. "You've done your homework."

"Trying to," Drew said. *Still trying to live it,* he thought.

Twining dismissed the men, and Drew went straight to motor

pool. He hadn't had a chance to contact Sienna; neither she nor Antonio's restaurant had a telephone.

The rain had let up by the time Drew steered the jeep out the front gate. Mist rose from the pavement as the sun burned through the clouds and began to heat the ground. The sea heaved iron gray swells against the shoreline. Drew assumed Sienna would be at work by now, getting ready for the lunchtime crowd, so he drove into Brindisi and parked outside the restaurant.

Raindrops from the morning's shower still clung to the restaurant windows. Drew placed his hand on the wet doorknob, gathered his thoughts, and pushed open the door. The aroma of garlic and peppers greeted him. No other customers had arrived yet. Antonio stood wiping glasses at the bar, a white apron around his waist. He looked up from his work, stared for a moment, and broke into a gap-toothed, tobacco-stained grin.

"Sienna," he called.

From the kitchen, Sienna answered in Italian. At the sound of her voice, Drew felt the glow down in his gut.

"Sienna," Antonio repeated.

She made a scoffing sound, as if frustrated. She entered the dining room with a ladle in her hand. When she saw Drew, the ladle clattered to the floor. In an instant, she was in his arms. She squeezed Drew so hard, his ribs ached. He breathed in the scent of her hair, lingered in her embrace. Finally she released her tight hold around his chest. She held him at arm's length and looked up at him. Her eyes welled.

"I'm so glad you're safe," she said. "Can you tell me where you were, what happened?"

"No, but it was good. That's all I can say."

"Well, yes. If you are in one piece, it was good." Sienna wiped her eyes with the back of her hand. "It is now, anyway," she added.

Antonio shuffled around behind the bar. Glasses and bottles clinked as he arranged them. "Take the day off, Sienna," he said.

"Thank you, Uncle Antonio."

Outside the restaurant, Drew offered his hand, and Sienna

took it without hesitation. Hand in hand, they strolled the old-town section of Brindisi. Gulls, shearwaters, and terns fluttered over rooftops. Street smells, both foul and pleasant, filled the air: rotting trash on one corner, grilling sausage on the next, dog droppings, fresh lemons, coffee, and cigarettes.

In the marketplace, vendors plied fruit, vegetables, and fish. At one stall, an American private and a corporal loaded crates of cabbage onto an army truck. Drew bought two cups of cappuccino from the same man he'd seen in the market before. Business must have been good. The man now gave out paper cups instead of the clay mugs that had to be returned.

*"Grazie, signore,"* the vendor said when Drew tipped him an extra fifty lire.

At the columns that marked the end of the Appian Way, Drew and Sienna descended the steps down to the harbor. Out on the water, a fisherman readied his boat. He began unfurling a white sail from the boom. The man steadied himself against the varnished wooden gunwales. Drew had nearly finished his cappuccino; he took the last sip as he sat on a bench that overlooked the marina. He crushed the paper cup in his hand.

*Memento mori,* he told himself. *Find your courage while you can.*

"Sienna," Drew said, "would you ever consider life in America?"

She looked at him with a serene expression, with no sign of surprise or joy. No sign of shock or apprehension, either. The breeze scattered locks of her hair across her face.

She looked out across the harbor. Wind swelled the fisherman's sail, and the boat began gliding out to sea. With her eyes still following the boat, she said, "I might. It would depend on the reason."

Drew considered his next words with care. Finally he said, "Maybe if we get to know each other better, we'll know if you have a reason."

The fishing boat receded toward the horizon. With distance, its sail shrank to a postage stamp.

"That's a nice idea," Sienna said. "I like that idea."

Drew watched the boat reduce to a dot in the Adriatic, barely discernible. Like a future you could imagine, but not count on.

She leaned into him, let her hair fall across his chest. The breeze rose and spread ripples across the harbor. By now, the fishing boat had vanished. An unbroken blue line marked where the sea met the sky.

# CHAPTER 36
## All That You Love

$V$ASA'S FIRST VIEW OF THE OCEAN TOOK HIS BREATH AWAY. THIS SHADE of blue he had seen only in Aleksandra's eyes. He'd imagined God made only that much of it, just those two small orbs. But here it stretched to infinity, as if nothing existed but a narrow strip of beach and a world made of water. To see this color again left him awed but saddened.

Clouds with flat gray bases and sunlit white tops rode the wind. The sea breeze felt good on his face. The salt air smelled nice, too, just like that first night when he'd flown in. Now, at the water's edge, the scent carried even stronger.

Vasa sat in the backseat of an open motorcar the Americans called a "jeep." Bogdonavich and two others had sneaked him out of the base hospital when the nurses weren't looking. For weeks, while Vasa lay immobilized in traction, the Yanks had promised to take him to the beach. They'd asked what he wanted, and he could think of nothing else. Nothing else, at least, that was in their power to give.

His leg remained in a cast, and he still couldn't walk. But without the cords and pulleys holding his leg aloft, he became more mobile. The fliers had lifted him into a wheelchair, rolled him out to the vehicle, and raised him into the backseat. All the while, these older men laughed and bantered with one another like schoolboys on a caper.

Now that they were parked at the beach, Bogdonavich leaned on the vehicle, next to Vasa. The other two Americans walked down to the surf and began picking up seashells.

"Thank you," Vasa said in English. During his recuperation, he was beginning to pick up a few words and phrases: "yes," "no," "bathroom," and "please." But he reverted to his own language when he pointed out to sea and asked Bogdonavich, "Yugoslavia is that way?"

"Yes, Vasa. Yugoslavia is that way. We flew you across the Adriatic."

"And you will fly me back?"

Bogdonavich took a long time to answer. Then he said, "If that is what you want."

"I have to get back to fight for my country."

This turn of the conversation seemed to change Bogdonavich's mood completely. He no longer laughed and smiled. The flier looked at Vasa, then stared out over the water.

"You have already done more than your share, Vasa," Bogdonavich said. "And you won't be in fighting condition for a long time. You're lucky you still have that leg. No matter what you do, you'll always be a hero."

Vasa liked those words, and, at least in the beginning, he had sought glory above all. But now that he had it—or now that people *said* he had it—he didn't feel so glorious. He just missed his country, his village, his family, and his friends. He missed his detachment, though he knew he was its only survivor. He knew his family and most of his friends were probably gone, too. But if he could just get back to the land where they'd lived, maybe he would feel closer to them. Until he could find them again in the hereafter.

"Serbia is where my heart is," Vasa said.

"I know it, Vasa," Bogdonavich said. "My father feels the same way, but he lives in America."

"My country needs me."

Bogdonavich sighed, folded his arms. He looked off into the distance before he spoke.

"Someday soon, the Germans will be gone from Serbia and all of Yugoslavia," he said finally. "But then you still have the Partisans, Vasa. You do not know if they will win, or if the Chetniks will win. It could become very dangerous for you if Tito's side wins."

"They cannot win. They are Communists."

"I agree. But in this war, we have already seen things that cannot be. Things that should never be. I understand how you want to get back in the fight. But you need to open your mind to other possibilities."

At Vasa's bedside, Bogdonavich and the other Americans had talked about those possibilities. In time, with the right arrangements, he could come to America. Or he could stay in Italy. Or he could go to Britain or France. Powerful people knew what he had done, and they could help him.

Vasa's eyes focused on the blue horizon. Haze blurred the line between sea and sky, but he imagined he could see Yugoslavia's green hills in the distance. In reality, that was too far to see even on a clear day. But in his mind's eye, he could almost reach out and touch his homeland.

The summer's heat yielded to fall. Nearly all the men rescued in Operation Halyard had gone home, but Bogdonavich remained behind at the air base in Bari. He longed for home, too, and he looked forward to telling his father what he'd seen and done. But his language skills had caught the attention of Captain Marich and others who worked in the shadows. In military parlance, Bogdonavich had been "CHOPPED"—Change of Operational Control—from the USAAF to the OSS. Neither he nor anyone else had gotten into trouble for bringing Vasa out of Serbia; the brass seemed to have looked the other way. And now Bogdonavich had a new job.

He couldn't tell Vasa why he'd stayed in Italy when most of the other rescued fliers had left. But the boy didn't ask many questions; he just seemed happy to have a friend to converse with him in Serbian. Bogdonavich was working on several options for creating a new life for Vasa. President Roosevelt's War Refugee Board had set up camps in Italy, North Africa, and the United States. Allies such as Britain and Australia were welcoming fighters who had aided their cause. For someone like Vasa, an orphan and a minor, but an ex-guerrilla and not a child, things got complicated. Still, Bogdonavich felt he could eventually cut through the red tape. Vasa might settle anywhere, get an education, train for a job.

The problem was Vasa himself. He didn't want any of that. He just wanted to go home.

Bogdonavich finally relented, and Captain Marich said Vasa could fly back to Serbia on the next C-47 that was landing there.

The aircraft lifted off at dusk, bound for a dirt airstrip not far from General Mihailovich's headquarters in Pranjani. Bogdonavich had read the airfield survey: This new airstrip was longer than the first one, and thus safer for night operations.

Vasa sat next to Bogdonavich, upright on a seat made of canvas webbing. His crutches lay on the floor beside him. He could walk short distances without them now, but the nurses made him promise to keep them until he'd fully recovered. He wore a new leather A-2 jacket and a set of flight boots, courtesy of the fliers at Bari. A supply officer had also given him a duffel bag filled with clothing and toiletries. If Vasa had to resume life as a guerrilla, he would at least start with fewer privations.

Unlike his previous flight, this time the boy could see out a window. Bogdonavich watched him press his nose to the glass as the aircraft crossed the shoreline and climbed into the night.

"I can see the stars coming out," Vasa said.

"*Da,*" Bogdonavich said. "They are beautiful from the air."

Bogdonavich's voice conveyed little enthusiasm. In fact, he fought tears. Intel reports from Serbia didn't sound good. The Germans were retreating, and that was fine. But in the concurrent civil war, the Partisans were gaining the upper hand.

Through a borrowed headset, Bogdonavich monitored the interphone during the flight. He watched the navigator and the radio operator at work, their faces bathed in yellow glow from instruments, tuning dials, and utility lights. The navigator fixed a position over the water, marked his chart, and updated the pilots.

Bogdonavich tried to think of some final words for Vasa, but there wasn't much left to say. Maybe "Godspeed" or "Be careful," shouted quickly over the sound of engines. "Have a nice life" seemed too flip, but that's what Bogdonavich wanted for his young friend.

The fuselage's vibration lulled Bogdonavich. In the dark cargo compartment, he began to feel drowsy. But then he noticed something that brought him back to alertness. The radio operator, who'd been slouching at his seat, sat straight up and reached for a pencil.

"We're getting a message on the liaison set," the radio operator said.

Bogdonavich couldn't hear the Morse code coming in, but he watched the radio operator scribble onto a notepad. The man tapped a reply on his Morse key, then ripped off a sheet and passed it up to the cockpit.

"Operations wants us to return to base?" the pilot said on the interphone.

"Yes, sir," the radio operator said. "The landing zone's too hot."

"I thought the Germans were out of that area."

"They are, sir. Message said this is related to the civil war. Chetniks and Partisans got themselves into a bit of a firefight down there."

"How did Ops know all this?"

"The report came from an OSS team on the ground. They transmitted on their W/T set, and then beat feet out of there."

Several seconds passed with nothing but electronic hiss on the interphone. Then the pilot said, "Damn it. All right, boys, we're going home. Nav, gimme a heading."

Bogdonavich explained the situation to Vasa as the aircraft banked into a turn. Even in the pale light of the cargo compartment, Bogdonavich could see the teenage guerrilla's face fall.

"Are they lying?" Vasa asked.

"No, Vasa. They are not lying. If we wanted to trick you, we wouldn't go to the trouble of flying you halfway there."

Vasa stared at the floor for a long moment. Shook his head.

"The priest told me everything I loved would pass away," Vasa said. "Losing my family and friends isn't enough? Now I lose my country, too?"

"Vasa," Bogdonavich said, "your life is just beginning, and you have opportunities ahead of you that you can hardly imagine. I know it's hard to see now, but it's true."

"Maybe you can fly me back tomorrow. Or the day after that. Whenever this battle ends."

"We have no idea when it will end, Vasa. And we fear it will not end well for your side."

Vasa stared out the window. From over Vasa's shoulder, Bogdonavich saw a three-quarter moon rising over the sea. The moon glowed copper, the color of a new penny. From this angle, an optical illusion gave the appearance of the moon riding the water's surface.

When the C-47 rolled out of its turn, the Italian coast sparkled: a distant silver necklace against a night of black silk. Towns, with all their lights on now, twinkled against hillsides. The engines hushed from a roar to a whisper as the pilot eased back on the throttles, and the aircraft began a gentle descent. The flight remained smooth; the calm night air offered not even a hint of turbulence.

"It's a big world down there, Vasa," Bogdonavich said. "It has a place for you, somewhere. A new home. A girl you have yet to meet."

Vasa looked away from the window. Wiped his eyes with his sleeves. After a few minutes, he gazed out over the dark ocean again. He nodded, almost imperceptibly.

Below, moonlit waves lapped at the shore. As the C-47 continued its drift-down for landing, fields and houses took form. Vehicles crawled along roadways. Streetlamps threw pools of light throughout towns and villages. This part of Italy, at least, had begun a transition toward peace.

The aircraft banked to set up for final approach. In the turn, the right wing came up, and with it, the windows on the right side where Bogdonavich and Vasa were sitting. The windows framed the stars, revealing a sky strewn with the fires of distant galaxies. A moment later, the wings leveled and the landscape returned to view, nearer now.

The earth rose. The runway lights beckoned. The air lay calm and still. The C-47 flared, and its wheels kissed the pavement. The aircraft rolled into the ramp area, parked, and shut down. As the propellers spun to a stop, Vasa popped the release on his seat belt and hoisted his duffel bag. A ground crewman opened the cargo compartment door and positioned a set of steel steps at the exit. Vasa climbed down from the airplane into circles of light cast by floodlamps, and a fresh breeze from the west.

# Historical Notes

Real events inspired this novel. In the summer and fall of 1944, American aircrews flying C-47s rescued more than five hundred downed Allied airmen in Yugoslavia. They flew into dirt airstrips built with hand tools, as described within these pages. For narrative purposes, I took artistic license with certain details. Primarily, this novel compresses events. Its timeline covers approximately eight weeks. The real Operation Halyard began in August of 1944 and continued almost until the end of the year, using multiple improvised airfields. Some aircraft flew in at night. Some sneaked in unescorted. Some flew in with fighter cover. At least one dinged a wingtip on a haystack.

The Chetnik guerrilla leader, General Draza Mihailovich, is a historical figure, as is the Fifteenth Air Force commander, General Nathan Twining. The scenes depicting them in this story are imagined. However, Twining's backstory is not. As mentioned in Chapter 25, he survived for days in a life raft on the Pacific before being rescued by a Navy flying boat.

General Mihailovich did not live long after this rescue operation. His side lost the Yugoslav civil war, and Josip Broz Tito went on to become the Communist leader of postwar Yugoslavia. Tito's government captured Mihailovich and put him on trial for treason and war crimes in 1946. Some of the rescued aviators protested on his behalf outside the Yugoslav consulate in New York. Others flew to Washington, DC, to lobby the U.S. government to intercede. Their efforts could not save him. On July 17, 1946, the Tito government executed Mihailovich by firing squad.

Mihailovich's legacy remains controversial. However, in 1948, President Truman posthumously awarded him the Legion of Merit, Chief Commander, for his role in the rescue and in resistance efforts.

Most of the other major characters are fictional, though some were inspired by real people. My OSS officer, Captain George Marich, is based on one of the actual organizers of Operation Halyard, George Musulin. Because I placed that character in so many imagined situations, I thought it fairer to Musulin to change the name. But it must be said that the real-life Musulin played a central role in Operation Halyard, one of the greatest rescues in military history. He retired from the Central Intelligence Agency in 1974, and he died in the Washington, DC, area in 1987. Two of his teammates, Mike Rajacich and Arthur Jibilian, are represented within these pages by the characters Mike Racanin and Arthur Jezdich.

Two real-life figures inspired my character Vasa. One is Nick Petrovich, a seventeen-year-old guerrilla fighter who helped protect the downed fliers. In the nonfiction book *The Forgotten 500*, author Gregory A. Freeman describes Petrovich's role in Operation Halyard.

The other is one of my old teachers. At the University of North Carolina at Chapel Hill in the 1980s, I took a course in Russian novels. Dr. Vasa Mihailovich led the class—and kept us students spellbound. As a teenager in Yugoslavia, Mihailovich took up arms in a civil war raging within a world war. Eventually he escaped to Italy and spent five years in refugee camps.

After he made his way to the United States, Mihailovich paid his way through college by working on the assembly line at Chrysler. He earned his doctorate and became a literature professor at UNC. His works include an English translation of the Serbian epic *The Mountain Wreath*, mentioned within these pages. When not in class, he marched for civil rights, wrote poems and short stories, and became an avid, even fanatical, follower of Tar Heel basketball. This brave and gentle man left us in 2015.

(Mihailovich is a common Serbian surname. I do not know of any close family relationship between Dr. Vasa Mihailovich and General Draza Mihailovich. The actions of my character Vasa Petrovich are fictional and do not represent those of Dr. Mihailovich or Nick Petrovich.)

The firefight in which Vasa is wounded while protecting the airfield is a product of my imagination. However, I didn't have to use *much* imagination. According to *The Forgotten 500*, a garrison of 4,500 German troops lurked only twelve miles away from Pranjani, and another unit of 250 troops was only five miles away. Historical accounts report firefights between guerrilla and German forces to keep the enemy away from downed airmen.

My scene depicting an airdrop of supplies to Mihailovich's forces is also fictional, with a basis in fact. According to historical accounts, Halyard flights were meant to rescue downed airmen and not to aid the Chetniks in any way. However, *The Forgotten 500* describes OSS personnel bending the rules to get medicine and shoes to the guerrillas. In a similar manner, my scenes with the nurse Katarina are imagined from a grain of truth: The fictional Katarina stands in for villagers who provided whatever care they could manage for wounded airmen.

The real name of one of the downed airmen appears in this novel as a minor character. Pilot Tom Oliver, the "Mudcat driver," helped encode radio messages that facilitated the rescue. My scenes depicting him are entirely made up. But his efforts, described in *The Forgotten 500*, were so ingenious that I placed his name in print here.

This story mentions massacres at Kraljevo and Velika, and the infamous Jasenovac concentration camp in Croatia. All of these, sadly, are real. Between October 15 and 20, 1941, the *Wehrmacht* killed two thousand people in Kraljevo. On July 28, 1944, Albanian SS members killed more than four hundred civilians in Velika. Both massacres were reprisals for resistance activity. The number of people killed at Jasenovac is not clear. However, the United States Holocaust Memorial Museum in Washington, DC, estimates that at least 77,000 Serbs, Jews, Roma, and others died there. In the sordid history of concentration camps, Jasenovac stands out because of the personal nature of the murders. Jasenovac was not a death factory with gas chambers. According to some accounts, most of its victims were slashed, hacked, or beaten to death.

The sexual assaults by French colonial troops described by my character Sienna, sadly, are also real. The attacks are mentioned in Rick Atkinson's book on the Italian Campaign in World War II, *The Day of Battle*. These incidents, called the *Marocchinate* by Italians, were also the subject of a 1960 film starring Sophia Loren, titled *Two Women*.

In a scene near the end of the novel, Drew and his crewmates learn they are not about to receive medals for Operation Halyard. Though some of the participants did eventually get decorated, their story was kept hushed for political and security reasons. Drew, by the way, is entirely fictional. I found no record of any Operation Halyard pilot facing a flight review board or having a checkered past with other operations.

I've tried to provide technical authenticity to the novel, extending to some of the aircrew's navigation procedures. The Rebecca and Eureka radio system described in the story represented the cutting edge of technology in its day. It's the great-grandfather of the GPS-based systems in use now.

The depiction of departing airmen throwing their boots and jackets out of the airplanes before takeoff is also based on actual events. According to *The Forgotten 500*, many of the rescued fliers left their coats, footwear, and even socks and shirts as gifts for their hosts.

Though Operation Halyard remains an obscure corner of World War II history for many, it's not entirely forgotten. The Halyard Mission Foundation seeks to keep alive the memory of this rescue. The foundation's efforts include a permanent memorial site at Galovica Field near Pranjani. Other efforts involve historical research and film projects, along with recognition plaques for the families of those who assisted with Operation Halyard. Inside a church in Pranjani, an icon depicts events of the Halyard mission, including the image of a C-47 aircraft. You can learn more on the foundation's website at halyardmission.org.

Tito's Partisan forces also took part in rescues of American airmen. The history of Yugoslavia during and after World War II is a complex and bloody story. If you look for a faction that's entirely heroic and innocent of war crimes, you'll search in vain. Ethnic tensions that had seethed for centuries exploded during and after the war. They exploded again in the 1990s as the old Communist regime fell apart. I saw some of the results firsthand as a young Air National Guard crewman flying into Bosnia and Kosovo during that time. Homes gaped open from mortar fire. Bullet holes marred buildings. At one airfield, I was warned not to venture outside the fence for fear of land mines.

The former Yugoslavia is a beautiful, tragic, mystifying, and fascinating part of the world. I pray it finds a future more peaceful than its past.

Tom Young
Alexandria, Virginia
June 2021

# Acknowledgments

Getting any book into print becomes a team effort, and that's especially true of a historical novel. Though fiction requires imagining certain scenes, you still want to stay within the broad guardrails of actual events. In your research, you turn to nonfiction books, museums, historical organizations, and other sources of expertise in an effort to paint an accurate portrait. Once you have a rough draft on paper, trusted manuscript readers provide a sanity check on your work. And, of course, no book happens without the dedicated efforts of editors and literary agents. As this book moved toward completion, their jobs became even more challenging due to the social distancing required by the COVID-19 pandemic.

As always, first thanks go to my wife, Kristen—history buff and manuscript critic extraordinaire. I can't say enough about her support during all that led to this novel, which includes her courage and patience during multiple deployments while I was in the military. She comes by her editing skill honestly, from a good first teacher: her mother, Laurel Files, UNC-Chapel Hill Professor Emeritus. Laurel also helped polish the manuscript. This novel benefited greatly from her thorough review and attention to detail.

After Kristen and Laurel read my manuscripts, the next person who sees them is my old friend and squadron mate, Lieutenant Colonel Joe Myers, Retired. Joe's an avid student of history—and during his distinguished career in the U.S. Air Force and Air National Guard, he helped make some of it. I had the privilege of sharing a flight deck with him many times, and his sharp eye benefited this story.

Another sharp eye—one that has critiqued my writing in one form or another for forty years—belongs to Professor Richard

Elam. Our friendship began during my student years at UNC and continues to this day. So does his ability to seek and destroy unnecessary verbiage. Dick's also a veteran; he served his country for many years in the U.S. Naval Reserve.

I've enjoyed other lasting friendships in the literary community; that's one of the best things about being a writer. Friends who helped me polish this book include Jodie Tighe, Fiona Shrimpton, K.C. Potter, and Elizabeth Lee.

If you enjoyed this book and you'd like to learn more about World War II, you can do more than read and watch films about it. Thanks to dedicated volunteers, you can see the planes up close, hear the engines, smell the exhaust—and if you're intrepid enough—feel the opening shock of a parachute. The World War II Airborne Demonstration Team, based in Frederick, Oklahoma, brings living history to air shows around the country. Using authentic equipment and uniforms, the team wows audiences with troop drops from its C-47 and C-49. If you're so inclined, you can join them and sign up for their nine-day Parachute School. My thanks to WWIIADT's Matt Anderson and Ray Steeley for valuable technical information.

I also received technical help from another fine living-history organization, the Commemorative Air Force. Jane Copeland of the CAF's Gulf Coast Wing, along with Bobbie Carlton and Jim Olivi of the CAF's Arizona Wing, provided valuable information on WWII bombers.

As I mentioned in the Historical Notes section, the Halyard Mission Foundation does excellent work in keeping alive the memory of Operation Halyard. My thanks to the foundation's president, John Cappello, for helping make this work of fiction true to the spirit of actual events.

You'd never have held this book in your hands if not for the dedication of my literary agent, Michael Carlisle of InkWell Management. Our association goes back more than a decade now, and he's never steered me wrong. Michael introduced me to the fine folks at Kensington—and it's a pleasure to work with my editor, Wendy McCurdy, and all the rest of her Kensington team.

My thanks to Wendy for her particular interest in military history. With World War II more than three-quarters of a century behind us, we have fewer and fewer members of the Greatest Generation left with us. We'll never repay the debt we owe them, but we can at least pass down their stories.